ST

The Four Horses

Also by Chapman Pincher

NOT WITH A BANG
THE GIANTKILLER
THE PENTHOUSE CONSPIRATORS
THE SKELETON AT THE VILLA WOLKONSKY
THE EYE OF THE TORNADO

The Four Horses

CHAPMAN PINCHER

Michael Joseph
LONDON

First published in Great Britain by
Michael Joseph Limited
52 Bedford Square
London WC1B 3EF
1978

ISBN 0 7181 1683 6

Photoset by D. P. Media Ltd, Hitchin
Printed in Great Britain by
Tonbridge Printers, Tonbridge

To Jack and Roslyn, who love Venice

Contents

Episode 1 *Violence in Venice*
    Chapter 1   11
    Chapter 2   31

Episode 2 *Creation in Corinth*
    Chapter 3   39
    Chapter 4   55

Episode 3 *Reincarnation in Rome*
    Chapter 5   61
    Chapter 6   78

Episode 4 *Crusade to Constantinople*
    Chapter 7   95
    Chapter 8   102
    Chapter 9   110
    Chapter 10   116
    Chapter 11   129

Episode 5 *Plunder for Paris*
    Chapter 12   147
    Chapter 13   162
    Chapter 14   174
    Chapter 15   179
    Chapter 16   194
    Chapter 17   203

Episode 6 *Vengeance in Venice*
    Chapter 18   215
    Chapter 19   239
    Chapter 20   244
    Chapter 21   266

EPISODE 1

Violence in Venice

'Unbitted, unbridled, stampeding through time,
Have you in our story seen reason or rhyme?'

Chapter One

The Piazza San Marco had never looked more peaceful as the white-haired Venetian in the dove-grey suit, cream silk shirt and Gucci shoes conducted the young couple towards one of the outside tables of the Cafe Lavena, near to the Basilica of St Mark.

'Well, there they are,' he said as they sat down. He pointed to the four bronze horses above the gold-mosaiced main entrance, where they had stood in splendour for seven centuries. Believed to be threatened by bronze disease, joint product of Venice's salty air and local industrial pollution, the proudly stepping stallions had been removed for restorative treatment in the Basilica's laboratory. The last one had been winched back into their alcove, the Loggia dei Cavalli, very early that morning. As the symbols of Venice's former power, independence and prestige, their return was to be celebrated that evening in a nostalgic festival, which would resurrect the old carnival spirit that had served as a substitute for greatness after the rot had set in with the decline of the Republic's maritime supremacy.

'They're not in bad shape after two thousand years are they, Paul?' the Venetian asked his young American friend, who was inspecting the horses through binoculars.

'They are perfect, Luigi, just perfect,' Paul replied as he scanned the close-cropped manes, the thin collars round the arching necks and the verdigris stains of the once over-lying bridles—the only remaining evidence that they had ever drawn a chariot.

'Not perfect,' Luigi responded with a cautionary wag of a delicate finger. 'Nothing in art is perfect and I think the man who made them would agree with me.'

Paul acknowledged the correction with a smile. Luigi Scarpaccia, an internationally renowned art critic, connoisseur and

11

professor at Venice's Institute of Architecture, was an old family friend and performed occasional commissions for his father, Samuel J. Kline, the Jewish banker and art patron.

'Who was the sculptor?' Paul asked, as he passed the binoculars to the Israeli girl he had married in New York three weeks previously.

'There's argument about it, especially since the scientists got to work on them with their chemicals and their probes,' Luigi said with some distaste. 'But I support the view that they are almost certainly the work of Lysippus, one of the greatest Greek masters. The detail is marvellous, as you'll be seeing in a few minutes.'

Ruth Kline, who was not stirred by plastic art, did her best to look impressed as she handed back the binoculars.

'They really are beautiful,' she murmured. 'They look as though they have been gilded.'

'They were—by the Romans. The Romans could never resist gilding lilies. For them everything had to be brighter, bigger, more impressive. But now that most of the gilding is worn away the mixture of green, bronze and gold is quite splendid. Only Nature can "improve" a great work of art and get away with it.'

'What do you reckon they are worth?' asked Paul, whose father had spent millions of dollars acquiring so many choice Italian paintings and sculptures that several American galleries had been enhanced by generous donations from the Kline Collection.

'Worth! Worth! My dear boy, they are the last surviving quadriga of antiquity. Their extraordinary history alone makes them priceless. They were made for Alexander the Great, then they belonged to Nero, Constantine and, for a short time, to Napoleon!'

Ruth's interest quickened at the mention of such names. A sabra of Russian immigrant parentage, she had majored in history at the Hebrew University of Jerusalem, where her father, Isaiah Yacob, a former army general and now leader of the most hawkish political party, had lectured, specializing in the archaeology of the Old Testament.

'How did the Horses get here?' she asked.

'We stole them,' Luigi answered with a shrug. 'But we weren't the first to do that. In fact they have been filched four times.'

He held up his left hand, on which he was wearing a thick wedding ring, though his wife had been dead more than twenty years, and counted the events with some flourish on his fingers.

'The first time was when the Romans stole them from Greece, the second when Venice stole them from Constantinople, the third when France stole them from Venice, the fourth when Austria stole them back for us. . .'

'Gosh, Ruth, what a history!' said Paul who, with his athletic physique and casual attire, contrasted sharply with his slightly built and elegant companion.

'And a very violent history too,' Luigi added. 'They've witnessed a lot of suffering, seen a lot of terror—in the burning of Corinth, in Nero's Circus, in the sack of the Hippodrome in Constantinople. . .'

'But not here?' Ruth asked.

'Yes, here too, at least out of the corner of their eyes.' Luigi pointed towards the lace arcade below the rosy brickwork of the Doge's Palace. 'See those two columns that look reddish while all the others are white? That's supposed to be because they've absorbed so much blood. The people of Venice would often wake up to find a butchered corpse suspended there—a warning from the Inquisitors to the rest to behave themselves.'

Mentally, Paul shuddered. A dove by disposition, like so many big men, he detested cruelty in any form or for any reason.

'What do you reckon the Horses' main conclusion would be after watching *Homo sapiens* for two thousand years?' he asked as he filled his large-bowled pipe.

'That human nature hasn't changed, not even marginally.'

Paul did not accept that view and sensed that Luigi, cynical as he might be, was deliberately exaggerating, but Ruth who had spent most of her twenty-five years in Israel was inclined to agree with it. The shameful history of Jewish persecution which hopefully had ended with world reaction to Belsen,

13

Auschwitz and the rest, had been revived with new refinements in Russia, and through her army service in the Yom Kippur war she had experienced more savagery than most of her age.

'The use of terror as a political weapon certainly hasn't changed,' she said bitterly, with a trace of Hebrew accent.

'The Horses would emphatically confirm that, if they could talk,' Luigi said. 'Ruthlessness still pays. Softness never has and it never will.'

'Yes, there's only one thing to do with terrorists,' Ruth added almost fiercely, her blue eyes constricting as she stared at the cloudless sky. 'Stamp them out. Kill them, even if innocent people have to suffer in the process.'

To Paul, who had been sheltered from the bloody impact of barbarity, though touched with the threat of violence after his father's vocal stand with other New York Jews in calling for international action against terrorists, it seemed strange in that peaceful piazza to hear Ruth, who was so warm and compassionate, taking such a merciless stand, but he thought he knew what was in her mind and it disturbed him. Ruth's first fiancé, Yigael, had been killed in 1972 at the Olympic Games in Munich when eleven Israeli athletes had been massacred by Palestinian gunmen. She had taken it so badly that until she had met Paul on a holiday visit to New York she had never had another serious boy-friend, though she had dallied with many.

Yigael, who had been the only son of one of Yacob's closest friends, was so mourned by the General that the murder had been a major factor in making him so uncompromisingly tough against all Arabs. Paul had not been a welcome successor, in spite of the friendship between Yacob and Sam Kline. Yacob considered him immature for his twenty-eight years but was more dismayed that a future son-in-law should not be an ardent Zionist or even an ardent Jew. He had been appalled to learn that young Kline had been named Saul at birth but had insisted on changing it when entering Harvard on the grounds that he had never liked 'Saul'.

'More likely he has been defiled by the Christian ethic,' the General had remarked bitterly when first hearing about it.

14

Sensitive to his father-in-law's chilliness, Paul wondered whether he would ever fully replace Yigael in his wife's affections. He knew it was silly to be jealous of a dead man, especially one who seemed to have been rather fine, but there it was.

In fact at that moment Ruth's retrospect was concentrated far from Munich at an Israeli village called Ma'alot, where Palestinian terrorists, cornered in a school, had butchered more than twenty children, throwing their bodies out of the windows. The corpses had been removed to a makeshift mortuary before she had arrived there with her father, who had been diverted to the scene while they had been travelling together, but he had made her see them. The piteous sight of such a massacre of innocents had branded itself on her memory and the wails of the parents were still loud in her mind's ear.

'Come back, darling, wherever you are,' Paul said touching her hand. 'We've come to Venice to forget all about violence and fear.'

'That's right, my dear,' Luigi said with an affectionate smile which displayed several gold teeth. 'I'm talking about the past. Venice has finished with bloodshed. That's one of the advantages of being a backwater.'

Luigi had been delighted when the Klines decided to end their honeymoon in Venice after spending most of it in Israel, and was determined to show them everything. He had deferred the Basilica, his prime love, until the early afternoon because it was then going to be closed to the ordinary public to allow final preparations for the festival. The Church was deeply involved in the occasion because the Four Horses were its property, and through Luigi's influence his guests could not only tour the unique building in comfort but would even have the honour of meeting the Cardinal Patriarch in his palace adjacent to the Basilica. All three were content to relax first over coffee after an exhausting tour of the Correr Gallery in the piazza.

'You know, it looks just like a stage-set,' Ruth observed, gazing at the fairy-tale façade of the Basilica with its glittering mosaics, gothic pinnacles and oriental domes.

15

'Every visitor says that,' Luigi acknowledged. 'It's fair comment. A lot of exciting dramas have been enacted here, but not since that monster, Bonaparte, made us into a museum. You can't expect dramas in a museum.'

Ruth had noted that Luigi, who claimed descent from the fifteenth-century Venetian painter who had become known as Carpaccio, had been visibly saddened as they had stood before the glass case containing the linen skull-cap of the last Doge— who had so ingloriously ended the Republic's thousand years of independence when terrified by Napoleon in 1797—though he had seen it many times. She had not met Luigi before but shared his feelings more intensely than her husband. Born in Jerusalem, she had spent most of her life surrounded, not by expressionless concrete, but by weathered stones saturated with tribal history.

The Festival of the Four Horses had been advertised for months in the tourist brochures, so the city was full in early June, a time not normally regarded as the height of the Venetian season; but the great crowd which had been moving slowly about the sunlit piazza, chatting, rubber-necking, clicking their cameras or sitting languidly at the cafés or on the steps, was beginning to thin as visitors disappeared into the restuarants and hotels. The itinerant vendors were packing up their wares—metal and plastic models of the Horses; T-shirts with the Horses emblazoned across the chest; and chalk-white carnival masks, copied from those which had offered such licence to both men and women during the final centuries of the Republic's decline and which were now giving great merriment to the children sporting them in the piazza.

'They're not much good for the tourist trade,' Ruth remarked, pointing to two groups of rather scruffy-looking people with bed-rolls, hold-alls and rucksacks who had settled round two of the splendid bronze bases for the three flagpoles in front of the Basilica. One thickset man with a black Zapata-style moustache and wearing jeans, a denim peaked cap pulled over his eyes, was handing round sandwiches to four companions. In the other group of three a flaxen-haired girl had produced a bottle and was pouring Chianti into plastic cups.

16

'No, I'm afraid we're getting a lot of day-trippers,' Luigi said. 'Most of them come on bus tours—from Germany, France, Yugoslavia, you name it. As you can hear, their behaviour leaves a lot to de desired.'

The blonde girl had a cassette player which was blaring out the current hit song 'The Four Horses', which had been commissioned for the Festival celebrations and had become an instant success with its galloping chorus:

Oh, welcome back Horses, brave emblems of Pride,
Reminders of conquests and boundaries wide,
Unbitted, unbridled, stampeding through time,
Have you in our story seen reason or rhyme?

'I'm sick of that song already,' Luigi remarked.

'It's a catchy tune, though,' said Ruth, swaying her suntanned shoulders sensuously to the rhythm, a movement which caught the eye of a young Italian. His lecherous look was not lost on Paul, who responded with an angry stare.

'But why does it always have to be so loud?' Luigi asked, cupping his hands to his ears. 'It's supposed to be one of the virtues of living here that you don't have to shout to make yourself heard in the street. Some of these vistors think they own the place.'

'What nationality would you say they are?' Paul asked.

'The group with the fair-haired girl are German. They were in the gallery with us and I heard them talking. As for the man in the peaked cap—he could be Spanish, Mexican, Algerian, anything. All nations meet in this piazza. They always have. Originally they came to trade. Now they come to relax and enjoy themselves and thank God they do. It's only through tourism we can keep this whole museum going.'

He indicated the splendours of the piazza and the innumerable glories beyond with a graceful movement of both arms, then as one of the bronze figures on the clock-tower behind him hammered one stroke on the bell, he looked towards the Basilica.

'Ah, I see the doors closing,' he said. 'Come on, let's go.'

While Luigi settled the bill, Paul knocked out his pipe and gazed at his wife admiringly. Tall, honey-blonde, she had the

17

right figure for her well-cut cream slacks and caramel-coloured shirt, which were set off by his wedding-gift, a heavy gold medallion hanging from a neck-chain. Ruth smilingly registered the affection which her nature had always craved, but which in recent years had been restricted by her father because of his preoccupation with war or politics.

She knew that her choice of a husband belied the belief that women tend to marry their fathers. The dominant figure to date in her life had been a dynamic cutter and thruster, an eye-for-an-eye man with such need to see each day fulfilled by meaningful action that to many he was a hard-line fanatic. Yigael, with the lean face, burning eyes and impelling energy, had been in a similar mould.

Her new man, who appealed to the less physical side of her nature, was quiet and gentle, ready to turn the other cheek, a soft touch to the impecunious, content to live much of his time vicariously through books or as a spectator, but she knew that, while his fortune could command all material requirements, he had need of her. He would surrender himself completely to her while Yigael would never have surrendered to anybody. There was also much to commend a mate who was more predictable, less impulsive and less moody than Yigael and who could make her laugh. Sure, Paul would never be a ball of fire in business but with a realist like herself to push him, big changes were possible, even in his lukewarm attitude to the Jewish homeland.

A rather skinny black and white cat jumped on to the seat vacated by Paul and he bent down to stroke it.

'You know what they say about Venice's cats?' Luigi remarked. 'They are like the Venetian people—amiable but sceptical, detached and selfish and not prepared to take anything seriously except love.'

'I've heard worse testimonials,' Paul said with a laugh which creased his strong features in such a way that, fleetingly, they disclosed his Semitic origin.

As they ambled slowly towards a back door of the Basilica, Luigi pointed to the two huge granite columns in the piazzetta, the smaller square leading past the Doge's Palace to the waterfront.

'That column on the left with the lion on top is the Column of St Mark. The one on the right with the statue is the Column of St Theodore. He used to be our patron saint, until we relegated him after a couple of our traders stole the remains of St Mark from Alexandria and smuggled them here in a crate labelled "Pork". You must never walk between those two columns. It's unlucky.'

'Why?' Ruth asked.

'Because so many criminals have been executed there—burnt or buried alive head down for endangering the State or its treasures. No self-respecting Venetian will pass between them.'

'But you don't really believe in it?' Paul asked naively.

'Of course I do,' Luigi smiled, raising his arms in protestation.

Ruth was sure he was joking until she noticed that on his left wrist he was wearing a copper bracelet—a charm to protect himself from rheumatism.

They passed out of the piazza round the north side of the Basilica, where a small boy trailing a red balloon and wearing a carnival mask was sitting astride a marble lion. He was being watched by his parents, who were neatly and nicely dressed for working people, in contrast to so many of the tourists.

'I did that when I was a boy,' Luigi said. 'So did my father and his father. The marble has been polished by millions of Venetian backsides.'

'Alessandro,' the woman called musically to the child, who obeyed reluctantly. The father, an off-duty member of the carabinieri—the para-military police based nearby in the Campo San Zaccaria just off the waterfront—hoisted the boy on his shoulders, helped by his wife, Sofia.

'What a relief to be shot of the tourists for a bit,' Sofia exclaimed with some bitterness.

'Yes, everything is for the tourists and nothing for the people who live here,' the husband, Filippo, replied, almost shouting so that the American couple must hear.

Luigi eyed them with his inveterate curiosity. Filippo had the prominent Venetian nose, as he had himself, but was rather dark and olive-skinned, while Sofia was also dark with heavily-lidded eyes and high cheek-bones. He could tell by the way they spoke the dialect that they were Venetian-born but they could also have had distant Greek or Byzantine blood.

'I'm afraid there's a lot in what they say,' Luigi explained. 'We are losing our people to the mainland because there are just not enough homes and jobs here. The tourists are partly to blame but these poor people's expectations have been raised too high by politicians touting for votes.'

'It's the same in the States,' said Paul.

The family disappeared towards the smelly *calle* behind the Campo San Zaccaria, where Sofia's mother lived. Venice might be called the City of Light but the two dank, ground-floor rooms she occupied never saw sunshine. And because the tourists pushed prices so high, the only way she could feed herself was by being in the Rialto Market at five o'clock most mornings when the previous day's produce was offered at cut rates. Her daughter and son-in-law could not help her much. The carabinieri were so poorly paid that Sofia had a part-time job in a supermarket.

★   ★   ★

Proceeding slowly, to help his guests absorb the unique atmosphere of the Basilica with the cool gloom of its recesses and its mosaics sparkling in mote-laden shafts of sunlight, Luigi led them towards the chancel with so many entertaining anecdotes that Ruth was in wonder at such learning so negligently worn.

'Now you understand, sweetheart, why the first Italian I ever learned from Luigi was that quotation from Dante, which is on my father's desk in his office,' Paul said. '*Nella mia mente potei far tesoro*—Of my mind make Thou a treasure-house.'

'If I remember rightly there's another quotation on your father's desk—in Hebrew,' said Luigi who, having secured some really choice Italian works for Sam Kline, had made several visits to the Kline mansion in New York.

'Yes indeed. "If I forget thee, O Jerusalem, let my right hand forget its cunning." That has been an even greater influence on his life.'

'And quite right too,' Ruth commented, catching hold of Paul's fingers, for she liked to touch and be touched.

A devout Catholic, Luigi genuflected as they paused in front of the marble rood-screen, which was surmounted by a magnificent crucifix flanked by sculptures of the Virgin and apostles.

'Those statues date from 1394. They were . . .'

He stopped as he became aware of someone moving in the nearby St Peter's Chapel and recognized the short, shadowy figure as the man in the denim forage-cap, which he was still wearing.

'That man shouldn't be in here,' he whispered to Paul. 'Nor should he be wearing his hat in the House of God. I must go and tell him . . .'

'Scusi . . .' he began.

'Excuse nothing,' the man rapped in English, producing a pistol from inside his jacket. 'Put up your hands.'

Believing he was about to be robbed, or had disturbed an art thief, Luigi, who had learned respect for guns by using them, obeyed.

Paul and Ruth were too unsure of what was happening to respond, and before they could understand, two of the man's comrades appeared behind them with machine-pistols.

'Sit on the floor, all of you,' the man with the cap commanded. 'Then, perhaps, you may not get hurt.'

'What's this all about?' Paul asked as he sat on the chill marble floor which had been crazed by repeated flooding. 'If it's money you're after we don't carry much—only credit cards . . .'

'We want no money from you, Mr Kline, at least not directly.'

'How do you know my name?' Paul asked.

'Because we have made it our business to. We know all about you.'

Ruth, who had been studying the faces of the three men was certain that two of them who had dark complexions, long black hair and thick eyebrows were Arabs but, though their leader was sallow-skinned with a Semitic looking nose, he seemed European, possibly Spanish from his slight trace of

21

accent. His round face with heavy jowls, thick lips and large ears flat against the skull was vaguely familiar. Spanish! He could be South American! Could he be . . . ? The possibility chilled her.

'If you are thinking of holding me to ransom, why don't you let my wife go?' Paul said. 'Her folks haven't any money.'

The man with the cap smiled and his lips behind the thick moustache seemed thicker than ever. 'Maybe it's not just money we want, Mr Kline. Until three weeks ago your wife was Ruth Yacob, wasn't she? We have several scores to settle with her father and his murderous gang. "No quarter!" he advocates, doesn't he? "Two eyes for one eye!" '

Ruth now had no doubt about it. 'You are Santos, aren't you?' she asked with trepidation.

'It's as good a name as any other,' the terrorist replied almost casually.

Paul knew enough about 'Santos' to appreciate the extremity of their predicament. 'Santos' was an alias of a South American who espoused the Palestinian cause and was probably the most daring and wanted terrorist in the world. A guerrilla hero to those supporting him, to most people he was a fanatical assassin who seemed to enjoy killing.

'The rest of you must be Palestinian terrorists then,' Paul blurted out, recalling that there had been five of them.

'We are freedom fighters for the liberation of a country you Jews have seized by fraud and held by force,' Santos replied almost haughtily. 'Ask Professor Scarpaccia. He knows about freedom fighters, don't you Professor?'

Luigi scowled. This man seemed to know everything about all of them. During World War II the connoisseur, who looked so gentle, had been a remorseless partisan fighter against the Nazi occupation forces after the Allied armistice with Italy, but always declined to speak about his searing experiences.

'What do you propose to do with us?' he asked quietly.

'I want you to come with me, Professor,' Santos answered harshly. 'On your feet! The others stay here.'

Luigi stood up, flicked the dust from his immaculate suit, smoothed back his hair and was directed at gunpoint up the

22

steep steps leading from the portico to the Loggia dei Cavalli. He was horrified to see what was happening there. Two other Arab terrorists were wiring up sticks of gelignite, arranging them like garlands round the Horses' necks and girths and linking them through a long coil of wire to a plunger-exploder. No mean hand at setting demolition charges in his day, he could see that the men were highly professional.

'Why are you doing all this?' he asked.

Santos smiled. 'This is going to be our headquarters. Your friends will be brought here and tied to these pillars.'

He indicated the supports on which the Horses were mounted. 'Unless we get our demands in full, they will be blown to bits.'

'God Almighty!' Luigi exclaimed, knowing that with the Basilica so regularly undermined by flooding, the entire structure could be made unsafe by such a blast. 'What are your demands?'

'All in good time, Professor. Right now we'll go down again. I think you'll find we have another hostage.'

As they re-entered the nave Luigi could see two more men sitting on the floor, one slight, the other ponderous, while the two terrorist guards had been swollen to five.

He was appalled to recognize the large figure in a black cassock with scarlet piping, buttons and sash topped by a round, black velvet hat as Cardinal Talamini, the Patriarch of Venice. The thin man was his Jesuit chaplain. He also recognized the additional terrorists as the three Germans from the Correr Gallery and the piazza. Ruth was sitting cross-legged slightly apart from the others and the flaxen-haired girl was standing over her, a gun in one hand and her captive's medallion dangling from the other. She had removed it as a possible weapon, as Paul had also been relieved of the penknife he used for scraping out his pipe. It was only after some argument that the German girl, who sounded the most vicious of them all, agreed that the Cardinal should not be relieved of his pectoral cross.

Luigi bowed deferentially to Talamini, an old friend, beloved of most Venetians, even the anti-clerical Communists. A portly extrovert whose origins were humble— he

23

was a fisherman's son—he cared greatly for the poor of the city, did what he could for them and made them laugh. The three Germans had surprised him while he had been discussing the details of a *Te Deum Laudamus* Mass, which was to be sung in the Basilica to celebrate the return of the Horses.

The Jesuit, thin to the point of emaciation and with the protuberant eyes of a hyperthyroid, continued to argue with his captors in spite of their gun-waving until quietly silenced by the more realistic Cardinal.

Santos turned to Luigi. 'Now here is what you must do, Professor. Go to the police and any other authorities who need to be told and inform them that Cardinal Talamini, Mr Kline and Ruth Yacob, as I prefer to call her, will be held hostage until all our demands are met. Our first demand is that television services must be allowed into the square immediately but no nearer than fifty metres from the front of the Basilica. That's about level with the Campanile according to the way I paced it out. I will announce our main demands later this afternoon. I want you to be our go-between, Professor. I know you have the courage and you also know the penalty for a double-cross.'

As Santos pointed his gun at the back of the Cardinal's neck Luigi bit his lip, recalling a situation which the terrorist seemed to know when he had been obliged to order the execution of a fellow partisan caught spying for the Nazis.

'And take this garrulous priest with you,' Santos commanded. 'We can do without him.'

'I prefer to remain with his Eminence,' the Jesuit, whose face was wrinkled like a walnut, said quietly.

'No, Father, you must go,' the Cardinal insisted. 'I order you to.'

'But your Eminence . . .'

'Go with Professor Scarpaccia. You can't do any good here. Go and pray for us. For all of us.'

Luigi looked at the three remaining captives with a shrug of helplessness. 'Just do what they tell you,' he advised them. 'Somehow we'll get you released.'

'Somehow?' Santos queried. 'There is only one way to accomplish that, Professor—fulfilment of *all* our demands. Tell the police that if there is any attempt to attack us we all go

24

up in smoke. You must know from your own experience that we are prepared to sacrifice our own lives if necessary.'

As Luigi and the cleric hurried out of the nave, the terrorists and their hostages climbed the stairs to the Loggia dei Cavalli. It was a strenuous haul for the Cardinal, who had no option but to ignore the prodding of the gun at his back and pause for breath after each few steps, but he looked the least perturbed of them all when he sat down alongside Ruth and Paul below the Horses. He laid down his hat and mopped his brow.

'Don't be afraid, my children,' he assured them. 'The blessed St Mark is watching over us.'

He pointed towards the statue of the patron saint high above them. 'He has seen Venice and her people through far worse situations than this. And you have every reason to trust in him,' he added, hoping to induce a smile. 'After all, he was Jewish, you know. Why, in this city we even have Saint Moses!'

*   *   *

While the Chaplain disappeared to a private chapel to pray, Luigi used his office to telephone the Chief of Police, Guido Fanti, at his headquarters, the Questura, which was close by on the Fondamenta San Lorenzo. Fanti, a slim, dark man with piercing eyes and a thin moustache, could not believe what he heard until he called Luigi back to eliminate the possibility of a hoax.

'Stay where you are, Professor. I'll be with you as soon as I've made a few dispositions.'

Before leaving by fast patrol boat, always at the ready on the canal outside, he alerted his Squadra Mobile, the armed emergency group which, as in most cities, had been trained in anti-terrorist operations. He also alerted the chief of the carabinieri and the local detachment of the Bersaglieri, the crack, feather-hatted troops detailed to strike the flags in front of the Basilica. They were ordered to seal off the piazza and mount marksmen as surreptitiously as possible in the towering Campanile, in the clock-tower and within the Basilica itself but with strict instructions not to fire until further order, even if fired on themselves. The Police Chief also informed the

25

Mayor, the American Consul and, through a deputy, the Israeli Embassy in Rome.

Among those of the carabinieri suddenly recalled to duty was Filippo, who was just sitting down to the lasagne cooked by Sofia's mother when a colleague, smart in his khaki uniform and peaked cap, called to give him the astonishing news. Sofia was terrified, but as Filippo gulped down the oven-hot meal with the help of some cheap wine they had brought he was excited at the prospect of witnessing some action, if perhaps not taking part in it. The news had spread through the *calles*, and Filippo and his comrade had to force their way through a vociferous crowd of neighbours demanding information.

Disembarking on the Fondamenta de la Canonica behind the Basilica, Fanti was quickly in the piazza arcade and satisfied himself, with a quick look through binoculars from behind one of the square pillars, that terrorists were indeed occupying the Loggia dei Cavalli. He could see the man he had been told was Santos holding an automatic pistol.

'It looks like a Czech high-velocity job—that fits Santos,' he dictated to his assistant, who was taking notes behind the pillar. He had a clear view of the Cardinal, for whom a chair had been found in the Basilica, and what he could see of the terrorist leader's profile as he bent over to speak to Talamini was certainly not unlike the photographs he had been shown. The age group was right too. He seemed to be in his thirties.

Luigi filled him in with further details and Fanti decided that, futile though it was likely to be, he would have to go through the motions of urging the terrorists to surrender. For public relations' sake this would be better attempted outside the Basilica than inside. Sidling as near to the main door as he dared, he addressed the terrorists above through a loud-hailer, so that at least some of the public within earshot, apart from policemen and soldiers, could hear him.

'This is Guido Fanti, Chief of Police,' he shouted in heavily accented English. 'In your own interests I order you to surrender immediately.'

The command was received with raucous laughter.

'You have nothing to be laughing about,' Fanti continued.

26

'Your position is hopeless. You are being surrounded by marksmen. All possible ways of escape are being blocked. Surrender now before you get yourselves into deeper trouble.'

Seizing Ruth roughly and pushing her in front of him as a shield, Santos leaned over the balcony to shout, 'Do you think we would be here if we were worried about "trouble"? We are prepared to sacrifice our lives if necessary. Furthermore we are prepared to sacrifice the lives of our hostages—one by one unless our demands are met. You have our first demand—full television coverage. Get on with it.'

'Why do you want that?' Fanti asked.

'We want the world to see all that is going to happen. We give you two hours to get television crews here—until four p.m. by that clock.'

He pointed to the ornate clock-tower on his right. 'I guarantee the crews complete safety but to make sure that all the action is being relayed, I want a portable set provided for our use here in this alcove. I also want a loud hailer. I'm going to have a lot of talking to do. We have a rope to haul them up, so have them here within two hours. That is the deadline for issuing our further demands. Any delay and the world will hold you responsible for anything that happens to the Cardinal and the Klines.'

'Understood,' Fanti replied. 'But won't you consider releasing his Eminence, the Cardinal? You have no quarrel with him and he is old and not well. Holding him will only alienate public opinion.'

'We don't see it that way,' Santos replied curtly. 'We will consider the Cardinal's release when you have considered our demands.'

It was the response Fanti had expected. Talamini was in line to be the next Pope. Next to His Holiness himself, the terrorists could hardly have grabbed an Italian personage less expendable or more guaranteed to invoke international pressure for his release.

Back in the Chaplain's office Fanti telephoned the local television headquarters, where cameramen were already assembling in the hope of coverage after hearing the news flashes.

'It's obviously a move to get maximum publicity for the Palestinian cause,' Fanti explained. 'It's a complication. But we'll have to comply with it.'

As events would quickly show, there was much more behind the television requirement than just that.

★   ★   ★

'This could be a lengthy business,' Fanti said to Luigi as they left the Basilica together by a side door. 'We must have an operations room with first-class communications close by. We'll have to commandeer the Hotel Danieli. They won't like it but it's in the danger area and should be evacuated anyway. I'm afraid you'll have to stay on hand there, Professor. From what you say, Santos seems to trust you and we may need your help in raising the ransom money. That's what I imagine they are going to demand.'

'There shouldn't be much difficulty about that,' Luigi said; thoughtlessly, as it transpired. 'Paul Kline's father is immensely rich. If I know him he'll pay anything to rescue his only son. I'm going to telephone him now, though I expect he's already heard the news. I certainly hope he has. I don't want to have to break it to him. He's an emotional chap. He'd have been upset if it had only been the Horses that were in danger.'

The combination of Santos, the Cardinal, the Klines, the Four Horses and the demand for television coverage was beginning to convince Fanti that what he was facing was the 'Big Show' which police chiefs everywhere had been dreading: the Palestinians' spectacular revenge for the humiliation at Entebbe, the abortive hijack at the Uganda airport when Israeli commandos in a brilliant airborne operation had killed the terrorists and rescued the Jewish hostages. German terrorists, including a girl, had been shot to death there and it could be significant that the team now in the Loggia included Germans, one of them a girl.

Though well briefed from Rome on this possibility, Fanti had never anticipated that Venice, the acme of tranquillity,

28

would ever be involved. But on reflection he realized that it was just the kind of soft target the Palestinians preferred.

The situation would have to be resolved quickly and without shooting. That was the standing instruction from Rome and was particularly relevant to a city so dependent on tourism. He was determined to accomplish it without outside assistance if he possibly could. What was needed, he told himself, was firm action with the minimum of domestic disturbance. He must avoid overreacting, as the authorities had at Naples during the typhoid scare there when they had destroyed the mussel beds, depriving hundreds of their livelihood with the inevitable violent response.

'How do you think the girl will stand up to it?' he asked Luigi. 'Her husband looks tough enough but the girl . . . I hope she doesn't get hysterical.'

'She'll be all right if I'm any judge.'

It had been Luigi's experience in the partisan struggle that most women disciplined by military training, as Ruth had been, faced violent death more calmly than men. And the warmer they were in their normal relationships, the more they seemed inclined to be ice-cold in an emergency.

*   *   *

Luigi managed to contact Sam Kline just before he set off for Kennedy Airport. His immediate reaction on being telephoned by the US State Department had been to get to Venice to parley with the terrorists directly, if possible.

'I feel terrible, Sam,' Luigi confessed. 'If I hadn't taken them into the Basilica . . .'

'Nonsense. It's not your fault. Those people would have grabbed them somewhere in Venice. That's what they came for. I've just had a call from Isaiah Yacob, Ruth's father. You can imagine how he feels. We're both in a hell of a spot if they start demanding money.'

'How's that?'

'Neither of us can be seen doing deals with terrorists. I've gone on record time and again saying that anybody who gives

29

in to terrorist blackmail only encourages more. Now I realize what it's like when your own are involved. Isaiah's in an even worse situation. You know how hawkish he is. Politically it could be disastrous for him if he gets involved in any deals with an election on the way. He's only recently managed to get into the coalition government. But we've got to save our children somehow, Luigi. What are we to do?'

'I wouldn't encourage your Israeli friends to try any of their fancy rescues, Sam. What I saw of these guerrillas they look very professional and determined. Any shoot-up like Entebbe and I wouldn't give much for the lives of the hostages.'

'That's how I feel, Luigi, and Isaiah agrees with me. I hear the Israeli Cabinet is going to meet as soon as the terrorists issue their demands.'

'What time are you due in Venice?' Luigi asked.

'Just before eight p.m. your time. If I get my connection.'

'O.K. I'll be there to meet you with the latest news. God bless you and safe journey!'

As Kline was whisked to the airport past Brooklyn, where he had been raised by severely orthodox parents, he shook his head in disbelief. That this should happen to Paul of all people! Paul, who had argued with him so vehemently that countering violence with violence only engenders more! Paul, who was convinced that the Israelis' extraordinary run of military successes had corrupted their judgment, and whose reaction to the Entebbe rescue had not been proud elation in being Jewish but sadness for the innocent Ugandan soldiers who had died, and fear for future consequences.

He wondered what his son was thinking now, especially if the terrorists turned out to be thugs who had been bought off by spineless governments before. Perhaps he would understand, at last, why savage things had to be done to preserve the land which Sam devoutly believed, in mind as well as heart, had been promised to his people by God in person.

30

Chapter Two

Guido Fanti moved with speed and efficiency in commandeering the Danieli Hotel, formerly a palazzo of the distinguished Dandolo family, as his headquarters for dealing with the terrorist situation, which he was calling Operation Equi. The hotel offered not only the best communications in the area through its switchboard but access to food and drink if Fanti, his staff and the others involved had to spend the night there as they anticipated. By speedboat it was but a few seconds to the back of the Basilica via the canal under the Bridge of Sighs, and it was near enough to the piazza for cables to be run there for closed-circuit television from cameras already mounted on the Campanile, which was once again fulfilling its ancient function as a watchtower. This would enable the Police Chief to monitor the proceedings in the comfort to which he was notoriously accustomed. Had Santos not demanded television coverage Fanti would have installed it, illuminating the Loggia at night with searchlights and infra-red equipment. And he would even have offered the terrorists a monitor set. The more they knew what was going on the less they were likely to behave irrationally or with desperation.

The distracted manager of the Danieli had done all he could to point out that the hotel was out of blast and firearms range but Fanti invoked all his powers, demanding that the guests and staff be moved to other accommodation, mainly on the Lido, except for a few servants who would be required to look after the hotel's new temporary guests.

Well before the four p.m. deadline all was ready and the sandbagging of the windows of threatened buildings like the Marciana Library, with its priceless manuscripts and books, was under way. It was not just the front of the Basilica that was menaced by the tons of shrapnel the disintegrating Horses might produce.

31

Keen to secure his share of the publicity, which was clearly going to be world-wide, with Eurovision links and satellite transmission in which scores of countries were already showing interest, Fanti called a press conference in the operations room.

'I think we can be sure that this is an effort by some branch of the Popular Front for the Liberation of Palestine. Eight is the usual number of a PFLP cell and the presence of Germans is typical. While I cannot be sure that the leader is Santos he certainly could be. The short, compact build is right. The trouble is that nobody is really sure what Santos looks like. Some of the published photographs are definitely of other men. His girl friends give conflicting descriptions. So do his former hostages. "Santos" could of course be the *nom de guerre* of more than one man. I should be able to give you a more definite opinion after he has made his demands.'

After posing sternly for photographs, which he hoped would offset some of those occasions when he was snapped with people of dubious reputation, Fanti, with Luigi the designated go-between, moved to the piazza to join another small group including the Mayor, Piero Pizza, a prominent Communist equally determined to be in the picture.

Pizza and Fanti, who disliked each other, made a constrasting couple, the Police Chief slim, dynamic and meticulously smart, the Mayor, who was also in his early fifties, as trapped in his own fat as Venice was in her former glory. With as much weight padded behind his shoulders as in front of his stomach, Pizza seemed almost spherical. His large head, topped by half-grey curly hair was exaggerated by the small, narrow-brimmed, black trilby hat he wore almost as a trade-mark. His braces were so overstretched by his paunch that they hitched his trousers too high, displaying his fancy socks as the small group walked down the centre of the piazza towards the parley point in front of the Loggia.

Luigi waved encouragingly to Paul and Ruth, but could not tell if they had seen him as all three hostages were being kept out of camera-shot while Santos held the stage.

As the clock-tower bell rang out the hour of four, Santos placed a piece of paper on the parapet, using a pistol as a paperweight, then raising the loud-hailer Fanti had provided along with the television set, he began to read:

'I speak to you on behalf of the Arm of the Arab Revolution. These are our demands and they must be met in full by this time tomorrow:

'First, we demand a million American dollars. This is not for our personal use but for the liberation of Palestine from the Zionist tyranny. The money will be delivered in used, repeat used, hundred-dollar and fifty-dollar notes in 10,000-dollar bundles packed in two suitcases.

'Second, we demand the release of the following freedom-fighters held by the Zionist aggressors in their concentration camps.'

Fanti's assistant took down the names though the whole statement was being recorded in the operations room. The list included Kozo Okamoto, the Japanese 'Red Army' student sentenced to life imprisonment for a murderous machine-gun attack on civilians at Israel's Ben-Gurion Airport in 1972; Archbishop Demetrios Tabbucci, the former head of the Greek Catholic Church in Jerusalem, serving twelve years for assisting Palestinian terrorists by smuggling in explosives and weapons; a German; and seven Palestinian Arabs. At the mention of the Archbishop, Luigi realized that the Cardinal's position was particularly intriguing. One high priest was to be exchanged for another.

'All these men are to be delivered here in this square into our safe custody,' Santos continued.

'Third, we demand that the money be handed over in person by Samuel J. Kline, father of our hostage, Paul Kline, and the released prisoners be delivered to us personally by Isaiah Yacob, the notorious Arab-baiter and father of our hostage, Ruth Kline.'

Fanti looked at Luigi and they appreciated more fully why Santos had insisted on television coverage. The world was to witness the extreme humiliation of two prominent Jews who had been among the loudest in advocating no deals with terrorists. Santos was determined to make them grovel before an audience of millions, and being seen to be the man who had made them do it would be supreme personal gratification.

33

Vanity was a key feature of his recorded character. Yes, this was the Big Show all right, perhaps the arch-terrorist's last, considering how he was so unconcerned about being seen.

'Fourth, we demand that the freedom-fighters be brought here from Venice Airport in an Italian helicopter big enough to take us all, including our hostages, back to the airport. There an Italian airliner must be waiting to take us to Dar El Beida Airport in Algiers. The Italian Goverment must make arrangements with the Algerian Government to receive us, and in return the hostages will be freed and can be brought back to Venice in the same Italian airliner.'

Fanti had little doubt that Santos or the men who manipulated him had already made their dispositions with Algeria. Dar El Beida Airport had been used by Arab kidnappers before, and always they were allowed to go free.

'We have a fifth and final demand,' Santos continued. 'To show that we mean no harm to the people of Venice and to compensate them for the inconvenience, we also demand a written guarantee from the mayor that an extra thousand million lire will be made available in the coming year to improve the housing of the poor of this city, many of whom are living in squalor in homes endangered by water and decay while tourists wallow in comfort.'

Pizza's lower lip pouted at this jibe at his Council, but Fanti rather savoured the spectacle of one Marxist-Leninist poking public censure at another, for the terrorist's dossier showed he had been trained in Moscow.

'Millions are being spent on monuments like these Horses and on palaces and hotels to please tourists, while so many homes are rotting that thousands of workers are having to leave the city where they were born,' Santos cried, warming to his unique opportunity for a party-line tirade. 'Is Venice for the families who live here or for the foreigners who drop in for a few days? Venice must be liberated from the shackles of the foreign invader!'

'Oh God, another liberator!' Luigi murmured as the terrorist paused to let his goodwill message to the Venetian people sink home.

'All our demands must be met by four p.m. tomorrow,' Santos concluded. 'There will be no negotiation for any extension of deadlines. All our demands can easily be met within twenty-four hours.'

He gave a clenched-fist salute and cried, 'Long live the Arm of the Arab Revolution!' to which his colleagues responded with a similar defiant gesture.

Santos watched suspiciously as a policeman carrying a sheaf of telegrams and other messages ran across the piazza to his chief. Fanti read the top message, which was addressed to the guerrillas from the Pope, urging them to release the Cardinal on the grounds of his age. He passed it to Luigi while he skimmed through the rest, which were mainly from people willing to offer themselves in exchange for Talamini. Through his loud-hailer he relayed the Pope's message and the replacement offer, but Santos was unyielding.

'I have just said there will be no negotiations. We will not release the Cardinal until the Zionists release Archbishop Tabbucci. You are wasting valuable time.'

It was no more than Fanti had expected, but he had to be seen to be doing all he could with so many millions watching.

'I suppose that *is* Santos,' he said with a note of doubt as they walked towards the north side of the Basilica. 'His English sounds so good he could be anything—even another Arab, a Lebanese, perhaps. Anyway we'll soon know. A French Secret Serviceman who has seen him at previous incidents is on the way here from Paris.'

'Do you think his demands can be met, Questore?'

'That depends on the Israelis. They obliged us once before, in 1968 I think, by releasing some of their terrorist prisoners as a goodwill gesture after we had resolved a hijack for them. But they weren't the men the hijackers had demanded and they certainly weren't notorious characters like Okamoto and Tabbucci.'

'On the other hand, they've never been faced with a situation quite like this before,' Luigi countered hopefully.

To his mind, if the Four Horses and the front of the Basilica were demolished with the world watching, simply because the Israelis refused to release ten prisoners, the artistic

35

loss would be a permanent reminder of unforgivable intransigence.

*   *   *

While Luigi was being driven back to his flat in a police speedboat to collect an overnight bag, he had never felt so fearful and depressed since the bleakest days of the war, when the Germans, retreating northwards out of Italy, were not only killing his countrymen but demolishing Renaissance bridges and other irreplaceable monuments. Fanatics—and the hordes they could always rouse to do their destructive bidding—had been the curse of civilization down the ages.

The thought of the Four Horses, the very symbols of liberty with their air of dynamic freedom, now shackled with explosives, sickened him. That such mean, despoiling hands should even touch such treasures . . . He would never have confessed it, save to himself, but he was more concerned about the fate of the Four Horses and the Basilica than about the hostages, fond of them as he was.

Whether this was the consequence of his own childlessness or an intellectual conviction that the sanctity of human life was an unrealistic concept in an overcrowded world, he had never stopped to consider, but had he been asked which would be the greater disaster, an explosion destroying St Mark's or a bomb killing a hundred people, he could have answered without hesitation. His recompense for this wayward attitude, had his conscience troubled him, would have been that he genuinely rated his own life no higher, as his wartime record had proved.

Having done so much to save the Four Horses from death by corrosion from industrial fumes generated through money-grubbing greed, he thought it would be hideous if he was now to see them perish in a flash to fulfil the needs of such an insensitive and half-crazed creature as Santos. Yet human greed of some kind had dominated their existence, even their creation . . .

EPISODE 2

Creation in Corinth

'What force dominates all the love and the hate?
Which is it? The drive to destroy or create?'

Chapter Three

On that brilliant October morning in 336 BC, Corinth had never looked more entitled to its reputation of being the most beautiful city in Greece. Below the stupendous backdrop of the Acrocorinth, the sacred citadel so high on its rearing rock that it outrivalled the Acropolis of Athens, the terraced gardens, colonnaded walks, temples, stadium and busy marketplace basked in the sharp sunlight. The Gulf, with its blue waters, which had made the city the maritime and commercial centre of Greece and provided easy access to the lustful pleasures for which Corinth was notorious, was so calm that it seemed like a vast Alpine lake, with the distant peaks of Bœotia and Parnassus itself showing the first sprinkling of fresh snow through a bluish haze.

To the two horsemen trotting out from the city centre with a small bodyguard of cavalry at a discreet distance behind, life had never seemed more delightful nor more promising. The younger, who had just passed his twenty-first birthday and whose name was Alexander, was not only King of Macedon but two days previously had been hailed at the Gate of Corinth as 'Leader of the Greeks and Captain-General of the Hellenes'; this was in preparation for a venture which already in his extraordinary mind was to be nothing less than the conquest of the known world.

His comrade, Cleitus, who regarded himself as a foster-brother because his sister had nursed the King as a baby, was a member of the 'King's Companions'. These were the exclusive band of Macedonian noblemen, the 'bravest of the brave', who commanded crack cavalry units and were expected to be the first, save only for Alexander himself, to engage the enemy, ford the rivers and rush the breaches.

'My Lord, tell me more of this fellow we are going to see,' he said.

Alexander certainly merited the title. As he sat there—proudly mounted, strong, elegant, ardent; his fair skin clean-shaven; the straight, almost bridgeless nose that was to adorn so many coins; the fiery, full-lidded eyes, beneath pronounced brows that were topped by longish curls—he did indeed look like a god.

' "Fellow" is hardly the word for Lysippus of Chios,,' he replied. 'He is the greatest sculptor in bronze since Phidias, perhaps the greatest ever. Aristotle says he is among the few to represent men as they are, not as they ought to be. He taught himself by studying nature, and his statues are so lifelike that you could mistake them for living beings struck into immortal postures by the gods.'

Cleitus, who was older than Alexander, was not impressed. Unlike the king he had not been tutored by Aristotle, and to him sculptors were no more than artisans whose wares were to be paid for by the pound. Had not Socrates given up his original calling as a sculptor because it was 'low and ignoble', while in Plato's ideal republic wasn't the artist regarded as the basest order of citizen? Citizenship might be bestowed on exceptional artists but they were still no more than labourers. However, it was wiser not to argue with Alexander, even from his privileged position, a precaution which, had he always observed it, would have saved him from an early death at his master's hand.

'What is Lysippus making for you this time, my Lord? Another portrait?'

'No, Cleitus. I've portraits enough until there are more victories to celebrate. Who knows, I might commission him then to make one of you? This time he's making a four-horse Chariot of the Sun. It is Apollo who is being honoured, not I.'

'And is it to be left in Corinth?'

'Yes—and very fitting too. After all, it was here that the great god came riding in on a dolphin. In fact, I've commissioned a double tribute—to Apollo and to my father, who between them have made all things possible. Two tributes for the price of one!'

Cleitus smiled. Had he dared he would have asked, 'Why not make it three and include Olympias?' referring to the

40

young king's mother, who had almost certainly been responsible for the murder of her ex-husband, King Philip, with, it was widely believed, Alexander's blessing.

'Where will the chariot be sited?' he asked instead. 'By the Temple of Apollo?'

Alexander pulled up his horse as Cleitus looked towards the temple, with its fluted Doric columns standing on the terrace dominating the market-place. 'No, it's going in front of the South Stoa.'

He indicated the long, two-storey building, one of the largest in Greece, set up alongside the vast market-place to accommodate the delegates to the Congress of Corinth. The Congress had been organized by King Philip in the previous year, to consolidate his conquest of the Athenians by establishing a confederacy under Macedonian rule. Having decided to make Corinth his administrative centre for Greece, Alexander had come to summon the delegates again before setting out on the plundering conquests that would make him master of two million square miles.

'If I set the statue up by the Temple, only the worshippers who trouble to climb the steps will see it,' Alexander explained. 'Outside the Stoa it will be seen by everyone—to remind them that I can be back as quickly as Apollo drives across the sky if they don't behave themselves.'

'These people won't misbehave, my Lord,' Cleitus said scathingly. 'They've no stomach for a fight. They are just a city of shopkeepers.'

'And whore-mongers,' Alexander added in disgust, looking up at the Acrocorinth with its temple dedicated to Aphrodite, where more than a thousand carefully-selected prostitutes followed their calling. Alexander, who had privately committed himself to total domination of his own emotional compulsions, had been horrified to learn that Corinth owed much of its opulence to the notorious whore-house, which attracted rich merchants who sometimes parted with the profits of a year for one night's sexual pleasure. Indeed, the unremitting activity of these courtesans had made the city so rich, not only through their direct earnings but by the maritime trade their attraction generated, that the Corin-

41

thians could afford to pay mercenaries to defend their territory, a situation which to Alexander, who regarded war as man's most glorious activity, was contemptible. That these whores should be held in such honour that after the Greek naval victory at Salamis, which saved them from the Persians, it was to them that the Corinthians expressed their thanks, he found particularly offensive. He loved wine and song, but at that stage of his life he affected to despise women, particularly unchaste women, believing that they drew the sap from men.

'Each man has only so much drive, Cleitus,' he pronounced. 'And those unable to resist diverting it into carnal channels are useless for our great purpose. As Aristotle says, those intent on conquest must first conquer themselves. As for woman, any woman, her creative capacity lies exclusively below the belt.'

Cleitus smiled, but not simply at the aphorism, which he imagined must also derive direct from Aristotle or from one of the other philosophers or poets with whom King Philip had filled his court to rebut the Greek jibe that the Macedonians were barbarians. He knew that though Alexander regarded himself as descended from Achilles through his mother, Olympias, daughter of a half-barbaric king, he had never taken kindly to the knowledge that his father had met her during a wild orgy while both were being initiated in some mystic rites on the island of Samothrace.

Cleitus also suspected that through the weight of adulation already heaped upon him after his earlier victories, Alexander was more than a little in love with himself, and had once remarked when both were in wine: 'The overwhelming advantage of being in love with oneself is that it eliminates all risks of being cuckolded.' As for his passionate inclinations, Cleitus knew they were naturally channelled more towards men, especially fighting men.

Alexander expanded his chest and filled his lungs pleasurably. The cool air was heavy with the smell of horse, but that was so usual in all big towns that he would have noticed it only if it had been missing.

'We must get on,' he announced peremptorily, as his sandalled heels kicked his horse into a canter. Lysippus's workshop was still further out near the potters' quarter on the edge of the city, and the King was anxious to see how the massive sculpture was progressing. It was important to him not only as a tribute to Apollo, with whom in exultation in his looks and physique he half identified himself, and to whom he regularly offered sacrifice, but for political reasons. With precocious insight nurtured by the tutelage of Aristotle, he appreciated the value of impressive displays of permanent public art as an instrument of rule after conquest. There could be no mass leadership, still less worship, without charisma, and the fount of charisma was showmanship.

*　　*　　*

The choice of an equestrian group had not been left to the artist. Not only had four-in-hand racing been immensely popular for two hundred years, but the horse had long been established in Greece as the symbol of military power and aristocratic privilege, even Athena herself being also Athena Hippia; and Alexander, already a successful horseback general, was aware of the debt he would owe the animal in all the future victories of which he was so confident.

Lysippus was the sculptor he favoured above all others, ever since that talented Greek had portrayed the future king in bronze as a child, but he had to assure himself that the work was going well and on time. As he was to show again and again in his brief but glorious career, he had little confidence in the determination of others to carry out projects over which he did not exercise the closest personal control, and he was time-conscious in the extreme, as though aware that his years might not be long.

*　　*　　*

It had not needed the imminent arrival of the King to drum up an air of bustling activity in the foundry and school which Lysippus had established on the outskirts of Corinth. The bronzes of Lysippus, who was then in middle life, were in such demand throughout the country that he, his artisans and his

43

slaves were working in shifts. Already he was in trouble with other patrons, for holding back on their commissions to fulfil this latest command from Alexander for a Sun Chariot even more magnificent than the famous group he had made for the people of Rhodes. Those people had commissioned it as a votive offering to Apollo of Delphi, where it now stood resplendent on a pedestal. The subject might be the same, the glorious Sun God with four splendid stallions in hand about to drive his car across the heavens, but it could be no mere copy of the Delphi achievement. It had to be different and, if possible, better.

Three of the horses had already been completed. Each six feet high, they stood proudly in the sunshine with one hoof raised, glowing with the red-gold of freshly cast bronze containing an unusually high proportion of copper. The arched and inclined heads were extraordinarily expressive, the mouths half-opened, nostrils flaring, ears pricked, the eyes, with their comma-shaped pupils, vivaciously alert. The detailed precision of the hide, creased by the rippling muscles beneath, the short-trimmed manes, the surface veins and the calluses on the fetlocks were superbly reproduced, as the metal had forced its way into every crevice of the moulds as it solidified. While Lysippus had first achieved fame through his statues of the gods and humans, he was also celebrated for his interpretation of the horse.

The head of the fourth horse, and the collar which would mask the eventual joint with the torso and parts of the ornate two-wheeled chariot, were lying nearby awaiting the attention of the chisels, hammers, files and other finishing tools; but the centre of activity that day was a large shed, where the body of the last horse of the quadriga was almost ready for casting.

First, Lysippus had modelled the body in all its detail in clay, and when this had hardened he had taken a plaster mould in sections which could easily be removed from the clay and later fitted together to reconstitute the body. Each mould section had then been lined with a layer of wax as thick as the sculptor wanted the final bronze to be to ensure its rigidity and strength. Meanwhile, in a sloping casting-pit dug into the

44

earth floor of the shed, his assistants had built a cage of iron rods to provide support, and filled it with specially seasoned clay to make a core capable of withstanding the intense heat of the molten metal. Then, when vents and jets had been inserted to provide escape holes for air and steam, the mould sections had been assembled round the core and the whole packed round with clay.

A great heap of dry faggots had been piled over the entire structure and lit to melt out the wax, creating a space into which the bronze could run and to raise the clay to such a temperature that the molten metal would not solidify too rapidly. Near by, a relay of slaves was attending the furnace in which the pigs of bronze had been melting. As each horse would weigh two tons when completed, the size of the melt was formidable and the slaves, naked to the waist, the grimy sweatbands round their heads so saturated as to be useless, were weary with their continuous effort of piling on the logs and working the huge bellows. Their only respite until the casting was complete would be the flagons of salted water and food prepared and brought to them by the women slaves in the compound.

The look-out ran to warn Lysippus that his royal patron was at hand, and as Alexander clattered into the yard closely followed by Cleitus, the sculptor was quickly on one knee.

'Welcome, my Lord, to your servant's workshop.'

Alexander dismounted, rejecting the service of the slave who had been instructed by Lysippus to hold the horse, and summoned one of his bodyguard to take care of it. As the cavalryman slipped from his mount he handed the King a spear, which Alexander had adopted not only as a staff of office and personal weapon but for use in walking. As he stood there, he was the shortest man in the yard but his personal beauty and aura of restless energy commanded attention for what he was, not solely for who he was.

The slave, who was spindle-shanked and had an olive skin, straight black hair and dark eyes, stood by nervously, not knowing what to do. 'Get back to the fire, Philip,' his master called out roughly. 'Get back to the fire.'

'You are doing well, Lysippus,' Alexander remarked as he

45

strode over athletically to one of the completed horses and patted its withers. The finish looked so lifelike that the flank muscles could almost have shuddered to throw off the flies which had settled on it.

'I like this modern art. What do you think, Cleitus? Will Apollo approve?'

'You know what I think about horses, my Lord. It's not what they look like but how they ride. Look at Bucephalus. Hardly a beautiful beast!'

Alexander smiled. It was true enough. Bucephalus, the name he had given his black battle stallion, meant 'ox-head', which aptly described the somewhat bovine features of the oriental charger which was to carry him in action for twenty years and become the best-known warhorse in history.

'How is Bucephalus, my Lord?' Lysippus inquired.

'In splendid shape. I'll shortly be putting him to the test again. He didn't do badly last time.'

Alexander was referring to the cavalry charge he had led in the decisive battle when the Macedonian Grand Army, under his father, had broken the power of Thebes and of the Athenians.

'I must sculpt you one day astride Bucephalus, my Lord,' Lysippus suggested.

'That you shall do. But not until after we have defeated the Persians. I will do even better for Bucephalus if he carries me victoriously. If he dies in battle before I do I shall found a town to his memory.'

Lysippus smiled but said nothing. Alexander had already founded his first city, Alexandropolis, in his search for permanence and would found more to perpetuate his name, but to found a city for a horse! Surely this was but the unbridled extravagance of youth.

'I can see that the horses and the chariot are well advanced but what about the Apollo?' Alexander asked.

'Come this way, my Lord,' Lysippus said, indicating a small wooden shed. 'The men will not be ready to pour the bronze for some little time.'

After Alexander and Cleitus had entered the shed Lysippus carefully removed a white sheet from a full-scale clay model of the god, which immediately drew the King's approval.

'Excellent, Lysippus! Most excellent!'

Lysippus smiled and bowed.

'Cunning old bastard,' Cleitus thought. The features strongly resembled those of the King. There was even a suggestion of the 'Alexander look', the intense gaze with the slight turning of the head, a consciously adopted affectation already widely imitated.

'Do you see how true to nature this is, Cleitus?' Alexander said. 'Look how the left testicle hangs lower than the right. That's the usual thing in right-handed men.'

Lysippus nodded approvingly as the King inspected the god's genitals more closely.

'But there's one thing wrong,' Alexander observed. 'The testicle that hangs low is shown bigger than the higher one. Paradoxically, in real life it is the smaller testicle that hangs low.'

Lysippus said nothing but clearly doubted the assertion.

'I assure you it is true, Lysippus. Examine yourself some time and you'll find I am right. You too, Cleitus. It will convince you of the importance of first-hand inspection of all that we do, especially in our preparations for war. According to common sense the heavier testicle should hang lower, but it doesn't. You see, common sense is not always right.'

The sculptor was not prepared to argue with the King, who put his hand on his shoulder.

'Never mind, Lysippus, nobody is perfect. Not even the gods,' he added, pointing to the figure.

This was a consolation he frequently expressed to himself when disappointed with his self-control, particularly in respect of that private compulsion which, he suspected, sapped a man's strength even more than a woman.

'What about a stallion's testicles, my Lord?' Cleitus intruded. 'How do they hang? Can you tell us that?'

Alexander's eyes narrowed, expressing his irritation with the remark, but he said nothing.

'My Lord, that option is still open to you if you have changed your mind,' Lysippus interrupted, as he replaced the dust-sheet over the sculpture.

The King looked at Cleitus. 'He wants to put a figure of me

47

in the chariot instead of Apollo. What do you think of that?'

Cleitus thought he had almost done that already but replied half-jokingly, 'I think the old villain has another customer for an Apollo.'

'Not so, my Lord, I assure you,' Lysippus protested.

'Well, let us not risk offending the great god, Lysippus. He may even punish you for the thought. I must admit though, that had you suggested Achilles I might have been tempted to change.'

Achilles was Alexander's prime hero, preceding even Hercules, and the indifference to the enemies' weapons he displayed in battle suggested that he so identified himself with the mythological warrior that he regarded himself as virtually immune to injury.

As they left the shed, the foundry foreman approached deferentially to announce that the bronze melt was ready for pouring. Though the sculptor had supervised massive pours of metal many times before, it was always an anxious time, particularly in this case. His tin supplier had failed him and he was so short of the imported metal which, with a little lead, made copper into bronze, that the alloy would not flow anything like as easily as it should. Had it not been for the King's insistence on seeing the work before he left Corinth, he would have delayed the whole project until fresh tin supplies arrived. But the severe problems of casting bronze with only two parts of tin and lead to ninety-eight of copper, compared with the usual proportions of about eleven to eighty-nine, were preferable to the problems created by disappointing the impatient Alexander.

Lysippus led his visitors into the foundry, where they were hit by a wall of resinous heat radiating from the hard-baked clay and the wood ash, which had been scraped back from the top of the structure. Channels of baked clay had been built to conduct the molten metal from the bronze furnace to the runners—the cavities of the mould into which it would pour—and the moment for tapping the furnace had arrived. The foreman had calculated the weight of the melt so that there was certain to be enough to fill the mould and more. As he bored through the clay plug at the base of the furnace with a

48

long-handled augur held near the heat by Philip, the top slave, the fiery metal began to flow, illuminating the faces of Alexander and the rest in the half-darkness of the building.

They watched fascinated as the metal raced down the channels into the mould, while smoke and hot air hissed through the vents. A staccato shout from the foreman warned that he had detected a crack in the edge of one of the clay channels where the bronze, sluggish through lack of tin, was crusting. Within seconds, a small section of the rim collapsed and molten metal began to seep over the edge into the pit.

'Plug it, Philip, plug it,' the foreman bellowed to the slave, who was crouching by a mound of damp clay set there for such an emergency.

Seizing as much of the clay as he could in two hands, Philip crawled towards the hot channel on his belly and packed it hard against the rim. The overflow was stopped, but as the metal hit the wet clay steam was expelled with such force that it scalded his hands. The slave rolled away with a cry of pain and slipped over the edge of the pit into the glowing ashes.

While the others hesitated Alexander leapt to the edge and, shielding his face from the heat with his left arm, thrust down his spear for the slave to grasp. Then, bracing his legs, with their almost outsize calves, he pulled him out with one great heave.

Immediately the King began to strip off Philip's burning loincloth, assisted by one of the women who had rushed to help.

'Will he live, my Lord?' the woman, whose name was Sophie, asked anxiously as she comforted Philip.

The King took a closer look at the scorched and scalded areas of skin which were beginning to erupt in blisters.

'He should live if he wants to,' Alexander replied brusquely. 'Is he your man?'

'Yes, my Lord,' she answered tearfully. 'Thank you my Lord, for saving him.'

Philip, moaning in pain, was carried outside by fellow slaves to the shade of a cypress tree.

'My Lord, you should not have risked your life for a slave,' Cleitus remonstrated. 'He could have pulled you into the pit.'

'That is surely right, my Lord,' Lysippus agreed, though the fault had really been his for running short of tin. 'The man was extremely stupid to fall into the pit like that. He should have known better. I'm afraid the world is largely populated by dolts.'

'For which we should all be grateful to the gods,' Cleitus murmured.

Alexander knew he had acted impulsively but impulsiveness, seizing circumstances by the throat while others wavered or saw nothing, was life's sweetest gratification—and materially its most rewarding. Unless he showed contempt for all the dangers he knew he would face in the incredible enterprise he had set himself, and shared them with his men, it could never succeed. This had been his first opportunity of facing fire.

'Cleitus, if we are to succeed we must show disregard for danger but never for our men.'

'For *our* men, I agree, my Lord, but not for other people's and particularly not for their slaves. Slaves are cheap.'

Indeed they were. So cheap that in Corinth captured slaves had made the poorer workers redundant, so that they had to subsist on hand-outs provided from the money earned by the prostitutes. But this was irrelevant to Alexander's argument.

'At that crucial moment that slave was the right man in the right place at the right time,' he said decisively. 'He plugged the breach. He deserved consideration. Were you not of lowly origin yourself, Lysippus?'

'I was, my Lord,' the sculptor admitted, grudgingly. 'The casting goes well now . . .'

The accident had robbed the operation of all interest for the King. He walked out into the sunshine and over to where Philip was lying naked while Sophie swabbed his hands and loins with cool water. Kneeling by him he asked: 'Your name is Philip, is it not?'

'Yes, my Lord,' the slave whispered.

'The same as my father. And have you a son?'

'Yes, my Lord,' Sophie replied for him.

'And what is his name?'

'Alexander, my Lord.'

Cleitus, who had followed the King, laughed, while Lysippus was horrified by this familiarity with a slave. Alexander looked up at them. 'Don't begrudge your slaves their names, Lysippus. It's all they own. Give me what money you have about you.'

Lysippus opened his pouch and gave him four drachma coins, which Alexander pressed into Philip's hand. The slave's palms were so scorched that he dropped the silver coins in anguish. As Sophie snapped them up the King took a closer look at her. Above her high cheek-bones and heavily-lidded eyes her dark, straight hair was drawn forwards and loosely knotted over her brow. Her thin black dress, reaching only to her knees, clung to her skin, outlining an ample bosom and well-fleshed abdomen and thighs. She was perhaps in her late twenties but, like most slave women in Corinth, looked older than her years.

Sophie returned the King's gaze with intense curiosity. She had never seen anyone quite so handsome. His body, which was always liberally anointed with spice, smelled so sweetly that she felt he could be a god. With his locks falling into a natural, central parting he certainly looked different from any mortal she had seen.

'Give me more money, Lysippus,' Alexander commanded.

Looking at the King's outstretched palm Lysippus saw that it too was burned where it had beaten out the flames from Philip's clothing, but he was even more horrified at giving the slave more money. Four drachmas was two days' wages for a skilled workman! Like anything for nothing it would only be wasted—probably on wine!

'We must take care not to make them greedy, my Lord,' he protested. 'Give them expectations and there's no knowing where it might lead.'

'Everybody is greedy for something,' Alexander said as he handed the extra coins to Sophie, who had never held so much money at once.

'What are you greedy for, my Lord?' Cleitus ventured, as the King stood up and brushed the dust and ash from his tunic.

Alexander knitted his brows deprecatingly at this further familiarity. 'Not for baubles,' he responded, pointing to the bronze horses. 'I agree with Diogenes on that score.'

Cleitus knew that was true. Alexander almost disparaged the idea of private ownership, as he had attested during a brief discussion with the philosopher, who believed that a man was rich in the smallness of his needs and who, to show his contempt for private possessions, was living in a tub in a Corinth suburb. Territory was what he coveted, and once he had acquired it the next conquest and the fame of it were his motivations. A pathological competitor, cities were the target for his acquisitive instinct, and with conquest already engendering conquest his appetite was to prove so insatiable that legend would say he had tried to conquer Paradise by harnessing two hungry griffons to a chariot, with liver suspended over their heads on a spear as incentive to keep flying.

'You are certainly not greedy for women, my Lord,' Cleitus averred, looking rather longingly towards the Acrocorinth, which the King had refused to dignify even with a curiosity visit when his companion had suggested it. 'For what then?' Cleitus persisted.

Alexander looked at the sky with the demonic fervour that was to blaze in the eyes of so many men with the vision of world conquest when their creative fantasies had distended into destructive delusions, and which was to make people say he was thinking, 'You, Zeus, hold Olympus but the earth is under *my* rule.' But he was not prepared to admit his cupidity for personal glory, heroics and recognition—to be 'Ever the best and stand far above all others', as Homer had put it in one of the young King's favourite lines. It was an ambition which was to express itself in the unprecedented concept that the gulf between Greeks and 'barbarians' could be bridged by statesmanship, marrying East and West into one vast Hellenic civilization united by trade and culture. This was a concept which even Aristotle had dismissed as impossible but which his pupil was to achieve so thoroughly, ruthlessly using terror to stamp out revolts, that it was to last a thousand years.

'Come, Cleitus, we must go,' the King announced.

'A moment, my Lord, I have a gift for you,' Lysippus said, hurrying into the small building which served as his private office. He returned with a superb bronze statuette of Hercules in a sitting position and handed it to the King.

52

Alexander held it up and turned it round in the sunshine. He so admired the mighty hero who, through his deeds, had become a god, that he wore a similar lion head-dress in battle to advertise his invincibility both to his troops and to his enemies. 'It is magnificent, isn't it, Cleitus?'

Cleitus, who cared nothing for plastic art, though so well-versed in literature that too apt a jibe from Euripides was to launch the fatal shaft from Alexander's hand into his heart during a drunken row, replied, 'Indeed it is, my Lord.'

'It's just the right size for carrying on my campaigns, Lysippus. I'll use it as a table decoration to remind me of civilization while we are dealing with the barbarians.'

That and the inspiration it would offer, would be the image's sole purpose. The King expected no favours from any god. His bedrock belief was faith in himself.

He handed the statuette and his spear to the guard holding his mount. Then he leapt on to the stirrupless horse with the grace of a born equestrian, easing himself on to the embroidered blanket which was all that separated rider from hide, and glanced over at Philip and Sophie.

'Make sure you care for that man, Lysippus. We can succeed only through people, and those who injure themselves in our service merit our special consideration. Remember that, as I intend to.'

'I will, my Lord, I will,' Lysippus said unconvincingly. 'I will send a message as soon as the chariot group is complete.'

'No. Just set it up outside the South Stoa when it is ready,' the King commanded. 'I will inspect it then. If it pleases me I have another commission in mind for you.'

It was a promise the King would fulfil many times, as his seizure of Persian gold led to a surge of spending on art and buildings by the rich, though the poor still remained near destitution.

'How long will it be before the group is finished, Lysippus?' Cleitus asked. 'Will you have it finished before we go north?'

'That depends on how well the casting has gone. Provided we don't run into problems . . .'

'A sculptor can do little in one day, Cleitus,' the King

53

interrupted. 'Neither can the builder nor the writer. But the fighting man can change the world.'

Watching from the gateway as the riders cantered towards the city, Lysippus marvelled that a body as small as the King's could generate such force. But that, he had noted, was often true of little men. He smiled as he thought how Pythagoras, whose writings had taught him so much about numerical relationships, might have expressed the theorem—the intensity of the fire in the belly is inversely proportional to the length of the body?

Chapter Four

Though the touch of the reins was agonizing to his blistered fingers, Alexander gripped the leather tightly as he trotted out of the yard. In furtherance of his total dedication to self-control he was determined to make himself insensitive to pain.

In the specific enterprise of ignoring personal suffering he was to succeed. So much so that his conviction that like Achilles he was virtually immune to enemy bolts and sword-thrusts was almost to be justified, though more than once he would owe that immunity to the devotion of others, as when Cleitus would save his life at the Battle of the River Granicus.

*   *   *

Alexander and his retinue left Corinth to travel north to Delphi, in preparation for his invasion of Asia. He needed an auspicious pronouncement from the Oracle there, if only to assure his troops that the gods were on their side in the battle to liberate their enemies from barbarism.

'You are invincible,' the priestess announced, under some duress from the forceful Alexander. And so it proved to be—in battle. But the one failure in his bid for victory over himself—his inability to avoid long bouts of barbaric drunkenness when celebrating with his officers and friends—was to lead to the painless wound that would kill him in Babylon at the age of only thirty-two. In June 323 BC, while considering his last campaign to bring the whole known world under his control, he was to die of fever transmitted by the bite of some noxious insect from the Euphrates swamps which he had been too drunk to swat.

*   *   *

Lysippus allowed two full days for the body of the last stallion to cool, before uncovering it bit by bit to see how the metal had taken to the mould. In shape it was near-perfect from the top knot, where there was a fitting for an ornament or plume, to the arched, trimmed tail and unshod hooves. There were numerous blow-holes and blemishes caused through the lack of tin but these would be rectified by patient filing and filling-in, an art in which the slave, Philip, had been specially trained.

With his hands heavily bandaged and in considerable discomfort about his loins, Philip had already been pressed into service for the dismantling of the mould. All hands were needed and, sick or not, slaves could not be spared from essential duty. Neither Philip not Sophie considered Lysippus harsh. That was the way of their lives and it did not occur to them that their conditions might ever improve. All they had was each other. To survive was their main objective, and each day they succeeded they thanked the gods for their full bellies.

*　　*　　*

Within the month the whole group was ready for transport to the platform in front of the South Stoa with its seventy-one splendid Doric columns, where it was to be erected as a permanent public monument. Lysippus had arranged the four horses so that the heads of the two inner beasts inclined towards each other, while the outer ones would lean away from the platform as though about to leap. The harness, all wrought in bronze, had been attached so realistically taut in Apollo's grip that he seemed poised to impel the steeds into a joyous gallop across the firmament.

'It is beautiful, Master,' the foreman said admiringly, when it was finally in position.

'That is because it is true to life,' Lysippus replied. 'Because we observed and calculated. Look after truth and beauty takes care of itself.'

'Yet King Alexander called it a bauble,' the foreman said. 'I heard him with my own ears.'

'What else would you expect from a man who's half a

barbarian?' thought Lysippus, who had never subscribed to the Macedonians' claim that they were of Greek descent. 'All that lofty stuff about caring for the wounded!' That was only so that they could be used again in the selfish game which he had heard the King call 'seizing life by the throat'. To Alexander this meant seizing by the throat anyone who stood in his way. This glamorous youth was prepared to see thousands massacred to satisfy whatever it was that was consuming him! Lysippus was too prudent to mouth such thoughts. Dangerous remarks travelled fast in Corinth, and he badly wanted to fulfil his own ambition of being formally appointed court sculptor. There was no surer way to the recognition he craved.

*   *   *

The latest creation of Lysippus was the wonder of Corinth, until it lapsed into just another of the bronzes which bejewelled the city in such profusion that they were barely noticed by the citizens. Alexander first saw it after returning from his Indian conquests and after capturing the golden treasure of the Persian and Indian rulers. It meant little to him then.

People from all parts of the Mediterranean world continued to admire the Sun God and his Horses as time and the weather embellished them with streaks of green, until the eye of Corinth's most significant visitor fell upon them. This was the Roman general Lucius Mummius who, in 146 BC when the group was already 190 years old, was dispatched there by the Senate to complete the 'liberation' of Greece and avenge an insult. Corinthian citizens had not only thrown mud at ambassadors from Rome but emptied chamber-pots over their heads. It was a typically Roman excuse to eliminate its last great trade rival after the magnificent city of Carthage had been razed in the previous year.

Mummius, a boorish but able soldier who was one of the Consuls of the year, obeyed the Senate's instructions to make Corinth an example to the rest of Greece. This he did with little opposition, the Corinthians paying the penalty for devoting so little of their resources to defending themselves. After ripping out hundreds of statues, including all those embellish-

57

ing the South Stoa, he set fire to the city and razed every building except the Temple of Apollo, which he spared only because he feared the vengeance of the god. Most of the men were killed, while the women and children were sold into slavery.

While anxious to secure himself the honour of a triumphal procession in Rome, for opening her markets to the whole Mediterranean and bringing back such spoils, Mummius revealed his inability to recognize an irreplaceable masterpiece. He warned the seamen who contracted to carry the statues from Corinth to the Imperial City that, should they lose them through shipwreck, they would have to replace them by 'others of equal value'.

On that note the Four Horses of Lysippus, their chariot and pagan driver, were transported to join the enormous collection of antiquities which were the public manifestation of military and political authority in the capital of the Empire replacing Alexander's.

EPISODE 3

Reincarnation in Rome

'Observing the pageants of rulers and Popes,
Spurred on by ambition, by fears and by hopes'

Chapter Five

The emperor who had been named at his birth in AD 37 Lucius Domitius Ahenobarbus, but became known as Nero on his adoption by his stepfather the Emperor Claudius, looked up with satisfaction at the immense triumphal arch that was complete except for the gilded bronze statuary group that was to crown it. A three-bayed structure of Attic marble with friezes, pillars and medallions in relief, it was much more than a monstrous conceit for the man who had ruled Rome and its Empire ably for twelve years, or a self-gratification for providing his numerous peoples with more peace than they had known for a long time. If the ceremonies of the next few days went well—and the arch was an essential component of them—then peace might be extended indefinitely to the most dangerous area of all. This was the border between Roman-occupied Armenia and Parthia, the kingdom of those superb Iranian desert horsemen who had killed so many Roman soldiers by their ability to release showers of accurate arrows while pretending to retreat at the gallop.

Nero's ploy, which was to prove to be an outstanding act of statesmanship, was to crown the King of Parthia's brother, Tiridates, as King of Armenia, thereby creating a friendly client-state and securing the support of the King of Parthia himself. Tiridates had agreed to come to Rome and go through the motions of bowing the knee in return for virtual autonomy, but Nero knew that if the full truth were known, the masses would see it for what it was, an admission of military stalemate if not defeat, a circumstance contrary to the popular requirement for crushing victory with the grand triumphal parade of spoils and vanquished. Hence the need that the occasion should be dressed up as a triumph both for Rome and its Emperor, a triumph magnificent enough to delude the mob and also overawe the visiting barbarian chieftain, who would shortly be arriving after a nine months' journey by horseback and by boat accompanied by his wife and three thousand Parthian cavalry.

It was a confidence trick, but long before he became 'His Highness the Head of State' at the age of sixteen, Nero had learned from his able tutor, Seneca, that the ability to gull the public and one's enemies was an essential component of the politician's art.

'You will find, my boy, that the world is largely peopled by fools,' Seneca had assured him, 'but it takes a really clever man to bend them to his purposes.'

Nero had also convinced himself through his own observations that to triumph through peace was more refined and more difficult than to triumph through war, an attitude with which the Roman patricians profoundly disagreed and which would eventually contribute to his downfall.

Still only twenty-eight, powerfully built and with the positive fitness sustained by a regular mix of athletic and intellectual endeavour, he felt it was particularly good to be alive that morning. It was barely five a.m. when he arrived at the gleaming structure spanning the commanding position where the Capitoline Rise turned sharply right towards the most sacred spot in the whole Empire, the Temple of Jupiter overhanging the Tarpean Rock on the Capitoline Hill. He looked through the central arch at the statue of the great god on its plinth outside the Temple, and smiled. There was no doubt about it. He had chosen the most select position in Rome for his triumphal arch, built to stand for centuries.

Who could say he lacked courage? No previous ruler had dared to pre-empt that location, which had occurred to him on his first official visit there for the dedication of the first shavings of his red beard in a golden casket. He did not fear the wrath of the deities, believing them to be indifferent to the fate of men. As he had put it to Seneca, 'Would gods worthy of the name be cajoled by the selfish wants of individuals?' No. The risk of retribution came from men—particularly from one's own relations and from the Senators whose animosity towards the Imperial authority, which had usurped the power monopolized by their predecessors, would be intensified by this new presumption. But the risk was justified. Every future hero making the solemn journey to the Temple would be reminded of the Emperor Nero's triumph, just as they would read his imperishable verses, which he had ordered to be engraved in gold inside the Temple.

The Emperor Nero? Not just the Emperor, perhaps. The Emperor and God Nero! Surely he would become as deserving of that supreme elevation as his forbear Augustus, the first Emperor who, like Hercules, had achieved deification through sheer accomplishment. The rebuilding programme he had almost completed at Pompeii after the earthquake four years previously, making it into an even more splendid city which should glorify him through the centuries, already merited some special mark of recognition. And now he was rebuilding Rome. Was that not Herculean?

He turned and nodded his approval to Sofonius Tigellinus, the Prefect and Commander of the Praetorian Guard who also served him as Master of Ceremonies. Tigellinus had accompanied him with a bodyguard detachment for the early morning inspection before the streets, which were always clear of carts by daybreak, became too congested with pedestrians.

'My arch is beautiful, Tigellinus. This morning all Rome looks beautiful. Worthy of a poem!'

He looked around with satisfaction at the new city, rising fast from the ruins of the fire two years previously which had destroyed two-thirds of the public buildings and homes. The city he was regenerating would be a more elegant, healthier and altogether better Rome, with wide streets, temples, colonnades and tenements limited to a height of sixty feet, much more like the Greek cities he preferred.

Even the strong smell of horse, itself a by-product of military and commercial power, which always pervaded the city, seemed invigorating as he placed his hands on his barrel chest and inhaled deeply. Before setting out, he had spent an hour carrying out breathing exercises with a lead weight on his ribs to improve the power of his singing voice, which he and thousands who had heard him believed to be not only good but great.

63

'You have done well, Severus,' Nero said to the architect who had joined them.

Severus bowed and took the opportunity to move back a pace. The Emperor's breath reeked of the onions he consumed in huge quantities, believing they were good for his voice.

'Don't you agree, Tigellinus?' Nero asked. 'It's going to be the most impressive arch in Rome when we get my statue on it? When will that be, Severus? There's not much time.'

Severus seemed so reluctant to reply that it was immediately apparent that all was not well, but he managed to get the words out before the peremptory order to explain.

'There's a problem with the gilding, Lord.'

'Problem? What problem? I don't like problems. We've enough already.'

'I was at the gilding factory half an hour ago, my Lord. They've worked through the night but they've run short of gold.'

Nero's freckled face and his bull-like neck were beginning to look even more florid than usual. The lips of his small mouth tightened and he hitched the loose, flowing garment he preferred to a toga over his shoulder, a nervous gesture which always denoted impending anger.

'Run short of gold! I understood you had personally made sure they had enough, Tigellinus. I do hope that none of it has gone astray.'

'I'll look into it right away, my Lord,' said Tigellinus, a Sicilian who had gained entry to Roman society as a trader in good horses for chariot races and then advanced himself through his attraction for well-placed women, holding on to his wealth and power through ability and ruthlessness. He restrained himself from reminding the Emperor that his order to cover the entire dome of the Pantheon with gold in preparation for Tiridates' visit had been bound to cause a shortage for other projects, especially when it had to be achieved in a single day. The Emperor did not take kindly to any suggestion that he could be at fault over anything. Tigellinus also knew well enough that Nero considered him a rogue, but one that he countenanced not only because he was convivial but also because he was ingenious at concocting the cruder revels in which the Emperor occasionally indulged, such as the notorious nocturnal orgy staged on a huge raft on Agrippa's lake. He had also been effective in nipping assassination plots in the bud, by bringing evidence obtained through an army of paid informers to his master's attention.

'The world's second oldest profession,' was how Nero laughingly described spying. He approved of it as heartily as he enjoyed the activities provided by the oldest, especially if his informers could be lodged in the houses of the less appreciative Senators. As Prefect, Tigellinus was able to make good use of other people's slaves to this effect. All slaves owed a debt to Nero, who had issued an edict requiring the Prefect to investigate complaints they made against their masters. So Tigellinus could approach them officially, and for anything really juicy that could lead to the sequestration of their masters' property he could promise freedom. It was a big advantage to have access to the refined methods of torture available to the Roman Police, which he had commanded before his last promotion.

'I find that whenever anything goes wrong it is always due to the stupidity of others,' Nero said sourly. 'I want to see my statue in position before I leave for Naples to meet up with this Tiridates. That's in four days. Understand?'

There was no need to add, 'Or else . . .' Tigellinus knew what the Romans said of the Ahenobarbus family: 'No wonder their beards are of bronze, because their faces are of iron and their hearts of lead.'

As Commander of the Praetorian Guard, Tigellinus wielded considerable power and it was through the support of the Guard that Nero had been acclaimed Emperor; but the wily Sicilian was well aware of his own unpopularity with the Roman masses, and that should he be the means of deposing the Emperor by assassination his own life would quickly be forfeit. He coughed nervously and rather raucously.

Nero gave him a steely look. 'You need to watch that cough, Tigellinus. It doesn't sound good and I can't have a man who isn't fit in charge of my Guard.'

*   *   *

The Emperor was particularly concerned about the equestrian group being prepared to top the arch, not only because he had provided it from his private collection, but because he knew it would be the finest on public view in Rome. Had it not been made for the great Alexander himself by no less an artist than the legendary Lysippus, creator of that other dynamic group of Alexander, Cleitus and the other victors of the Battle of the Granicus mounted so exhilaratingly in the Portico of Octavia?

As no mean hand with clay and marble, Nero appreciated the group—four horses drawing a chariot of Apollo—as outstanding art. He had acquired it from his close friend Otho, the extremely rich young general who was even more annoyed at having to part with it when Nero's greedy eye lighted on it during a visit to his country villa, than he had been at being required to give up his beautiful amber-haired wife, Poppæa, to become his master's second empress. Otho had obtained it through the estate of Sulla, the first of the big Roman collectors, whose greed for ancient sculpture was so insatiable that Cicero was to complain that they had 'stuffed their country estates as well as the city with looted art,' and then to observe prophetically, 'Will this artistic gluttony not make Rome a target for future pillagers?'

When Sulla, a great general, had established himself as dictator in the early eighties BC, he had seized the group along with the small Hercules statuette of Lysippus which had also belonged to Alexander, together with many more stolen masterpieces. As Nero's collecting enthusiasm burgeoned into pathological cupidity he had acquired the Hercules with particular relish, because privately he regarded himself as the reincarnation of that ancient hero.

He had gilded the statue in the Roman style, but following criticism of this by his artistic friends, such as the poet Petronius, the accepted arbiter of taste, he had deferred gilding the chariot group. Instead, it had been erected in its pristine condition as a free-standing ornament to his private circus at the foot of the Vatican Hill across the Tiber, along with other trophies like the great obelisk of Heliopolis. There he could appreciate their beauty as he practised chariot-racing, and so

66

they had escaped the flames which had consumed his palace on the Palatine Hill.

As a collector with exaggerated pride in ownership it was against his nature to part with any artistic treasure, but he did not regard the new arch as being anything but his own. So far as he was concerned, the whole of Rome belonged to the Emperor. Senatus Populusque Romanus? Rubbish! He despised the Senators with their chilly haughtiness, outdated prejudices and envy of his power. As for the bulk of the populace, what could ownership possibly mean to the poor?

It so happened that the horses and triumphal chariot on the Parthian Arch of Augustus in the Forum were gilded, like most of the bronzes there, and because the coronation of Tiridates in Rome was to be the Golden Day of all time the Emperor and his advisers had decided that, bad taste or not, the Lysippus group with Nero replacing Apollo as the charioteer and winged Victory alongside just had to be gilded too. Otherwise the mob would regard them as second-rate. And so might Tiridates.

'If that gold has disappeared it'll be no good coming crawling to the Fiscus,' Nero warned, referring to the private treasury which financed the public amusements and the corn supply as well as the army and the navy. 'It's cleaned out, so you'll have to find some of your own.'

'But you know I lost so much in the fire, my Lord,' Tigellinus protested.

Nero's face clouded and his blue eyes narrowed. He did not like being reminded of the fire.

'Don't make that excuse,' he thundered. 'You've had two years to make it up and I know you've been busy.'

Tigellinus swallowed hard. He did not relish such a remark in front of the architect and the Guards, who all knew it to be true.

'I'll report to you this afternoon, my Lord,' he said deferentially.

'No. Spare me the details,' Nero responded. He did not want his afternoon programme of musical practice disturbed. 'Just get me the results.'

★   ★   ★

67

The besetting problem of being at the top in Imperial Rome was not just staying there but remaining alive. So Tigellinus wasted no time in departing for the gilding workshop after conducting the Emperor back to the palace. If necessary he could grease his way back into Nero's favour by exposing yet another dangerous 'traitor'. And he had marked down a big one—Petronius, the clever-dick poet, who never lost an opportunity to score off Tigellinus by alluding to his humble origins and coarse tastes and was altogether too familiar with the Emperor. That could wait a while but on one thing he was immediately determined—he wouldn't be supplying the missing gold if he could humanly, or inhumanly, avoid it.

*　　　*　　　*

Filippus, the master-gilder employed by Nero for his private commissions—he had already gilded the Hercules of Lysippus—and by Tigellinus for the more sumptuous revels, was a short, sickly-looking man in his mid-thirties, which was middle-aged for a Roman. He was unaware that his symptoms of breathlessness, muscle weakness, tremulous hands and general irritability derived from his profession.

The Roman method of gilding bronze was to dissolve the gold in mercury to make an amalgam paste, and then brush this on to the statue after it had been cleaned in acid. The statue became silvery-white but when it was heated in a furnace the mercury was driven off, leaving the gold adhering to the bronze so securely that it could be burnished, giving an untarnishable and weatherproof finish. It was elegantly simple and technologically more refined than the Egyptian process of applying gold foil but unfortunately, though Filippus was aware that mercury was poisonous and insisted that all his workers wore a damp cloth over the mouth and nose when exposed to the fumes, he was not to know that the metal could penetrate the skin through the hair follicles, and since the start of his apprenticeship more than twenty years previously the slowly accumulated poison had caused considerable neurological damage.

In his stained woollen tunic, hitched up by a belt until it

68

hung just below his bare knees, Fillipus, dark and pinched, contrasted sharply with Tigellinus, whose intensely masculine presence and aura of physical strength were intensified by the moulded bronze cuirass, crested helmet and side-arms. He was not only miserable but frightened as he took the Sicilian to show him one of the Horses and the new bronze statue of Nero standing still ungilded. As a former horsebreeder, Tigellinus could admire the realistic stallion standing stripped of its harness in readiness for the gilding furnace, and the made-to-measure statue of the Emperor seemed adequate enough, but his artistic interest was cursory.

'Where is the gold that I provided?' Tigellinus demanded.

'You did not provide enough for all the commissions, Master,' Filippus said wearily, aware that he would not be believed. 'My wife, Sofia, has the only keys to the gold store. She keeps careful records of all the gold handled in this workshop, the amounts brought in and the amounts issued to the workmen. She is better at figures than I am. I will call her.'

He did so somewhat reluctantly, for Tigellinus had a notorious reputation as a man with an insatiable appetite for women—women of any class if they were handy. It was widely known that in the orgy on Agrippa's Lake, with its numerous bowers constructed for comfortable sexual indulgence, nobody had behaved more obscenely than Tigellinus. And Nero's joke—'Tigellinus's mother had a difficult birth because her son was born with the horn'—had gone the rounds of the winebars.

Sofia, a striking-looking woman in her late twenties, with wide brown eyes, high cheek-bones, sensuous lips and dark, straight hair parted in the centre and dressed in tight curls at the sides, came forward with a parchment roll, her full bosom outlined by the clinging garment she wore in the hot workshop.

'We are honoured, Lord,' she said in a rather husky voice which made her even more attractive.

Tigellinus, who had included Nero's mother in his conquests, was immediately interested, though not in the accounts Sofia had so carefully entered with a sharpened reed.

'You will see, Master, that every ounce, every aureus is

69

accounted for,' she said. 'I weighed it out myself. The figures are exceptionally high for this month because so much gilding has been required in a hurry for this ceremony, not only for the Pantheon but for the Theatre of Pompey. Even the stone seats there are having to be gilded. . . .'

'I know, I know,' Tigellinus growled.

He could hardly disagree. Nero was determined to make the visit of Tiridates so sensationally grand that he had been prepared to empty his own coffers and the city's in the belief that it would be a sound investment. As prodigal as Nature once he had set his mind on a project, and aware that his lavishness was the fount of his popularity with the masses, Nero's response to his head-shaking financial advisers had been, 'Money is made round to go round. Get on with it!'

If the Parthian border could be kept quiet, not only would resources be saved in the long run but he could then get down to the really serious business of writing poetry, singing and playing the harp, in all of which his interest was so much deeper than in territorial domain. To have to spend time and money conquering the same nation again and again, as Rome had been doing for centuries, seemed to him the height of stupidity.

'You agreed with the amount of gold I provided when you took on the commission,' Tigellinus argued firmly. 'Or at least your husband did.'

'I know I did, Master,' Filippus answered plaintively. 'I underestimated because you insisted so strongly that we mustn't over-order as gold is in such short supply. If you look at the totals, the weight runs into hundreds of pounds. It was only a small error to make. . . .'

'But surely the Emperor's personal group should have been given first priority,' Tigellinus interrupted angrily.

'Normally it would, Master,' Sofia said, wiping her brow with the sweat-cloth dangling from her arm. 'But we have furnace-space for only a few items at a time and the Emperor has made so many other immediate demands.'

Tigellinus gave a ritual glance at the parchment roll proffered by Sofia, but the only figure that interested him was hers. Always a pragmatist, he appreciated that he had no means of proving that the record had been falsified, and even if the rolls had been cooked there was not much time to do anything about it if the Emperor's deadline was to be met.

Putting Filippus to the rack might trace the missing gold if there were any, but then the gilder would be unable to finish the job and the others in Rome were overloaded. As for Sofia, the only other person who knew the truth, he could think of a more interesting place to lay her than on the rack, fun though that might have been.

'I am not satisfied,' he said to Filippus sternly. 'I have no time to examine these figures now. I have someone waiting to see me at my house. But they must be examined. I have to account to the Emperor this afternoon for every ounce. Therefore your wife must accompany me to my house with the records, so that we can go through them in detail as soon as my visitor has gone. If I am convinced that they are correct, I will provide the necessary gold at my expense. If not . . .'

He smiled at the suspicious fear showing on the face of Filippus. The reaction of the helpless husband was always part of the pleasure he extracted from seducing other men's wives, both before and after the event. He knew that with so much work to complete in such a desperate rush, Filippus could not insist on accompanying her.

*　　*　　*

Sofia, who had lived in Rome all her life, had never ridden on a horse before: any long journeys she had ever made had been in a cart. But Tigellinus was in a hurry, and one of his soldiers sat her sideways on his charger and led her on foot through the narrow streets, where the rapidly growing crowds were used to getting smartly out of the way of the Praetorian Guard. There was little hope of redress if a pedestrian was kicked or any of the stalls of the money-changers, barbers, tinkers or other tradesmen, whose activities tended to spill over into the street, were knocked down.

The walls of even the new buildings were plastered with notices in black and red paint about the coming Golden Day celebrations, slave auctions, lost property and graffiti, some

71

rude but a number wishing, 'Good luck to Nero Cæsar!'

'Good luck!' Tigellinus thought. 'By Jove, he's going to need it if he goes on insulting the Senate and the Generals.'

To the Establishment the word 'Emperor' meant 'military commander', and while Nero was not lacking in physical courage, as his chariot-racing proved, he was no horseback general and made no effort to conceal his preference for commanding respect and fame for his achievements as an artist. Privately, Tigellinus agreed with the Establishment that the Emperor's fanatical devotion to art, which drove him to evade his real duties and escape into a fantasy world of poetry, music and myth, was rash as well as degrading.

With the people still mindful of the paranoid Caligula, his penultimate predecessor, who had forced even his friends to kill themselves to amuse him before Rome was released by his assassination, Nero had begun sensibly. But as the sheer consciousness of his immense power corrupted his judgment he resumed the terror tactics, after anxiously consulting his soothsayer, Bilbilius, about the meaning of a comet which had suddenly flamed across the night sky followed by the birth of a four-headed baby to a Roman matron.

'Divert these bad omens away from your own person, my Lord, by substituting some of the nobles,' the diviner had advised.

Those selected by Tigellinus for this protective sacrifice had been men both of spirit and of wealth. Understandably the remaining Senators had become a cringing lot, but Tigellinus could see no harm in pretending to respect them so they could be jollied into supporting the Emperor's policies, and suggested it when both were in wine.

'You are wrong, my friend,' Nero had replied affably from his couch. 'You give the Senate a far longer shadow than its substance. The Senate is like a piece of rope. You can't push on it so you have to pull.'

Had he dared, Tigellinus would have answered, 'Mind it doesn't string you up,' but it would have been pointless. There was no talking Nero out of anything once he had taken a stand.

As the passers-by stared in some wonder and even commented at the sight of a working woman riding behind the

Commander of the Praetorian Guard, Tigellinus felt a certain sexual stimulus. The situation reminded him of the rape of the Sabine women.

★   ★   ★

The new house of Tigellinus was even more magnificent than his former palace, which had been destroyed in the great fire. Built with a priority second only to the Emperor's Golden House, which was so vast that it was never to be finished, it was resplendent in marble and stone, a far cry from the Sicilian cottage in which he had worked as a fisherman before turning his gifts to breeding horses.

He slipped off his helmet, handed it to a slave and ran his large hands through his black, curly hair. His skin was dark and the size of his large head was enhanced by a massive square jaw. He wasted little time after conducting Sofia to his bedroom, which was dark in spite of the open shutters. He was a busy man and while he expected no caller, as he had claimed, he was expected elsewhere for the midday meal.

Dismissing the proffered accounts roll with a contemptuous wave, he came straight to the point with no attempt at finesse. He pointed to his cushioned couch, the only large piece of furniture in the room. It was cast in bronze inlaid with silver and stood high off the mosaiced floor on ivory legs. As Sofia's eyes accommodated to the half-darkness, she saw that the mosaic was on a Bacchanalian theme, the central figure being Priapus approaching a nymph with an enormous erection. She noticed too that even the chamber-pot was of silver set with precious stones.

As she seemed reluctant to approach the couch, Tigellinus said coldly: 'Unless you are prepared to oblige me without fuss your husband will have to be racked and you too may suffer that indignity.'

Sofia, a virtuous woman, if only because she had had little opportunity to be anything else since marrying Filippus, was shocked and afraid.

'I don't understand, Master,' she stammered. 'I am a married woman. I am not one of the women of Tuscan Street,' she

73

added, referring to the notorious red-light district of the Forum.

'I should not be interested in you if you were,' Tigellinus said unfastening his belt, taking off his cuirass and kicking off his sandals.

Sofia crossed her hands over her breasts to display the circle of iron worn on the fourth finger of her left hand, because of the Roman belief that a nerve connected that finger directly with the heart.

'Don't start talking to me about your honour,' Tigellinus scoffed. 'I know women. When men speak of honour they are thinking of how they will look in their own eyes. To women it's just another word for reputation. How many children have you got?'

'None, Master.'

'None! Then how long have you been married to the gilder?'

'Eleven years, Master.'

'Eleven years and no children!'

Sofia looked at the floor. 'Every March festival I have prayed to Juno Lucina and offered sacrifices for the blessing of children but . . .'

'You are barren then?'

'I think not, Sir. You see my husband has never really been well since we married. He has difficulties due to his work . . .'

Sofia was too modest to say outright what she suspected, that chronic mercury poisoning had made Filippus impotent.

Tigellinus smiled broadly and grasped her by the hand, 'An unfucked wife!' he declared. 'The next best thing to a virgin. And they're at a premium in Rome! It's not the help of Juno you need. That's what you need.' He pointed to the massive penis of Priapus on the floor.

Sofia was not shocked. Replicas of outsize penes as fertility symbols were common enough in Rome.

'I may not be quite up to Priapus's standard, but you'll find I'm not bad,' Tigellinus said.

Though he was not then fully aware of it, he too was smitten by a debilitating and dangerous disease but its effect was to increase his sexual urge: he was in the early stages of tuberculosis.

74

He seized Sofia by the shoulder, hurriedly unwrapping the single-piece palla into which she had quickly changed from her working clothes, and gloatingly surveyed her near-nakedness. She was even more voluptuously proportioned to his taste than he had guessed. He untied the knot of his loincloth and threw the garment on to a large studded chest, then forced her on to the couch.

She saw that he had not been boasting unduly. With his dark, hairy body and lascivious face he looked like a satyr.

When she resisted as he tried to take off her flimsy loincloth he intensified his threat.

'You know the Emperor's reputation,' he warned. 'If I report that Filippus stole Imperial gold and confessed to it under torture, which he undoubtedly would, I've no doubt that the penalty will be the "ancient method".'

Sofia shuddered. In the ancient method of execution the prisoner had his neck fastened in a forked stake and was whipped to death.

'You see, my dear, neither of us has much time for pre-liminaries.'

Her tears as he achieved his purpose with considerable force, with refinements of which she had never heard, much less experienced, only heightened his animal pleasure. It was a novelty for him to copulate with an unwilling woman and it increased his sense of possession and conquest.

'You won't tell my husband what you have done to me?' Sofia entreated, as he lay on his back temporarily sated.

Tigellinus laughed. 'I just might do that. It would be interesting to see his face; I can't imagine it could look more miserable. He's a real whiner, isn't he?'

'He wasn't always like that. It's terrible what failing health can do to your nature. He was handsome and strong when I married him. And full of fun.'

'That's hard to believe,' said Tigellinus, who had failed to appreciate the recent changes in his own nature.

'Nevertheless it's true. It's the fumes from his work, from the fire-gilding, that have changed him. I've watched him slowly getting worse.'

'Why doesn't he give it up then?'

Sofia sighed. 'He has no other way of earning a living and the Emperor would not let him give it up. He's the best gilder in Rome.'

'I suppose you are right,' Tigellinus said derisively. 'Nothing must stand in the way of the Emperor and his art.'

'Please don't tell Filippus what you have done to me,' Sofia entreated again. 'It would hurt him very much and he's a good man: a kind man.'

Tigellinus laughed. 'Maybe that's why he's only a gilder and will never be anything else. Goodness gets you nowhere! You have to grab what you want in this world. Perhaps I won't tell him if you undertake to oblige me in future if the spirit moves me.'

She made no reply but her answer was of no consequence to Tigellinus. Once he had taken her in the devious ways he required that morning, she would be of no further interest. He would be looking for something fresh, motivated by the myth that the next woman will always be different and by a carnal covetousness that was insatiable even if his performance did not quite match his appetite.

*　　　*　　　*

It was approaching noon. The sun was baking the buildings and the city was at its noisiest, with ridden horses and crowds of pedestrians and idlers on the roads, when Tigellinus sent Sofia back with an escort and enough gold-plate recently inscribed with the initials ST to finish the gilding. He hated parting with it but, given time, there was plenty more where that had come from. When Tigellinus secured the execution of a conspirator, which was frequent enough since the Great Fire, he shared in the sequestrated estates.

*　　　*　　　*

Sofia did her best to hide what she considered to be her shame, but Filippus was not deceived. He was delighted and immensely relieved when she showed him the gold, but her excuses for her long absence were not credible.

76

'It took me a long time to convince him that the figures were genuine . . . He insisted on going through them all . . . It took him quite a while to find the gold dishes . . .'

'Well done, my dear, well done,' Filippus said, embracing her. 'I never expected he would be so reasonable. Perhaps he's not such a blackguard as people say.'

He had good reason to know otherwise. Tigellinus had been unable to resist the sadistic opportunity. The officer of the escort which had brought Sofia back took Filippus on one side and said, 'I am instructed to give you this message—Sofonius Tigellinus is not fully satisfied with the payment your wife has made for the gold. She may be required to make a further contribution.'

The soldier had smiled at the haggard look on Filippus's face. He fully appreciated what the message must mean.

'I must get on now, dear,' Filippus said, releasing Sofia from his embrace. 'There's not a moment to lose.'

There was time enough now that the gold was in hand and he had completed the complex incising and cross-hatching of the bronze surface, which was essential to give the statues optical contrast when they were gilded; but each knew that the other was near to tears and was glad of the excuse to be alone. Filippus adored his wife and in the past had often tried to express his love in the physical act, but it had always been a fiasco, so much so that to avoid mutual embarrassment they had not attempted it for years, pretending that it was of no consequence so long as they had each other. His belief that, superficially and as a matter of course, Tigellinus had accomplished something of which he would never be capable even in the height of desire, choked him as did the fear that the experience might have aroused in Sofia some longing he had hoped would remain suppressed. The only remedy was to immerse himself in work.

Chapter Six

Flanked by Senators and backed by a Praetorian bodyguard headed by Tigellinus in full armour, Nero sat in purpled and jewelled splendour on the New Rostra, the balustraded platform for public speaking in the Forum facing down the Via Sacra. His abundant reddish hair, crimped and piled in tiers in the style of the gladiators and the professional charioteers, and which he had adopted as a popular artifice, was encircled by a laurel wreath tied with a thin ribbon at the back of his bull neck. The early morning sun illuminated a ceremonial scene of extraordinary magnificence as the crowd awaited the arrival of Tiridates.

Nero, who had been taught by Seneca to yawn with his mouth closed, was usually bored with ceremony and would much rather have been practising with Diodorus, the virtuoso harpist or, better still, singing with his teacher, Terpnus. But as he sat in the curule chair of state, surveying the impressive lines of soldiers and the throng so great that hundreds were perched on the tops of those building which had survived the fire or been rebuilt, he could feel well satisfied. He had already made a friend of Tiridates by joining him at his beloved Naples and journeying back to Rome with him and his young wife, being delighted to find that both spoke fluent Greek, a consequence of the conquest of Parthia by Alexander so long ago.

The Parthian had been deeply impressed by Roman grandeur and might, and Nero felt that the Golden Day should set the seal. Then he could go to Greece and fulfil his ambition of taking part in the singing competitions. Unlike the Roman traditionalists, the Greeks did not consider singing or reciting to be degrading to the Imperial dignity, particularly when singing was an art sacred to Apollo. On the contrary, they admired an Emperor gifted enough to compose his own songs and sing them with a brilliance that outshone top professionals. The trouble with the Roman nobility was that they were overly suspicious of anything new, and Nero's sincere belief that creative art and its practice were superior to war and its results was blasphemy.

There was a roar as Tiridates, dark-skinned, handsome and taller than the rather squat Emperor, though less muscular, advanced through the double ranks of legionaries at attention with their battle-standards, plumed helmets and burnished arms, and mounted the ramp leading to the platform. As he reached the spot appointed for his homage, he could not fail to be impressed by the solid figure of the Emperor in the robes of a triumphator, which hid the slight paunch, the only visible side-effect of the occasional debauch when the graceless side of his nature took command.

Falling on one knee Tiridates declared in Armenian and then Greek, 'Hail the Emperor Nero, my master and my god.'

As the words were translated to the crowd and Nero raised him up and embraced him, there was such a tremendous shout that Tiridates looked momentarily concerned.

'Don't be scared,' Nero whispered in fluent Greek. 'The Romans have always been the noisiest people in the world.'

When Tiridates turned to acknowledge the cheers it was seen that he was wearing a scimitar, but Nero's security agents had seen to it that all the soldiers and enough people in the crowd knew that this was a concession granted only after the Parthian had agreed to have the scabbard fastened up so that the weapon could not be withdrawn.

After seating Tiridates beside him, Nero proceeded to that part of the ceremony which, as a stage-struck extrovert anxious for plaudits, he genuinely enjoyed—his speech from the platform where Augustus, Cicero, Mark Antony and many others had thrilled and swayed the mob with their oratory.

Nero's performances, whether in prose or verse, tended to be lengthy, but so much had to be crowded into this Golden Day that he had time only to praise Tiridates and his brave countrymen; and this he did in the strong voice and with the dramatic fervour that aroused his audience to thunderous acclamation, especially when prompted by the Augustani, the society of young patricians organized to encourage applause of the Emperor's artistic efforts. He removed the turban from the Parthian's head, and replacing it with a jewelled tiara declared him King of Armenia.

'We must remain seated a few minutes to give this lot time to make their noise,' Nero explained. 'Don't you find the masses unbearably stupid? Outward appearance means every-thing to them while the essence is ignored. All they want, apart from bread, is entertainment and the more lavish the better so long as they don't have to pay for it.'

He did not explain that the reason why most of them could not pay was because there was no work, since so much of it was done by the slaves who constituted a third of Rome's million-plus population.

'They are certainly getting entertainment today, Lord,' Tiridates said, making a gesture towards the bunting, banners and laurels decorating the Forum.

'Oh that's nothing. Wait until you see Pompey's Theatre, though I doubt whether these fools will enjoy it much. All they want is trash and nobody's going to be killed today. That's what Romans really like. Plenty of blood, so long as it's not their own.'

Tiridates smiled. He knew the Romans regarded the Parth-ians as barbarians, but his people did not indulge in savagery for entertainment.

'Personally, as an artist I hate unnecessary cruelty,' Nero continued. 'So much so that when I became Emperor twelve years ago I issued instructions that nobody was to be killed in the gladiatorial contests and the revolting fights with wild beasts. I stopped some of the gladiatorial shows altogether, particularly those held by candidates for office, because it was obviously a corrupt way of canvassing for votes. But was I thanked for it? I couldn't have been less popular. The people and the Senate thought it was a sign of weakness. Bread and blood! Give the Romans plenty of those and they are happy.'

Tiridates shrugged sympathetically as Nero added with a laugh, 'Still, I suppose I shouldn't complain. After all they *are* my public.'

He gave the crowd an imperial wave of his muscular arm, heavily bangled for the occasion though normally adorned

80

only with the snakeskin bracelet which, he believed, had magical powers to protect him from violence. Inwardly, Tiridates was disappointed. Out of curiosity he had been hoping to see a gladiatorial fight, but refrained from saying so. He did not know that, to crown the visit in the eyes of the people, the Emperor had arranged for a show later in which the highlight was to be combat to the death between teams of white men and negroes.

*　　*　　*

The two most splendid state coaches, each drawn by the standard team of four milk-white horses, were then driven to the rostra. Nero and Tiridates mounted the first while the Parthian's wife, her face covered by a golden mask, travelled in the second with the Empress, Statilia Messalina, a mistress Nero had married after Poppæa's tragic death following a miscarriage.

There was no sign of Nero's current love, the homosexual youth Sporus, who looked so strikingly like Poppæa. To increase the resemblance, Sporus had been castrated on the Emperor's instructions by the 'clean sweep' which removed both penis and testicles and then, having been dressed in the dead Empress's clothes, he was renamed Sabina, Poppæa's second name. The appearance of 'Sabina' alongside the Emperor on previous official occasions had further alienated the traditionalists, one of whom was responsible for a quip which went round Rome—'If only Nero's own father had had such a wife!'

Whatever the Empress Statilia Messalina thought about her rival, she kept her feelings to herself. There was no insecurity greater than that of women married or otherwise attached to rulers, and little they could ever do about it.

'I didn't know there was so much gold in the world,' Tiridates said, indicating the array of figures in front of the rostra and the several huge equestrian statues visible from the carriage.

'Oh they're not solid gold,' Nero explained. 'They're gilded bronze. The Romans have never been impressed with bronze.

81

But there is another reason,' he added with a twinkle. He made a gesture of tugging the red beard he had shaved off years before. 'With me on the throne they say there's enough bronze about already. My family name Ahenobarbus means "bronze beard", you know.'

The Emperor put his hands on his chest and laughed loudly. He liked to laugh and make others laugh, though it could be dangerous for them to laugh at the wrong time.

Tiridates obliged, but felt he would not take an insult so lightly in his own kingdom. Nero was an extraordinary man, he thought. Quite different from the stiff-necked autocrat he had expected. He had a sense of humour and charm.

As the procession moved slowly to the east end of the Forum, the Parthian's curiosity was aroused by his view of a large stone structure straddling the Via Sacra and topped by a huge gilded statue of a man driving a chariot pulled by four horses.

'What is that?' he asked in wonder.

'That is one of about eighty statues in Rome erected to the glory of Augustus, my great-great-grandfather—the one who called himself "The Liberator",' Nero replied somewhat sarcastically. He had the presence of mind to avoid mentioning that it was the *Parthian* Arch, which the first Emperor and god had set up to commemorate what he believed to be Rome's final triumph over its eastern enemy. But Tiridates knew well enough how totally the first Emperor's solution of the Parthian problem had failed, as had his boast that 'I have pacified the world.'

'I must respect Augustus, whose achievements have placed him with the gods,' said Nero, 'but creating peace by diplomacy instead of butchery is not only more elegant but likely to be more lasting. I totally disagree with our poet Horace that "To die for the fatherland is a sweet thing." To live for it is far more rewarding. No, my friend, I have no desire to be hailed as a conquering hero except through art, though I often need to pretend I have.'

Tiridates, an uncomplicated man of action, did not really understand what Nero was talking about, being intellectually

82

incapable of appreciating the yearnings of an artist for enduring recognition, but affected to agree.

The Emperor looked back at the Arch of Augustus. 'Yes, it is impressive, as it should be. But wait until you see mine. It makes those horses look like mules.'

The procession continued out of the Forum, past the Basilica Julia on the left and the Temple of Saturn on the right, to the start of the Capitoline Rise, which ran straight and steep and was flanked by masses of statues, columns and porticoes giving shelter and shade.

As the procession slowed with the horses straining laboriously on the gradient, Nero asked enthusiastically, 'Tell me, Tiridates, what do you think of my new Rome?' indicating the new buildings with his arm. 'All these blocks, shops, temples and arcades have gone up since the fire. Are the people grateful? Not a bit. All they say is that it's further proof that I started the blaze.'

'You?' Tiridates exclaimed.

'Yes, me. Set fire to my own capital! I was thirty-five miles away in Antium at the time and we've proved that the fire started in an oil store in the Circus Maximus, but the idiots still insist I did it—so that I could have the privilege of rebuilding it to my own artistic taste!'

Tiridates looked suitably astonished at the mindless calumny which had been spread by certain Senators as a means of undermining Nero's popularity.

'My personal losses were enormous,' Nero continued. 'My palace was consumed, with some of the glories of Greek art in it. So was my new market-place. After the fire I fed the homeless at my own expense. All this rebuilding has cost me millions of my own money. The architects and the builders are all feathering their nests. The Circus Maximus alone is costing me a fortune. But are the dolts grateful? You might as well ask if the pigs are grateful when you fill their troughs. The fire taught me that our poet Catullus was right when he wrote, "Cease to expect to win men's gratitude".'

'But it doesn't look as though any of then blame you now,' Tiridates remarked, indicating the cheering throng.

'Oh, some still do, though most of them now believe the

83

Christians did it,' the Emperor added with a mischievous smile.

'Christians? What are they?'

'Oh, they're a mad sect of Jews who disapprove of all enjoyment in this world and are always raving on about the next. I prefer the philosophy of my friend Petronius, "Man's life alas is but a span, So let us live it while we can." '

'That makes sense to me,' Tiridates agreed.

'Anyway, don't have the Christians in your kingdom at any price. They wouldn't raise a hand to put the fire out and were wandering round in ecstasy shouting that the world was ending and that their god, Christus, would be appearing any minute. They convicted themselves out of their own mouths and I had to deal with them.'

'What did you do?'

Nero laughed. 'I made the punishment fit the crime as it always should. They seem to like fire, so we wrapped them up in cloth steeped in pitch and oil, set them up on crosses in my private circus, let the public in and made them into torches. I believe that if people think they can shed light they should be given every encouragement.'

His shoulders shook with laughter which vanished as he realized that his joke had been lost on his guest.

'Actually I didn't really enjoy it,' he confessed. 'I drove my chariot around a few times in the glare but it was all rather crude for my taste.'

Tiridates grimaced in agreement.

'You'll never believe it, Tiridates, but some of these Christians are so mad that they *want* to be killed. They all think they'll be reborn again and the worse the death in this world, the better the life in the next. One of their chief men, a Jew called Petrus, insisted on being crucified upside down because Christus had been crucified the right way up! Naturally, we obliged. The mob thought it was an excellent idea.'

'Do you really believe they started the fire?' Tiridates asked.

'Frankly I don't. I think it just broke out in the oil store but it diverted suspicion from me. That was the object of the exercise. And they asked for it. They're mostly aliens and slaves, and we didn't ask them to come here. Yet they not only refuse to conform but have the impudence to tell us that we have to live their way. When they're in Rome they should do as the Romans do. I warn you, Tiridates, have nothing to do with them. They are fanatics.'

Dimly perhaps, Nero had foreseen that the strange teachings of the rebel Jesus Christ posed a more dangerous threat to the Roman Empire than any of the barbarian tribes.

He turned to the crowd to give a last broad smile and wave as the procession neared the summit. As the fate of so many of his predecessors had shown, and the future would confirm, popularity with the mob really was an essential insurance.

'Senatus Populusque Romanus!' Nero remarked to his guest, giving him a dig with his elbow. 'Let us pay them lip-service while it suits us but let us not raise their expectations too high! Money is far better invested in monuments to the gods than in mortal bellies.'

As the road turned sharply to the right on to the summit of the Capitoline Hill they were suddenly confronted with a huge three-bayed structure spanning it. Tiridates gazed in wonder while Nero looked at him with utmost animation. Under the ancient rules the Triumphator was supposed to keep his gaze concentrated on the Temple of Jupiter in front, but he was not made for rules.

'That's my arch, Tiridates! That's my new arch! Now isn't it better than the Arch of Augustus? Bigger? More beautiful? More impressive?'

'It's magnificent.'

It was certainly the biggest in Rome, eighty feet high and ninety feet wide. And the statuary group, fully gilded, was Rome's finest.

'Just look at that group,' Nero enthused. 'The horses belonged to Alexander. He too was a statesman as well as a general. They were made in Corinth, which we've rebuilt into a great commercial centre. I'm cutting a canal across the isthmus there to shorten the route between the Aegean and the Adriatic. The Senators say it's impossible but I like the impossible. So did Alexander.'

'The horses are certainly lifelike,' observed Tiridates. 'Your statue is good too. Who's that behind you?'

85

'That's Victory putting a wreath on my head. We have to do that to please the traditionalists. It's the custom, you know. It's not for my vanity, I assure you. It's for the people's. So they can feel big through their heroes.'

Nero was right. The people felt such security as they witnessed the plunder and slaves pouring into Rome that battles had sometimes been fought for no better reason than to justify another triumphal procession.

'I can assure you, my dear Tiridates, that it is not really me and you that this servile lot are celebrating. They are celebrating themselves.'

Tiridates nodded his understanding.

'There's another thing I would have you know,' Nero said looking up at the golden group. 'I'm in that chariot by professional right. Augustus was no charioteer. I once drove *ten* in hand and I won. And fairly, mark you, no favouritism! It's the same with my recitals. I compete on the same terms as anybody else: wear the unbelted silk robe; bend the knee to the judge.'

Tiridates looked suitably impressed but inwardly reflected that he would never do such things.

'Oh, the people love it when I win,' Nero enthused. 'You'll see what I mean when we get to the theatre.'

He was referring to the huge purple awning stretched across the open auditorium of the Theatre of Pompey in the Campus Martius to give shade, and which was embroidered with an enormous picture of Nero driving a chariot across a sky ablaze with golden stars.

'To show you I'm a man of my word I'll be giving you a display of chariot-racing tomorrow. In full competition with the best professionals in the world!'

Tiridates failed to see how the judges could dare to be impartial and declare anyone else the winner, and felt that their position was somewhat unenviable. Still, Nero seemed sincere if self-deluded.

They went through the central arch too quickly for Tiridates to see the details of the sculptured frieze showing Roman soldiers defeating the Parthians, with spoils being presented to Nero and prisoners being paraded in chains. Nor could he read

86

the Latin inscription recording that it was Nero's Parthian arch, a fact the Emperor omitted in his mistranslation.

'It commemorates the undying friendship between our two countries,' Nero explained. 'I wrote the inscription myself. I've also composed a poem in honour of it and will recite it at the banquet tonight. It begins . . .'

Nero struck a pose and declaimed:

> 'Proud monument of stone and gold endure!
> Proclaim how Mighty Rome and Parthia's Kings
> Shall live in friendship and forswear the lure
> Of War! . . .'

'I'll also recite for you my poem on the Fall of Troy. Ah, if only there was time for you to see my performance of Hercules in Chains or the Blinding of Oedipus. I even do Canace giving birth!'

Tiridates looked at Nero quizzically. He did not know the story of Canace, whose bastard baby by her brother was flung to the hounds, but to impersonate a woman giving birth! Surely that was going too far even for such an eccentric. How could soldiers approve of the sight of their Emperor moaning and bearing down?

'The reactionaries say the practice of art is unworthy of a gentleman and soils the Imperial purple,' Nero continued. 'They're always banging on about my public appearances, saying they are immoral and undermine the ancient Roman virtues of self-restraint, steadfastness and manliness.'

'Perhaps they are jealous because you are so popular,' Tiridates suggested, indicating the cheering crowd.

'You are absolutely right, my friend. The songs I compose are sung in every wayside inn but the speeches these windbags make cause not a ripple of interest. These Senators do not understand, as I do, that there is all the difference between having something to say and having to say something. I assure you, my friend, that their only effective form of creation these days is procreation.'

A true professional, he had learned to wait for his laughs, which were always forthcoming.

'Seriously though, Tiridates, these fool Senators are incapable of seeing that nothing, not even virtues, can remain the same, age in, age out. That the only certainty in life is change and that coping with change is the essence of statesmanship and, for that matter, of a satisfying private life.'

The Emperor could see that Tiridates was confused.

'What do you think is the greatest human virtue?' he asked.

'Courage,' Tiridates answered unhesitatingly.

Nero stroked his chin. 'I agree that all men need courage of some sort. I wouldn't dispute it. But for me the most important virtue is enthusiasm—being really keen on whatever one is doing. It's lack of enthusiasm—boredom if you like—that kills the spirit and destroys empires.'

Nobody could accuse the Emperor of lack of enthusiam or of being anything but truly Roman in the scale of his ambitions. His misfortune lay in the compulsion which drove him to divert so much of his energies to appease the intemperate demands of his addiction to art.

*   *   *

After the final ceremonies, in which a sacrificial ox was struck down with an axe and Nero deposited a laurel crown before the statue of Jupiter in the hope that the mob would interpret this as his final triumph over the Parthians, the procession returned by the same route.

'Just take one more look at those Horses,' Nero requested. 'The whole essence of horse frozen forever in time!'

'Forever?' he repeated, as he resumed his routine waving almost mechanically. 'I wonder. So much of the ancient world has disappeared.'

'I'll give you a permanent monument, my Lord,' Tiridates declared enthusiastically. 'I'll rebuild my capital and call it Neroneia.'

'Neroneia! How marvellous! To help you I'll send you some of our best architects and artists. There's nothing like being surrounded by great art.'

Nero was deeply touched by Tiridates' spontaneous tribute, but he had seen what the Romans themselves had done to

88

places like Carthage and Corinth and had no illusions about the permanence of piled-up stones.

'Everything decays or is destroyed,' he sighed. 'Nobody, not even Emperors, not even gods, can gain immortality through stone. As Ovid puts it, "Time devours all things".'

He paused, then asked, 'I wonder how I will be remembered centuries from now, Tiridates? As a statesman? As an Emperor who brought peace to the people? As a poet? Or might it be as a musician?'

*   *   *

'Qualis artifex pereo!'—'What an artist dies in me!' was the last recorded remark of Nero, convinced to the end of his genius. Hiding in a slave's cubicle he committed suicide to escape execution by the 'ancient method', after being deposed in AD 68 only two years after his Golden Day with Tiridates. For the Establishment the last straw had been the Greek-style triumph he had perpetrated in honour of his 1,808 victories in the musical and athletic festivals during his tour of Greece. The sight of the Emperor preening himself in his chariot with Diodorus the harpist alongside, while the accompanying soldiers were made to bear adulatory placards on the tips of their spears, had been too nauseating.

Nero's argument that Greek contests strengthened the body and mind while the Roman type destroyed both, cut no ice with the conservatives, who regarded them as diverting energies from training in the essential art of war. What better proof of the Emperor's infamy did they need than his announcement to the Greeks that he was liberating them from Roman rule? They preferred the liberation exemplified by General Lucius Mummius, who had shown the Greeks in Corinth the real meaning of Roman power. Softness never paid.

Time was to prove them right. Indulgent neglect of defence and Intelligence coupled with complacent faith in the Pax Romana, despite the baying of fanatical barbarian leaders determined to destroy it, would be a major factor in the Empire's decline.

*   *   *

Nero was only thirty-one when he finally stabbed himself, a year younger than Alexander had been at his death, and unlike the Macedonian, who succumbed in victory, he went in disillusion and despair. His passing ended the Julian line with its dynastic sanctity, laying the succession open to any opportunist who could drum up the loyalty of the Legions.

Under his successor, General Galba, who was soon replaced by Otho, the man from whom Nero had abstracted the Four Horses of Lysippus, most of the dead Emperor's monuments were destroyed. His arch was torn down as desecrating the Sacred Hill. The statuary group was dismantled and Nero's effigy smashed and cast into the melting-pot.

About two hundred and fifty years later the Four Horses passed into the possession of the Emperor Constantine, and when he decided to transfer the main capital of the Empire to the small port of Byzantium and build a magnificent New Rome, which quickly became known as Constantinople, they were taken there with many other treasures to adorn it. There they were to stand unbridled in pairs atop a high tower beside the royal box in the Hippodrome, the vast chariot-racing arena which provided the amusement factor in the bread-and-entertainment formula.

Constantine did not replace Apollo in the chariot because, following his vision of a flaming cross in the noon sky accompanied by the admonition 'By this conquer!', he had made Christianity the state religion. So the stallions stood proudly alone, as a tribute not to any god but to the spirit of the horse on which the conquests, commerce and administration of the Roman Empire had so depended.

During the nine centuries they remained there, undisturbed through sultry summers and winters chilled by winds from the Russian steppes, they witnessed many extraordinary events centred around a succession of extraordinary rulers. The Hippodrome was also the main centre for public announcements, the means of communication between authority and Constantinople's million inhabitants, most of whom never ventured outside the high city walls. Whether he liked it or not the Emperor, who was also Viceroy of Christ, had to attend the Hippodrome sports and show himself to his subjects. So it was also the centre for denouncements of officials, military chiefs and even the Emperor himself, leading to bloody brawls between rival factions, private murders, political assassinations and summary executions, sometimes of horrific refinement.

But nothing that happened beneath the Four Horses was to match in barbaric brutality or historic significance the events of 9 April 1204, the most shameful day in Christianity's violent history, which was once again to dispatch them on their travels.

Crusade to Constantinople

'Some sure to succeed, others destined to fail,
Does reason or primitive impulse prevail?'

Chapter Seven

His ears were getting bigger. Quite definitely. Or that was the way they seemed to Enrico Dandolo as he peered into his polished steel mirror on that fine spring morning in the year 1201, the eighth of his reign as Doge. Admittedly his sight was poor. It had been deteriorating for years ever since that failure of a mission to Constantinople, where he had suffered a head injury affecting the optic nerve. But it was clear enough to see his ears, pendulous chin-flap and nearly bald head.

Fortunately, the white linen skull-cap he was about to don would help to hide these penalties of his longevity. Perhaps, he thought, that was why the ducal headgear had been so designed by his predecessors, with its ear-flaps tying beneath the chin. And why the purple silk vestment covered his arms and reached to the ground, concealing the withered muscles, cross-hatched, mottled skin, varicose veins and other obscenities.

'Have you ever thought, Rinaldo, that man is the only creature that becomes ugly in old age?' he observed to the valet who was tying the strings behind the thinning beard.

'No, Serenissimus. But few of God's creatures are blessed with such long life as you.'

Dandolo laughed rather croakily. 'I owe my survival to steering clear of the doctors. The wisest thing the Blessed St Mark ever wrote was about the woman who "had suffered many things of many physicians, had spent all that she had and was nothing bettered but rather grew worse". But you are quite right, Rinaldo. I must count my blessings.'

He tested the string for comfort and the valet superimposed the horned cloth-of-gold hat. Then he stood up wearily and raised his arms while the jewelled belt was buckled. His gout was bad, his back ached and he had a niggling pain in his prostate, but this was one day when his infirmities would have

95

to be ignored. Dandolo had learned that the most effective way of achieving that was involvement in action. There was nothing like excitement for raising the pain threshold.

The meeting for which he was being prepared was big business. And big business was what the Dogeship and Venice were mainly about. Happily, he consoled himself, his mind seemed to be as clear and his acumen as sharp as they had ever been. The body of which he had once been vain in his days as a young patrician might have decayed, so that while he had never been tall he was becoming noticeably shorter as the discs of his spine continued to flatten, but there was no deterioration in his mental powers. Or so he assured himself as he strode with deliberate purpose out of his dressing-room to the audience chamber, where envoys from the most illustrious Norman princes and knights would shortly be admitted.

The commercial opportunity, which he was destined to exploit to such an extent that it would change the history of the world, had its roots in an event which had occurred when he had been in office only a year. The brilliant Arab ruler, Saladin, who had defeated the Second Crusade and forced the Third to accept a degrading truce in spite of the exploits of Richard Coeur de Lion, had died, and Pope Innocent III had promptly declared a Fourth Crusade to deliver Jerusalem and the rest of the Holy Land from the grip of the infidel. Many Christians would die in the endeavour, but it was all in the long-term interests of the true God and of His Church.

The Papal call had been well received, especially in France. Certain warlords were keen to 'take the Cross' for their Saviour's sake and for their own, because the contagious guilt of sin and the need to expiate it had spread from the monasteries and convents to the castles. Many among the impecunious and the seedy responded in the hope of booty, while others simply relished the chance of battle. So after many months of discussion, six envoys under the leadership of Geoffrey de Villehardouin, Marshal of Champagne, were dispatched with plenipotentiary powers to make arrangements with the Doge of Venice for ships to transport an overwhelming force of Crusaders to the shores of the Holy Land, with Old Cairo as the first and main gateway.

Sensing a deal that would give a whole year's work to the Venetian shipyards and restore the profitable pilgrim passenger trade, Dandolo had received the envoys with honour but without wasting time.

'We come in the name of the noblest barons of France who have taken the Cross to avenge the insults to our Lord, Jesus Christ and, if God will, to conquer Jerusalem. No other power on earth can aid us as you can . . .'

'On what terms?' the Doge had interrupted tersely.

'On any terms it pleaseth you to name if they be not too hard for us.'

He had given them time to be impressed with the splendour of the city, which proclaimed the wealth and power of its rulers, while he considered this promising windfall with the Quarantia, his Council of Forty; and on this, the twelfth day since their arrival, he was to tell them the terms. They were tough terms, tougher than the rather ingenuous envoys were to appreciate when they accepted them, and behind them was secret knowledge supplied by an army of spies, military and commercial, located in every city of importance to the Venetian state.

After paying their respects, the summoned envoys heard Dandolo's interpreter read from a parchment draft:

'These are the terms I will advise the people to accept. Transport ships, sufficient for 4,500 armoured knights and war-horses, 9,000 squires and their horses plus 20,000 foot soldiers, will be built and supplied complete with victualling for one year at the rate of four silver marks for each horse and two silver marks for each man, making in all 85,000 marks according to the mark-standard of Cologne.'

Villehardouin and the others were staggered at the price but then the Doge announced, 'And to show our approval of this noble enterprise and our deep concern that the Holy Sepulchre should be in infidel hands, Venice will furnish fifty-two war-galleys, fully manned to convoy the transports and assist in the attack.'

The envoys smiled at each other in appreciation but their chagrin quickly returned when the Doge added, 'And since we shall be taking active part in the assaults, providing weapons and engines of war for that purpose, the State of Venice will require half of all conquests in booty and territory.'

It was monstrous exactment, particularly as all the ships would eventually revert to the Venetians, and the envoys immediately went into whispered consultation. Some were for rejecting the offer but Villehardouin resolved their doubts by pointing out, 'We might get better terms elsewhere but would they be fulfilled? At least we can be sure that the Venetians will keep their word and honour their part of the bargain to the letter—and on time.'

Reluctant to leave empty-handed and sensing that Dandolo was not a person to be bargained with, the envoys quickly produced pre-signed agreements complete with the dangling seals of their Norman lords.

Dandolo could scarcely conceal his delight with the deal. If it progressed in the way he was beginning to think it might, in view of the intelligence he had received about the leaders of the Crusade, it would secure so much more than 85,000 silver marks for the coffers of the State he loved and served. The people of Venice would become shareholders in a gigantic enterprise for the continuous exploitation of the riches of the East.

'My Lords,' he announced, raising his hands, 'before I can affirm this contract there is an essential procedure which is much more than a formality. I have to secure the agreement of the people of Venice. So will you please publicly declare the great objectives of your mission to a General Assembly of as many of the people as can be mustered in the Basilica of St Mark?'

The envoys agreed with alacrity, and the following day Villehardouin addressed a tightly packed audience in the great Byzantine building. It was called a Basilica in the Roman tradition because it was not then the Cathedral of Venice, being the Doge's personal church, but served more as a public meeting-place and parliament—the centre of the Venetian Empire where rulers, clergy and people assembled in united purpose.

'Have pity on the Holy City of Jerusalem and help the barons of France to avenge the shame of Jesus Christ,' the

98

Frenchman implored. 'We have come to beg assistance from you because no people have such power on the sea as you.'

The envoys then knelt down, weeping aloud in supplication before the crowd. Stretching their hands high they urged the Venetians to grant their request.

Observing that tears were streaming down the pallid face of the old Doge, the people, caught up in the religious fervour, responded with a spontaneous shout which reverberated through the dark recesses, galleries and bulging domes of the ancient building.

Next day the agreements were sealed by the Doge and the contract consecrated in a High Mass in the Basilica, Dandolo and his Councillors pledging themselves to 'come to the aid of the Holy Land in the name of Jesus Christ', and the French voicing the old crusading cry, *'Deus lo vult!'*

'The ships are to be ready and the Crusaders' payments will be forthcoming by the Feast of Saint Peter and Paul next year,' the public was told, but the Crusaders' insistence that Old Cairo should be the first beach-head was not revealed. Dandolo required that secrecy concerning their precise destination should be preserved for operational security.

'News from spies can travel quickly,' he said darkly, with the secret carrier-pigeon service used by his own agents in mind.

But the devious Doge had no intention of ever delivering a rampaging army to Egypt. The import of grain from Egypt and its resale at inflated prices was one of Venice's main sources of wealth, and Dandolo had recently concluded a secret non-aggression treaty with the Sultan there. In return for monopoly trading concessions in spices, the ingredients of incense, which made the stench of the faithful bearable in packed churches, and other highly saleable commodities, the Venetian State had specifically undertaken to prevent any crusading army from attacking Egypt. And while Venice might be criticized for ruthlessness and greed, its commercial word was its bond.

It was more than Dandolo dared do to keep the truth from the Council, which was very much more than a cipher. The terror of the Inquisitors, who nosed into every hint of double-dealing against the State, embraced even the Doge.

'With Venetian admirals in command, including Vital, one of my own relatives, the Crusaders' ships will have to go where we decide,' he told the Councillors. 'Their secret orders will ensure that some maritime excuse can be found for by-passing Egypt and landing in Syria.'

But Dandolo already had a different landing site in mind—provided the situation could be safely exploited to that extent.

'We shall have to play it carefully though, won't we?' he asked the caged cock goldfinch he often addressed to excuse his habit of thinking aloud, which was becoming ever more compulsive with the years. 'These Normans might be simple soldiers but they are not exactly fools, are they? We shall need to cultivate some friends among them.'

The bird responded with a soft, sweet song, which the old man interpreted as an omen of success.

*   *   *

It did not surprise the Doge to learn that in order to provide two hundred marks as a token payment to start construction of the ships the envoys had been obliged to go to Venetian money-lenders. He expected a continuing struggle to secure the full payment, but that was an adversity which contained the seeds of rich advantage.

Both parties quickly dispatched ambassadors to the Vatican with copies of the agreement for the Pope's blessing, which he gave with joy. On Dandolo's part this had been no more than a formality. To him, as to all Venetians, St Mark was more important than St Peter.

*   *   *

Having set to work the shipwrights and chandlers of the Arsenal, which had so impressed the French envoys with its size and the efficiency and speed with which the galleys could be commissioned from standardized parts kept in store—one a day, complete with armament and rigging—Dandolo, impelled by a surge of enthusiasm he had not experienced for years, ordered the construction of a hutted encampment on the Lido, the island on the far side of the lagoon from the city. The rude Franks had a reputation for rapacity, especially when they became bored through idleness, and he had no wish to have any of them roaming Venice.

'Isolated on the Lido they will be dependent on our barges for supplying food and water, for which they will have to pay until the fleet sets sail and the victualling contract takes effect,' Dandolo told his Council with a sly smile. 'And if any of the money is not forthcoming they can be held there helpless until it is.'

Having secured a list of the barons and knights who had taken the Cross and had them checked out by his intelligence agents, Dandolo knew that many of them, far from being able to subscribe anything, were on the make.

Chapter Eight

Round about Pentecost of the year 1202 the men-at-arms began to collect on the Lido, arriving in small bands which had travelled for the most part over the Alps, and soon some twenty-five thousand had gathered. It quickly became obvious that the force was going to be much smaller than expected because the enthusiasm of so many had waned, either before they had set off or on the way, while others had decided that Genoa and other ports offered easier terms and a more direct route to the Holy Land.

Chief among the leaders who had kept to their sacred oath and had arrived in Venice were Count Baldwin of Flanders; Count Thibaut of Champagne; Simon de Montfort; the valiant Marquis of Montferrat, head of a distinguished Italian house and known to his troops as 'The Giant' because of his splendid physique; and Geoffrey de Villehardouin, who had headed the envoys.

The Venetians were on time and Dandolo took pride in escorting the chief crusaders to the Arsenal.

'My Lords, your ships!' he declared, indicating scores of war-galleys and transports nearing completion, with many more fully equipped and moored in the lagoon outside the crenellated security walls, the fifteen formidable towers of which encircled the largest naval dockyard in Europe.

There were murmurs of approval all round. The famous Arsenal—a corruption of an Arabic word meaning 'a place of industry'—had certainly lived up to its name. As the Crusaders inspected the quality of the ships and their fittings, from the workmanship of the decks and masts to the sails and ropes made on the premises, their faith in the success of their great enterprise soared. They smiled and slapped each other on the back as they congratulated themselves on their choice of an ally. Nothing had been skimped and they understood exactly why as they were conducted round the seemingly endless warehouses and yards, with the old, half-blind Doge astounding them with his agility, endurance and obvious enjoyment as he sniffed the scents of sawdust, paint and hot caulkers' pitch.

'There are sixteen thousand workmen here, all craftsmen or carefully selected apprentices,' they were told, 'and they use the best materials the world can provide.'

The Arsenal was the hub of Venetian wealth, the industrial complex where the merchant navy and war fleet were generated and where they returned bringing exotic timbers, hemp, metals and tar.

'As you see, my Lords, Venice has kept her word,' Dandolo said after they had re-embarked for the short journey back to the Ducal Palace, where the leaders were to be entertained. 'May we now have the balance of payment which is due?'

He did not have to observe the embarrassment of Montferrat and the rest to know, with so many absentees, what the answer must be.

'After collecting all the cash which has been brought in so far I am afraid we are still well short of the total,' Monferrat replied, his heavy, black moustache accentuating the dejection on his usually handsome face. 'All those of us here have kept our word and we can hardly be held to blame for those who have defected.'

The little Doge affected to be both surprised and deeply disappointed. His features were so fiercely stern that they were more like those of a *condottiere* than of a former merchant.

'That puts me in a very difficult position with my Council and the people of Venice, of whom I am merely the servant and spokesman. You will have to find the balance quickly, my Lords. We have put ourselves to great expense and you are the guarantors. See what you can raise.'

The Crusaders' plight did not induce the Doge to slow down the work in the Arsenal or cancel any of the ships, many of which would now be unwanted. A deal was a deal and Venice would fulfil her part of it down to the last plank. Besides, it suited him to put the Crusaders into a position of maximum personal embarrassment.

*   *   *

103

The Crusaders borrowed heavily from the Venetian money-lenders, and summoned over so much of their private treasure that day after day the idlers, stall-keepers, barbers, jugglers and fortune-tellers huddled round the base of the Campanile saw whole table-services, goblets and other objects of silver and gold carried into the Doge's Palace, where they were weighed, costed, entered into the account books and stored in the Treasury. The total value still added up to no more than fifty thousand marks, but not until the fleet was completely finished and furbished did Dandolo indicate the full extent of his implacability.

He summoned the Crusaders' leaders from the Lido and announced: 'My Lords, you have failed to keep your bargain. To us that is an extremely serious matter. As I see it we are under no obligation to transport you anywhere and are entitled to keep both the ships and the money you have so far paid.'

'The Giant' and the rest shifted uneasily, deeply regretting that they should ever have put their heads into such a noose. Used to walled towns and grim fortresses they had marvelled that Venice could be such an open city, but with their army trapped on the Lido and dependent on rapacious Venetian traders for food, they appreciated the effectiveness of the city's natural moats.

The Doge stared silently; then, with a despairing shake of the head, declared, 'I can see no other solution but I will consult with my Council to discover if some other way out can be found. Failing that, none of you will be allowed to leave the island nor will anybody bring you anything to eat or drink.'

Degraded and helpless the proud men bowed their way out, suppressing their anger, to return to the Lido, where their men were growing ever more restless.

With an outstanding capacity for judging how others would react to various situations—which he regarded as the kernel of accumulated wisdom—Dandolo already had a solution he believed the Crusaders would be unable to reject, but it would help to let them sweat for a few more days and give him time to deal with routine matters of State without overloading himself. He had learned, long ago, the essential survival art of pacing himself.

∗   ∗   ∗

The proposal he put to his Council could hardly be turned down by them either. The King of Hungary had removed from Venetian rule the port and city of Zara on the Eastern side of the Adriatic, not only eliminating an important trading post but establishing a constant threat to the Republic's shipping moving in and out of the Mediterranean.

'I suggest to you,' the Doge told his Councillors, 'that in return for an agreement to postpone payment of the thirty-six thousand marks still outstanding—though of course not to waive it—the crusading fleet should recapture Zara for us on its way to the East, a feat which we know is beyond the power of Venice alone.'

While the startled Councillors considered all the implications, Dandolo added, 'We have nothing to lose and much to gain this way. The alternative is the collapse of the Crusade which has the highest of all purposes—the recovery of the Holy Sepulchre.'

One by one the Councillors raised their hands in agreement.

The following day the Doge called the Crusaders' leaders to his presence again and explained the proposition, which he attributed solely to the Council. There were those among them who were revolted by it.

'We want no diversion,' Simon de Montfort declared stoutly. 'We have not staked our wealth and our lives to fight battles for Venice. Further, Zara is a Christian city and the King of Hungary is a Crusader himself, so the censure of the Pope for such an appalling act would be inevitable.'

'My Lords, I fully appreciate your objections,' Dandolo said deferentially. 'But solely because of your pecuniary problem it will now be October before you are ready to sail. I have consulted my kinsman, Admiral Vital Dandolo, who will be going with you. He says that the weather at sea cannot be anticipated at that time, and you may find you need somewhere to winter before the long voyage through the Mediter-

105

ranean to Cairo. The sea can be very rough there. If you capture Zara, which will be easy for such a force, it will offer you comfortable winter quarters and some early booty for you and your men.'

'And what if we refuse?' de Montfort asked haughtily.

'Then you winter on the Lido,' Dandolo replied grimly. 'That is unless you are all prepared to swim home.'

The Crusaders bowed their way out and returned to the Lido to consider this monstrous ultimatum. Their immediate response was to send the Cardinal whom the Pope had attached to the expedition, to reinforce their objections.

The Doge was even rougher with him.

'If you have come with any advice about the spiritual needs of the force, you are welcome; if you have come with advice about secular affairs you had better go back to Rome.'

To the further objections of the Crusaders, Dandolo made full use of the old man's privilege of being deaf or off-colour when it suited him.

*　　*　　*

Confined in the hot July sun on the Lido, short of food, women or any other comforts, the Crusaders soon accepted that they had no alternative but to comply, however grudgingly. When they returned to the Ducal Palace, Dandolo was ready with a dramatic announcement guaranteed to dispel any sullenness.

'My Lords, as we shall now be in this great venture together, I too have decided to take the Cross and will personally command the Venetian forces against the Crescent.'

Astonishment was the immediate reaction, quickly followed by apprehension. Could such an aged, purblind man even survive the journey, much less command an enormous fleet? Yet the apparent sincerity of the Doge, and his determination to risk his brief remaining time in fighting for the Saviour, was so heartening that Montferrat and his colleagues could not resist a cheer, which was loudly echoed along the Lido when the news was given to the troops. Perhaps they had misjudged the old fellow who, maybe, had been required to transmit decisions of the all-powerful Council with which he did not necessarily agree.

In fact at that stage the Council had no notion of the ultimate project in Dandolo's mind, a project which demanded his presence throughout the Crusaders' journey.

The previous Doge had taken the precaution of acquiring merit for entry to Paradise by retiring to a monastery. Dandolo, like most Venetians, had no morbid preoccupation with death, and though in the nature of things his time must be short, he still clung to the illusion that while death was inevitable it would not strike him in the near future. Glory appealed to him more than monastic contemplation, and if he could manipulate events as he hoped, glory was on the cards.

*   *   *

'I might be ancient, Rinaldo, but I am not senile,' the Doge said to his valet as he peered dimly at his bloodshot eyes in the mirror. 'My mind is clear and I have no diseases of indulgence. I've always kept myself spare and lived in moderation. At least for the last sixty years,' he added, knowing that Rinaldo had some knowledge of his reputation as a young blood. 'With God's blessing I shall live to return from this voyage.'

'I am sure He will grant you that favour, Serenissimus.'

'Grant *us* that favour, Rinaldo. You will be coming with me.'

Rinaldo was appalled. 'Me, my Lord?' He had never been on anything bigger than the ornamental barge which transported the Doge to the ritual Ascension Day festival of wedding Venice to the sea.

'Yes, Rinaldo, you,' the Doge replied with a touch of glee. 'You shouldn't have made yourself indispensable. You've become my tapping-stick so I can't possibly go into battle without you.'

Rinaldo gulped. Into battle! He wasn't a fighting man but he knew better than to argue with his master. 'It's all right for the old man,' he told the goldfinch, as he cleaned out its gilded cage. 'He hasn't got long to live anyway. I've got far more to lose if anything happens to me.'

107

The goldfinch inclined its crimson face and appeared to chirp in agreement, unaware that it too would be making the long voyage never to return.

*   *   *

On the following Sunday most of the Venetian nobles—some arriving by gondola, others on horseback—and many of the people, gathered in St Mark's. Before the Mass began, Dandolo, wearing the ceremonial horned cap adorned with pearls, diamonds, emeralds and one magnificent ruby, mounted his pulpit and said in as strong a voice as he could muster, 'Signori, you are now associated with the most important enterprise that men can undertake. I am old and feeble but if you consent that I take the Cross and that my son, in my stead, may direct the affairs of this city, I will go forth and live or die with the pilgrims, whichever God may destine for me.'

Such courageous words from the old man moved the assembly to shout their approval, and many wept as he knelt before the altar and the red cross was sewn on the front of his cap.

Only because the Doge would be operating far outside Venetian territory was he allowed to consider taking command of Venetian forces. At home the Council employed *condottiere*, foreign professional fighters, to lead their troops, to prevent any citizen from controlling armed power which might be misused to overthrow the State.

One man retained serious reservations about Dandolo's personal involvement—the Cardinal attached to the Crusade. Being privy to the Zara commitment he asked himself, 'With this avaricious old devil in command, who knows what else he may demand once we are on the high seas?'

But as the alternative might be the abandonment of the entire venture, which would certainly displease the thrustful Pope, he convinced himself that perhaps any means justified such a sublime end as the liberation of Jerusalem.

*   *   *

It was a proud and immensely formidable fleet which set sail from the lagoon of Venice in the first week of October 1202—some five hundred ships flying the coloured standards of the noblemen, their emblazoned shields hung on the deck-towers, and with the banner of Venice, the golden lion of St Mark on a red field, floating from the masts.

As the expedition eased out of the quiet water towards the despicable deeds it would accomplish, the Crusaders burst into psalms, while from the quays priests and monks chanted 'Veni, Creator Spiritus . . .'—'Come, Holy Ghost, our souls inspire . . .' with a following couplet of biting relevance for Enrico Dandolo, 'Enable with perpetual light the dullness of our blinded sight.'

Chapter Nine

In the following month Zara was stormed and captured after only five days' fighting. Dandolo took possession of it and divided the money, plate and other booty with the Crusaders. The weather was fine and the Crusaders were anxious to push on, but for the Doge's secret purpose the longer they delayed the better. So he returned to his ploy that because of the risk of sudden storms it would be wise for them to over-winter in the countryside round Zara, where provisions were plentiful for the taking, adding darkly that he had heard from agents who had reached Zara that there was famine in Egypt.

Again there was deep dissension, expressing itself in defections and some savage fights between the Venetians and the French, but with total control of the fleet, Dandolo once more had his way. He held on to it even when the Pope, on hearing that knights and men-at-arms wearing the Holy Cross had been misused to assault a Christian city, excommunicated them all.

To many of the Crusaders, even among the fiercest and most crude, this was a catastrophe, and a deputation was sent immediately to Rome to beg the Holy Father to lift the interdict.

Had they dared, Rinaldo and some of the other God-fearing Venetians would have quoted St Mark back at their leader—'For what shall it profit a man if he gain the whole world and lose his own soul'—but the effect of excommunication on Dandolo was no more devastating than a curling of his lip into a wry smile, which some who observed it interpreted as a snarl.

Dandolo was not in much fear of meeting his Maker deprived of the last rites. He was feeling fitter than he had done for years. The reconquest of Zara had rejuvenated him. And for the first time he appreciated the true meaning of his title

110

'Serenissimus'. With no Councillors, no Inquisitors, no other Venetians to challenge him, he really did feel 'Most Serene'.

★   ★   ★

While more defected during the stay at Zara, others joined the expedition there and among them was Alexius, young son of Isaac, the Emperor of Constantinople, which many still called Byzantium, who had been deposed and, it was believed, killed by a usurper. Dandolo affected to be surprised by the arrival of this high-born recruit just before the ships were due to sail, but secretly he had been in contact with him through agents while the youth had been visiting Verona, not far from Venice, before the fleet first departed. Montferrat, 'The Giant', also knew Alexius and for family reasons of his own approved of the potentialities Dandolo had in mind, a chance which provided the Doge with the ally he required.

As the Doge had anticipated, the pillage of Zara had not produced nearly enough for the Crusaders to pay off their debt and, as provisions were low after the winter and it was up to the Venetians to supply them, he took the opportunity of revealing the centrepiece of his ingenious design.

'My Lords,' he announced when sailing conditions were almost right, 'there is only one solution to the predicament in which we find ourselves. We cannot possibly sail straight to Egypt without supplies, so let us first go down to Constantinople. That city has owed the Venetian Republic 200,000 marks for many years in compensation for terrible wrongs to Venetian subjects living there. So we have every justification in taking whatever we need from its rich possessions around the city, which will offer little, if any, resistance to us.'

There were immediate cries of 'Twister!', 'Scoundrel!', 'Villain!', 'Judas!' and even 'Traitor!' As for going *down* to Constantinople, such a diversion would mean sailing five hundred miles north when Old Cairo was south.

Following the impact of the excommunication, which had been reluctantly lifted from the French but not from the Venetians on the strict understanding that the expedition would

111

proceed forthwith to Egypt, many were utterly revolted by this latest attempt to divert it.

'I for one will have no more of it,' Simon de Montfort declared resolutely and quit immediately, taking his men-at-arms with him. Others opposed to attack on lands belonging to the Emperor of the East, who shared with the Pope the distinction of being Vicar of Christ, prepared to follow him. But Dandolo was ready for their reservations and was not to be denied the ambitious scheme he knew would make Venice mistress of the East if he could seduce the Crusaders into accomplishing it for him.

It was Montferrat who took the initiative with his colleagues, after private discussions with the Doge.

'My Lords, remember that we have with us the rightful Emperor of Constantinople, Alexius. If we take him with us to restore him to his throne we shall have justice on our side because we will be entering his territory, and he has agreed that we can take whatever we need there to further our expedition.'

Dandolo immediately supported The Giant. 'Surely, my Lords, when the people of Constantinople see their rightful Emperor they will throw open the gates and welcome us as brother Christians—perhaps even join us in our assault on Palestine!'

The Doge and Montferrat knew that Alexius had no claim whatever to the throne of Constantinople. The crown did not pass by succession there. The people elected each Emperor, or rather approved of the man who managed to elect himself, on the principle—which had produced some outstanding leaders—that how the Emperor came to the throne was less important than the fact that he got there, which must, automatically, be by God's will. But most of the Crusaders were sufficiently ignorant of Constantinople and its customs to give credence to Alexius, who desisted from picking his nose for a few moments to confirm, 'I will be happy to give you all the assistance I can in return for your help in restoring the city and its empire to me, its rightful ruler.'

There were, however, seasoned warriors among them who realized that it might not be possible to put this brash Young Pretender on the throne without assaulting the City of Constantinople itself, the most fortified in the world, which had resisted attack after attack from Bulgars, Turks and other armies far stronger than theirs. And there was Rome to consider.

'What of the Pope?' Dandolo was asked. 'How will he react? It is all very well for you, who are already excommunicated. Nothing worse can befall you.'

The Doge was ready with his riposte. 'The Holy Father will be grateful, I can assure you. Constantinople has never accepted the rule of Rome. Indeed, I heard it said while I was there, not once but many times, that they would prefer the Turban to the Tiara!'

This was near to saying that the people of Constantinople were infidels, but there were many by then who did not trust Dandolo further than he could see them, which they knew was not very far.

Sensing that once again he was to get his way, Dandolo continued, 'You must remember that these people may claim to be of Roman origin—they are forever saying their ancestors came over with Constantine—but in fact they are Greeks. They speak Greek and behave like Greeks—treacherously.'

Villehardouin looked at Montferrat. What did that make Alexius then? He was a Greek. Why should he be trusted?'

It was true that Constantinople was in financial debt to Venice, but the Venetians had risen to wealth and power under the protective wing of the Byzantine Empire and recognized its ruler as the legitimate successor to the ancient Roman emperors. Indeed, never having been conquered by the mainland barbarians, as Rome and the rest of Italy had been, the Venetians regarded themselves as among the few remaining Romans, deriving their culture from the last Roman bastion, Constantinople, as their art and architecture, from the mosaics of Torcello to the cupolas of St Mark's, clearly showed. They also shared a dislike of the Roman Popes.

As his final throw Dandolo then revealed that Alexius was prepared to offer further tempting concessions if the Crusaders succeeded in putting him on the throne.

Producing a parchment statement in large script he had concocted with the Pretender, Dandolo, his long nose almost touching the document, read, 'The Emperor Alexius will revictual us for a further year and then accompany us to the Holy Land with a force of ten thousand of his own soldiers and man a perpetual guard of five hundred over the Holy Sepulchre!'

He paused to let the offer sink home, then when this had been welcomed by some he delivered his master-stroke to dispose of the qualms of those who still feared the wrath of Rome.

'Further he has promised to put Constantinople and all its territories under the supremacy of His Holiness, thereby uniting the Churches of East and West forever!'

A union of East and West after all those centuries of dissension! The ingenuous Alexius nodded smilingly, convinced by Dandolo and Montferrat not only of the righteousness of his cause but that all these splendid gestures were not merely possible but easy of accomplishment.

Montferrat and Dandolo looked at the Cardinal but there was no joyful expression there. He was now beginning to doubt that the expedition would ever reach Palestine, in which case he would be closest to the fury of Pope Innocent, who was a man to be feared.

Some of the Crusaders even suspected that this second diversion had been planned before they had set sail and asked themselves, 'Why should we be dictated to by a little old man in his dotage? Is there to be no end to his villainy and his greed?'

It was a question they would ask again and again but the answer would always be the same. The disciplined Venetian mariners would obey only the Doge, so the alternative to going where he wanted was to desert with nothing to show for their time and money.

The Crusaders' suspicions were even more justified than they appreciated. Dandolo did not disclose that Alexius had committed himself to repay the 200,000 marks owed to Venice. Nor did he tell Alexius or anyone else that the deposed Emperor Isaac, his father, was not dead but surviving in one of the imperial dungeons. Dandolo's spies among the large Venetian contingent living in Constantinople had informed him that the old man had only been blinded, an obscenity to which the Byzantines were addicted.

★   ★   ★

Shortly before the Crusaders left Zara, the Doge astonished and infuriated them further by sending in his men to pull down the walls, towers and even the city's splendid churches. He had never intended to reoccupy the ancient port, which had repeatedly revolted against foreign rule. He simply wanted it rubbed out, having more effective replacements in mind.

His action convinced them that they would never fathom this strange character who thought in a way which, they decided, must be Oriental. He never gave them much opportunity to study him, keeping himself to his fellow Venetians, who did not hide their arrogant dislike of all foreigners, and pleading age for his inability to carouse late into the night in the French style. But as they sailed down the Adriatic towards Corfu, with the galleys wallowing in the swell, so many of the knights suffered the indignity of being sea-sick that they convinced themselves that Dandolo had been right in delaying the voyage until after the winter storms.

As soon as they reached Corfu many of the men were so relieved to be on dry land that they proposed to defect and offer their services in a closer war in Sicily, but after Montferrat and their other leaders had sworn on Holy Relics that they would sail them direct to Palestine, they agreed to stay with the Crusade.

Dandolo's only commitment had been to quote from his favourite gospel, naturally that of St Mark, 'If a house be divided against itself, that house cannot stand. Surely that is even more true of a Crusade!'

Once the grumblers were embarked and out in the open sea he ordered the fleet to turn left towards the Sea of Marmara and Constantinople, where all ideals and integrity were to be overwhelmed by greed and lust.

Chapter Ten

The first sight of the fabulous city of Constantinople, on the morning of Midsummer's Eve 1203, with its tiers of palaces, towers, lofty domes and enough buildings to house a million people, offered prospect of loot enough to send them all home so rich that in the minds of many all thoughts of the Holy Land evaporated. Others assured themselves that 'If we can repent in Jerusalem for our previous sins we can also repent for this.' Most, if they thought about it at all, took the view that matters were out of their hands, orders were orders and that they could not be held to blame by anyone, including the Almighty.

To the Doge, as he stood by the prow of his flagship, the picture in his mind was more detailed and more personal.

'Can you see a large palace standing to the left of a lighthouse?' he asked his kinsman, Admiral Vital Dandolo.

'I can, my Lord.'

'And behind that palace can you see a great, curving wall?'

'I can indeed.'

'That is the Hippodrome, the sports arena built by Constantine when he founded this city nearly nine hundred years ago. It was there that I lost my sight.'

The Admiral looked at the Doge with some surprise. Like most of his relatives, he knew that some incident when Enrico had been serving as envoy in Constantinople had been responsible for his progressive loss of vision, but there had always been some mystery about it and discussion of what occurred had never been encouraged.

'May I inquire what happened, my Lord?' the Admiral asked cautiously.

Dandolo's mouth tightened. Then he said with some venom, 'It was the Greeks, the treacherous Greeks. They have always been treacherous and they always will be. Remember

116

the Trojan horse, Vital! Never forget the Trojan horse. That was typical of the Greeks!'

The Admiral assumed that no further information would be forthcoming but Dandolo's face relaxed into a momentary smile.

'It's funny I should have said that,' he murmured.

'Said what, my Lord?'

'About the Trojan horse. There was a horse involved in the treachery against me. Or rather four horses. Can you see two towers in the Hippodrome, two towers, one topped by four golden horses?'

The Admiral shielded his eyes and looked hard beyond the Boucoleon Palace. 'No my Lord.'

'Well, they are there, unless they have been taken down. The Byzantines are very proud of them. They say they were made for Alexander the Great by some sculptor whose name escapes me. They are always going on about Alexander, though of course he wasn't a Greek at all; he was a Macedonian. Anyway, some Greeks I was involved with in negotiations about the ill-treatment of Venetian nationals in the city urged me to let them take me to see the horses in the evening sun—"the best time", they said. I was foolish enough to go with them and the place was otherwise deserted. As I was looking up at the horses I was struck on the head from behind, robbed and left for dead. The Greeks said we had all been set upon by robbers and that they had managed to escape, but I am sure they organized it and the robbery was just a cover.'

'Why did they want to kill you?' the Admiral asked.

'Because I had discovered proof of their treachery against our nationals. They had been extracting money from them and I was about to expose them to the Emperor, who could well have had them put to death.'

'And did you expose them when you had recovered?'

'Yes, but the villains argued that I was out of my mind as a result of the head-wound I had received. Anyway, I was so ill that our ambassador made me return home.'

The Admiral looked at the Doge standing erect with his arms folded, gazing in the direction of the Hippodrome.

'And now you have returned, my Lord.'

117

'Yes, Vital. Now I have returned. I hope to some purpose, if God continues to spare me.'

The Admiral, who alone had been told what was in the Doge's mind, wondered why God should spare any of them for such an enterprise but said briskly, 'I am sure He will spare you, my Lord. Considering the long voyage, you look remarkably fit.'

'That may be so, Vital, but there are things about age that can only be felt in the bone.'

Dandolo regarded the infirmities of age as a monstrous imposition. Surely, in a properly ordered system, there should be some reward for overcoming the appalling hazards of infancy, youth and middle age? Instead, all one could expect was diminishing health and strength.

*　　*　　*

The mighty walls and sea defences of the city dismayed many of those with experience of besieging smaller fortresses, but at their next meeting Dandolo was able to allay their fears.

'The Greeks won't fight,' he predicted confidently. 'At least not with any strength that should dismay us. They have no fleet left to defend their waters. All that remains of it are a few old galleys rotting in the Golden Horn.'

He pointed to the horn-shaped, deep-water inlet which stretched seven miles and would glow golden when the sun set. For centuries the greatest war- and merchant-fleet in the Mediterranean had sheltered there behind an enormous protective chain, which could be quickly lowered to let the fleet out to fight off an invader. But, as Dandolo knew from his spies, a succession of weak and decadent emperors had allowed the fleet to degenerate. They had even forbidden the cutting of wood to repair the warships because this damaged their hunting forests. Everything movable from anchors to ropes had been sold off by a succession of corrupt admirals.

'The Army is no better,' Dandolo assured the Crusaders. 'Apart from the Emperor's Varingian Guard it has no will to fight and few weapons to fight with. If the people are prevented from throwing open the gates for us when they see

118

their rightful Emperor, the Army will soon surrender once we begin to scale the walls.'

Scale the walls! What was the old bastard perpetrating now? The Crusaders had never seen such formidable fortifications, for there were none like them in the world. Immense walls rose sheer from the fast current sweeping down the Bosphorus, and on the landward side the city was protected by a succession of three walls with fighting towers behind a moat. And the man who was now talking so glibly about scaling them had assured the Frenchmen that with Alexius among their number there would be no need for an assault!

There could be no going back on the enterprise now, but more and more of the Crusaders realized that they had been duped by an incorrigible entrepreneur using French power and lives for Venice's commercial purposes.

But Dandolo soon mollified them. Like the taking of Zara, any attack involved another sea-crossing, so once again he held indisputable command and the detailed plan he discussed with Montferrat and the other leaders reassured them.

'I still hope that the gates will be thrown open to us, but should we be forced to take the city I have no intention of trying to assault the main walls. We Venetians will force the entry to the Golden Horn where the defences are much weaker because, in the past, so much reliance was placed on the fleet which was anchored there. And we Venetians will then attack the weaker walls there—*from our ships.*'

From their ships! The Crusaders wondered how this could possibly be done, but as Dandolo unfolded the details of his proposed operation they were even more astonished by the ingenuity and determination of the old man.

Privately, the Doge was wise enough to have some doubts about his judgment. He had witnessed in others how the faculty to distinguish between what is and what ought to be could diminish with age to the point of delusion. And, deprived of his Councillors, he was acutely aware of the weight of his responsibility under the corrupting circumstances of absolute power, and he used his valet to reassure himself.

'Rinaldo, you see more of me than anybody else and you see me off my guard. Tell me, because nobody else will dare to, do I seem to be behaving sensibly? I mean have you noticed anything about my behaviour that gives you cause to think I might be failing?'

'No, nothing, my Lord.'

'Come, Rinaldo. You must tell me the truth. I command you to.'

'There is just one thing, Serenissimus.'

'What is that?'

'You have developed a habit of telling people the same things twice, sometimes more. It's as though you have forgotten you have told them . . .'

Dandolo nodded. While his memory for the distant past seemed even to be improving—he found himself recalling the names of girls with whom he had dallied as a youth—he knew that his short-term memory was fading.

'You are sure that is all, Rinaldo?'

'There is nothing else, Serenissimus.'

'In that case I'm not doing too badly.'

Dandolo felt reassured, but he had intended to attack the city anyway.

★   ★   ★

When the Crusaders began to ransack the countryside for provisions, plundering the granaries and farms, the Byzantine Army showed itself on the walls; but the Emperor, with a million people behind him, made no attempt to destroy the ships or attack the invaders in strength when they landed on the shoreline below. When Dandolo sailed Alexius, the Young Pretender, close by the walls with a Greek-speaking sailor announcing that he was their rightful ruler come to liberate them from a usurper, all that the soldiers and the people did was to shout insults from on high.

As the Greek equivalents of 'Traitor!', 'Bastard!', 'Villain!' and 'Get lost!' came floating down from the battlements, expedited by obscene gestures, the Crusaders did not have to understand the words to appreciate the message.

'So much then for that little sod's assurance that the gates would be thrown open,' the Crusaders grumbled. But their spirits rose when a body of the Emperor's troops was quickly routed by a small contingent of Crusaders foraging for food. Clearly, as the Doge had predicted, the defenders had no stomach for a fight. And this was the fabled Byzantine Army which in its great days had conquered the Vandals in North Africa with only fifteen thousand men and protected the Eastern bastion of Christendom against Saracens, Avars, Bulgars and Turks.

Like the Romans before them, the Byzantine civilization was in the last stage of chronological senility, beset by lassitude and near-total loss of will to survive. So there were no further complaints about Dandolo's leadership of the conquest of the city which they now knew must be attempted.

*　　*　　*

Dandolo's first requirement was to capture the tower of the fortress housing the huge windlass which kept the great iron chain held taut a few feet above the harbour mouth. The Crusaders attacked it from a beach-head they had secured with little resistance, and the defenders stupidly came out of the tower to fight. The heavily armoured, mounted knights, fearsome in their barrel helms, quickly routed the Greek infantry, who were unable to shut the door of the tower in time to stop the enemy pouring in. The tower was stormed and the chain unshackled so that it rattled down to the bottom. With Dandolo on the prow of the leading galley, the Venetian Fleet sailed in over it to cries of 'Viva San Marco' and occupied the harbour of the Golden Horn. From that position the Doge then launched his cunning stratagem against the walls.

Wooden gangways more than forty yards long, fabricated from sailyards and planks, were hinged to the masts of the big galleys, so that when the ships ran on to the beach below the city walls they could be let down by ropes like drawbridges on to the battlements. Sailcloth awnings, fixed like tunnels above each gangplank, enabled the soldiers to run through them comparatively immune to arrows, bolts and stones raining down from the defenders. With these ingenious devices and with covering fire from catapults and other bombarding

121

weapons installed on their decks, the Venetians stormed the walls near the Emperor's vast Blachernae Palace, urged on by the purblind old Doge, who stood on his galley barely a couple of bow-shots from the enemy with the terrified Rinaldo beside him.

As the Venetians poured over the battlements Dandolo was helped on to the beach and saw the banner of St Mark firmly planted there. Then, when the fight seemed to be going badly for the Crusaders, who were finally attacked outside the main walls by the Emperor's troops, it was he who led a Venetian contingent to their assistance after that part of the city his forces had penetrated had been set on fire. His intervention was decisive and, forcing their war-horses through the ranks of the fleeing enemy, the Crusaders spurred through the main gates crying, 'Deus lo vult! Deus lo vult!'

The Emperor, who still had forces in plenty to repel the invaders, had the will to use them been there, escaped ignominiously, deserting his wife and all his children, save for his favourite daughter, but taking ten thousand gold pieces and as many gems as he and his friends could carry.

The Crusaders' belief that their puppet, Alexius, would now be declared Emperor and fulfil his promises to them, making further fighting unnecessary, was short-lived. The nobles of the city reacted by bringing out the deposed Emperor Isaac, the father of Alexius, from his dungeon and restored him to the golden throne, immediately informing the Crusaders that the true and undoubted Emperor was now in power.

Eyeless and enfeebled as he was by his eight years in the cold and damp, Isaac was dressed in the gold-embroidered imperial robes, jewelled head-dress and scarlet buskins, and reinstalled with his wife, Margaret, herself dripping with pearls and gold medallions, in the Blachernae Palace. Surrounding him were the nobles who had sided with the man who had deposed and blinded him, and visiting dignitaries including Agnes, sister of Philip, the powerful and unscrupulous King of France.

Margaret, who had not been badly treated, if only because she was sister to the King of Hungary, had retained her outstanding looks and resumed the position of Empress with both relish and resignation.

'It is God's will. He moves in mysterious ways,' she assured Isaac who, though physically weak, weary and at first bemused, clutched avidly again at the reins of his awful authority.

Like all women of her time, save those in nunneries, Margaret was hardened to the knowledge that her fortune could be reversed with appalling suddenness. As with plague and death it was in the nature of things, particularly for those married or otherwise attached to rulers. After her searing experience she was more aware than most that no place was so insecure as the point of a pinnacle, unless it was on the shoulders of a man poised on it. What was there to do but shrug, thank God for being alive and ascribe all to the inscrutable Divine will?

Agnes, with whom she resumed close friendship, had been similarly conditioned by experience. Her sister-in-law, the Queen of France, had been divorced by King Philip and then restored to queenship on order of the Pope, who declared the disunion void. That the only thing to do was to make the best of the unexpected pendulum swing while it lasted, was so self-evident to Agnes and Margaret that it did not have to be said or even thought consciously by either of them.

*   *   *

Margaret was hungry for the court gossip which had been denied her, and what Agnes could not tell her was quickly supplied by Sophia, the Greek woman, who dressed the hair of the court ladies, being particularly adept at the Byzantine style, ringlets piled high and held in place by pearl-strings, which visiting ladies were always keen to adopt.

Sophia's husband, Philip, a freedman, was responsible for the cleanliness and order of the Kathisma, the royal box in the Hippodrome from which the Emperor and his wife watched the chariot races and other sports. With seats for forty thousand, the Hippodrome was one of the great centres of life in the capital, providing the free entertainments essential to securing popularity with the masses. The Emperor had to show himself to his people at every performance, usually making some important announcements and hearing com-

123

plaints, so for security and convenience a long passage linked the Boucoleon Palace with the Kathisma, and this too was Philip's responsibility, along with the retiring rooms. He therefore had regular gossip with the guards and other servants of the Hippodrome, which he passed on to Sophia.

It had been through Sophia that Agnes had first heard of the sack of her brother's city of Zara during the previous winter, when news had filtered down through Greece, so when Margaret learned of it she and Isaac had the measure of the Crusaders' and the Venetians' ruthlessness.

'What do you think they will want now that the rightful Emperor has been restored?' Margaret asked Sophia as her long, fair hair was being dressed in her bed-chamber. 'Have you heard anything?'

'They should be getting on their way to the Holy Land, my Lady,' Sophia said, deftly manipulating the ivory comb, wooden rollers and gold-backed brush. 'But from what I've heard I don't think they'll go without the rewards the Prince Alexius has promised them.'

Margaret grimaced at Agnes sitting beside her. Alexius had not yet visited his parents, either because he was scared to do so or because the Crusaders were forbidding it, but a formal list of his promises had been quickly presented to the Emperor Isaac for his comments.

'Of course, my son made those promises in good faith,' Margaret explained. 'He really believed his father to be dead. I'm sure of that. I suppose the money can be found from somewhere, given time. But Alexius should never have promised that the Church here would agree to being under the control of the Pope in Rome. The people will never stand for that. But then Alexius has always been headstrong.'

Agnes could have thought of a better word. From what she had heard of Margaret's son he was something of a rogue as well as a fool, but with the Crusaders behind him and because of his recent marriage to the sister of the ambitious German, Philip of Swabia, he would have to be given a position of some power.

'Why doesn't your husband agree to reign jointly with Alexius?' Agnes suggested when Sophia had gone. 'Being half an empress is better than nothing.'

'It's never been done before.'

'Well, there has to be a first time and it would get rid of these dreadful Crusaders, providing your husband agrees to pay them off. After all he does owe them something. He would still be in the dungeon if it hadn't been for them.'

'I suppose that's true,' Margaret said. 'I can't see any other way of getting rid of them.'

'And there is another point, Margaret. Your husband is not young and his imprisonment has weakened him. He may not last long. Once Alexius is established as joint Emperor he would naturally continue when his father dies. And he could have a long life.'

Margaret nodded thoughtfully, appreciating the wisdom of the advice. After eight years of separation old Isaac was like a stranger to her, but callousness did not enter into her thinking. Margaret and Agnes were hard because the behaviour of men in a world made for men had made them hard.

* * *

At first the furious Crusaders refused to believe the story that Isaac was alive, though it was no surprise to Dandolo, and the leaders insisted on seeing him for themselves. A delegation led by Montferrat was allowed into his presence, and the sight of the resuscitated priest-king with his jewelled vestments, strings of pearls dangling from his head, and his throne surrounded by gorgeously dressed courtiers and heavily armed guards, sickened them. Not only had he survived his ordeal but as they looked at the expression around the sightless sockets they saw that his mind was clear enough to understand the embarrassing position his recall had created for them.

Isaac hardly looked the picture of health and strength, but Dandolo was in no position to make capital by suggesting that he was incapable of ruling because he was blind and old. He could not even express disgust at the way he had been blinded, for in the past the Venetians had blinded at least four of their erring Doges, the ritual act being accomplished with burning coals.

The sole comfort the Crusaders' leaders derived from the

125

solemn audience was the sight of elegant women, of which they had so long been deprived. Montferrat's eye in particular was caught by the Empress Margaret, whose beauty contrasted so sharply with her decrepit husband.

Dandolo had eyes only for the vainglorious trappings of unchallengeable power which, as a republican, he so despised.

'Why do you think that throne on Isaac's left was vacant?' he asked Monferrat after they had left.

'I have no idea,' The Giant replied.

'You won't believe it but it's reserved for Jesus Christ. For his Second Coming. To me that is nothing short of blasphemous.'

*　　*　　*

Baulked of any vestige of excuse for sacking the city, Dandolo and the Crusaders settled for the compromise foreseen by Agnes and quickly agreed to by Isaac with encouragement from his wife. There would be a joint coronation of Isaac and Alexius in Santa Sophia cathedral on 1 August 1203, and both Emperors would fulfil all the promises made by them.

Alexius, who remained in close contact with the Crusaders, regarding them at first as more reliable allies than the Byzantine nobility, produced all the wealth on which he could lay hands in a hurry, even melting down sacred vessels and ikons for the gold and silver. He also passed slivers of the 'True Cross' to the top Crusaders to carry in their sword-hilts, an offer which Dandolo declined, knowing there were enough pieces of the 'True Cross' to build a bridge over the Grand Canal. He imposed crippling taxes on his people, but with the imperial coffers emptied by the profligacy and indolence of his predecessors, including his father, he could not raise anything like the enormous sum he had pledged and he would have to wait for many months for revenues to arrive from the countryside and more distant possessions.

While the Crusaders still owed Dandolo a great amount on which he was threatening to demand interest, he had at least achieved his objective of keeping them away from Egypt. He knew that in the minds of almost all of them the thought of journeying further towards Jerusalem had completely faded.

Once they had grabbed their share of the booty prised out of Constantinople they would be making for home.

*   *   *

After months of waiting, with postponement after postponement and excuses which became ever more incredible, and with no progress whatever on the promise to submit the Greek Church to Rome, Dandolo and Montferrat demanded a final audience with Alexius.

Infected with the grandeur and autocracy of his imperial position, Alexius had decided to let the foreigners know that he was tired of their demands.

'You have already taken more than enough for what you have done,' he told them disdainfully. 'You want to strip us naked. We are sick of you. You are getting no more.'

'So that's it, is it?' Dandolo replied, before the Emperor's response had even been translated for Montferrat. 'Well, we dragged you out of the shit and you'll soon be seeing that we can drop you back in it.'

Alexius responded by waving the two envoys away from his presence and regarded the matter as closed. His father endorsed his hasty action as heartily as he was able, but the Empress Margaret was fearful of the consequences.

'Have no fear, mother,' Alexius snapped. 'These people have shot their bolt. They've foolishly given us time to repair the walls and organize our defences. Why do you think I have been stalling them so long? They won't storm the city a second time.'

*   *   *

The cold of the Byzantine winter had crept into the Doge's bones even more intrusively than the fogs swirling about the Grand Canal, and though time went faster for him than for the younger men, he too was bored with inaction. So, privately, he was delighted with the young Emperor's repudiation. It reopened all the glorious opportunities, and he lost no time in making another signed covenant with the Crusaders.

'Nobody can doubt that right is on our side now,' he assured the waverers.

They agreed that when they reconquered and occupied the city, Alexius and Isaac would be disposed of and be replaced by one of their number. Whoever that might prove to be would receive one-quarter of all the captured treasure. The remaining three-quarters would be divided fifty-fifty between the Venetians and the other Crusader leaders.

Beyond revenge, frustration and greed there was no valid excuse for using 'Soldiers of Christ' to capture the hub of Christendom. But so far as Dandolo was concerned it had to be done. The Venetian Republic had a way of dealing with failures, even if they were Doges. It offered no reward for a good try: success was all that counted.

In addition to underlining this to his admirals, captains and men, Dandolo played on their pride and their cupidity.

'Be valiant that the blood of your forefathers be proved in you,' he cried before the battle. 'By the help of Jesus Christ and of St Mark and by the prowess of your arms, let ye become masters of this city and enjoy its riches.'

Cynically, Dandolo and the Crusaders settled on Holy Week 1204 for the assault. Quoting St Mark as biblical justification, the Doge assured the battle conference, 'The sabbath was made for man, not man for the sabbath.'

The action was a quick success. Within a few days the Byzantine soldiers, who should have defended their families and homes to the death, started pulling down fortifications so that they could flee with any valuables they could carry.

The Crusaders' officers, intent on getting their hands on everything they could, realized that, Holy Week or not, they would have to scour and sack the city without delay. This meant that in the process their troops would be given rein to release their pent-up aggression, avarice and lust; but that did not worry Dandolo as he whistled encouragingly to his goldfinch in the privacy of his comfortable cabin aboard the flagship. In his experience the behaviour of most fighting men tended to degenerate towards brutishness unless disciplined by fear of pitiless punishment. His troops and sailors had been given their orders and they would not misbehave. What others did was not his concern.

Chapter Eleven

With shouts of '*Deus lo vult!*' the Marquis of Montferrat lost no time in leading a detachment of armoured horsemen and infantry to the place which he knew was not only the seat of power but the main treasure-house—the complex of living-rooms, reception-halls, chapels, workshops and gardens which constituted the ancient Imperial Palace of Boucoleon. Riding through the Forum of Theodosius and the Forum of Constantine in the acrid smoke from burning buildings, he picked his way past slumped and mutilated corpses. The screams of women, the curses of men and the groans of wounded rose above the din of doors being battered down.

'Holy Christ!' Montferrat mouthed the words inside his helm as he witnessed the wild savagery of the Crusading troops, the destroyer in their nature being so evidently in command.

He spurred on. There was nothing he could do. It was always that way for a while when a fortress was stormed.

There was no resistance as they entered the palace with swords drawn. The joint Emperors Isaac and Alexius had been murdered by their own people, and the man who had replaced them briefly had fled with the palace garrison. Only the ladies of the court, including Isaac's widow Margaret, remained with a few officials and servants about them.

The ladies did their best to conceal their terror, which Montferrat allayed with a respectful gesture to Margaret and to Agnes, as the sister of France's King. Then, leaving an officered guard to ensure the ladies' safety, he strode through the palace in wonder at the weight of treasure.

The five hundred rooms and thirty chapels held fabulous riches, accumulated over the centuries since Rome itself had served as the first art quarry for the new capital. The crown jewels and imperial robes were unparalleled not only in beauty

129

but in the number of pearls and precious stones which encrusted them. As they moved from room to room they saw that almost every one was embellished with gold mosaic, while even the hinges on some of the doors were fashioned of silver.

It was the chapels, and particularly the Holy Chapel, which impressed the ingenuous and basically religious Crusaders most. Never had they seen, for never had there been, such a collection of holy relics—pieces of the True Cross brought back from Jerusalem by Constantine's mother, St Helen; the nails and the head of the lance which pierced Christ's body; the Saviour's tunic; and even a phial containing some of his blood. Whether authentic or not they would be worth a welter of forgiveness when presented to the churches back home, in Italy and France.

When they had returned to the room where the ladies were gathered, after their cursory reconnaissance, Montferrat split his small force into groups, some under officers, others under sergeants.

'Search the palace thoroughly and deal with any resisting guards, then report back to me here. And don't forget,' he added loudly in French for Agnes to hear, 'you are bound by your code of chivalry. You have sworn not to harm any woman or cleric or defile any churches or holy relics. All legitimate booty must be delivered up. Anyone keeping anything for himself will be excommunicated and dealt with summarily by me. Remember you are soldiers of Christ. Officers and sergeants, I'll hold you responsible. Understand?'

The sergeants and the men believed they understood all right. The Marquis and his knights and those bloody Venetians were going to seize the lot for themselves, contrary to their promise that all would be divided with the troops getting the share they deserved. As for the threat of excommunication, they had observed the behaviour of their leaders over the past year and a half only too clearly for that to have much impact.

They noted too that The Giant had removed his frightening helm and was staying with the ladies, behaving more courteously to the ex-Empress Margaret than mere chivalry

130

warranted. He was, they knew, unmarried and the daughter of the King of Hungary would not be a bad match, particularly when she was so easy on the eye.

'It's all right for The Giant,' the sergeant of one of the detachments said roughly, when he was out of earshot. 'He'll get his share of the loot, Crusader's oath or not. And he'll nail one of those women before the day's out. Maybe more than one!'

His men smirked. The sergeant's lascivious eyes were always bigger than his balls, and he assumed that everyone else was the same.

'I can see us getting bugger-all out of this,' he went on. 'Yet it was us, the infantry, who got through the walls. Bloody horses couldn't do it but you've only got to get yourself astride a horse to be better than the next man. Let's get on, lads. There might be a drink handy and there could be some women in it.'

They had been detailed to search every room in the area connecting the Palace with the Hippodrome.

★   ★   ★

As the Crusaders continued their wild rush through the city, grabbing what they could to pile on carts, guzzling what wine they could find and butchering anyone in their way, Philip, the caretaker of the Imperial Box, decided that rather than take to the streets, he and Sophia would lock themselves in there, hoping they would be safe until discipline had been restored. Their only son, Alexander, had been staying with Sophia's parents, and there had been no opportunity to collect him or even find out if he was still alive in the blazing city.

Peering cautiously through the closed curtains of the Box into the Hippodrome beyond the deserted terrace of the Guards below, they were shocked to see what the Crusaders were doing. Mindlessly and under the influence of the strong, resinous Greek wine, they had set fire to some wooden structures which were burning fiercely in the spring sunshine. Several of the magnificent bronze statues, including the gigantic Hercules by Lysippus and the original of Romulus, Remus and the She-Wolf brought from Rome, had been hacked down and were being smashed so that the metal could be carted to melting-pots for conversion to coinage. If the city's coffers were short on coin for share-out they were going to make their own. There was no way of sharing out a statue.

The Four Horses of Lysippus, which Constantine had brought from Rome, were set too high on their tower on the right of the Box to be pulled down easily, and a guard of Venetian soldiers had been placed round them. Dandolo, who had a personal score to settle, had given orders that they were to be taken to Venice intact.

The Doge had also stationed a guard around another object he was determined to acquire—a stone relief depicting Alexander the Great in his legendary attempt to conquer Paradise by flying there in a chariot drawn by griffons. As he had remarked to Admiral Dandolo, 'It is tailor-made for the north façade of the Basilica to remind our people that the powers of even the greatest men are limited.'

The Admiral had concurred, but the subconscious reason for Dandolo's interest in the tenth-century sculpture was the indirect link between the Basilica and the mighty Macedonian. It had been from Alexandria, the most important of the many cities to which the warrior-king had given his name, that the Venetians had stolen the precious relics of St Mark in AD 829.

As the Venetians watched the wanton destruction they were appalled, but what the barbarians did with their share was their business.

*   *   *

Philip and Sophia had not been in the Imperial Box more than an hour when there was a great hammering on the door. The lascivious sergeant and his detachment, somewhat unsteady with altar wine, had climbed the spiral staircase leading from the Chapel of St Stephen. There they had stacked a score of gold reliquaries, including one containing the head of the stone-martyred saint himself. The locked door filled them with visions of further treasures, some perhaps small enough to be hidden in a belted jerkin, where the sergeant had already secreted a solid gold figurine of the Virgin. So, break-

132

ing off a marble pedestal, they began to use it as a battering ram.

There was no escape for Philip and Sophia. To have run down into the Hippodrome arena filled with rampaging soldiers would have been fatal. There was only one hope.

Philip lifted the purple cover which hung down inside the Box from the balcony. 'Quick,' he whispered. 'Inside here and keep absolutely quiet whatever happens.'

There was little of value in the Imperial Box, so perhaps the soldiers would not tarry there.

*   *   *

'Christ, take a look at this,' one of the soldiers cried, as he flung back the curtains of the Box and looked out into the smoking Hippodrome. They had never seen anything like the arena for size, magnificence or content. It had been a veritable museum of precious art, most of it looted originally from Greece. Mounted on the spina, the central stone reservation around which the chariots raced, was the great bronze column of three entwining serpents which had once stood at Delphi, and the huge Egyptian obelisk from Karnak. There were sixty statues which formerly had graced the Fora of Rome, many already toppled and some under the breakers' hammers.

'Just look at those horses,' the soldier said, leaning out and pointing upwards to the stallions of Lysippus glinting in the flames. 'Look at the size of them! Do you think they're solid gold?'

'Nah, gilded bronze,' the sergeant replied. 'Not even these crazy Greeks have that much gold.'

'Well, they'd still make a hell of a lot of coin.'

'Huh, we'll be lucky if we get the balls of one of them as our share by the time these bloody Venetians have finished with us,' the sergeant said. He looked down at the Venetian guards and spat derisively. 'Talk about being hooked, caught and filleted!'

One of the soldiers had turned over the central throne-chair and saw that it was studded with gems.

'These would prise out,' he exclaimed, taking out his dagger.

133

The sergeant glanced at the broken door and listened. There was nobody there.

'All right, but make it slippy,' he said.

Three of the soldiers got to work and put the semi-precious stones on the marble floor, along with those silver mountings which could easily be removed. After sharing them out the sergeant ordered, 'Right now, destroy the evidence. Two of you throw that bloody chair over the parapet, and then those greedy buggers below will get the blame for it. See if you can land it on that Venetian lot guarding those horses.'

The sergeant had been involved in several scuffles with the Venetians, both at Zara and during the winter camp around Constantinople.

As the soldiers lifted the chair to heave it out, one of the jagged settings caught in the drapery of the balcony, pulling it up to reveal the crouching form of Sophia.

'Hello, what have we here?' the sergeant said, pulling her out by the arm. 'Who said there was nothing for us? She's a beauty. She couldn't have shown up at a better time.'

Any woman was welcome to these men who, unlike so many of their comrades, had been denied the opportunity of sexual assault in which others were revelling.

'Keep watch on that door,' the sergeant ordered the youngest of his men, who was relieved to be spared taking part in the violence, though unable to resist watching it. 'Now let's see what she's like under that dress.'

While one soldier held her arms the sergeant ripped off the garment, to reveal a nicely covered, olive-skinned body in its middle twenties. The sergeant cupped his hands under her breasts as though weighing them, and her dark desirability was heightened by her trembling fear.

'I go first,' the sergeant said tipsily. 'Take her into that room where the big couch is.'

He indicated one of the retiring rooms, and two of the soldiers grinned at each other as they dragged Sophia towards it. The sergeant was given to boasting about his sexual prowess, larding his stories with tales of rape during the previous Crusade, when he had served with Richard Cœur de Lion at

134

the capture of Acre thirteen years previously. Now they would see if he could live up to his claims.

Philip, who might have remained unseen, could not stay silent.

'Leave her alone,' he shouted in Greek as he crawled from his hiding-place.

One of the soldiers grabbed him and held his dagger at his throat. 'Who the hell are you talking to, you Greek bastard?' he shouted. 'Shall I slit him?'

'Not yet,' the sergeant ordered. 'Bring him too. He can watch.'

They dragged Sophia away and three soldiers held her down, legs wide apart, while the sergeant struggled heavily on top of her, bruising her flesh with his coarse leather breeches and the figurine of the Holy Virgin secreted in his jerkin. He ejaculated within seconds and though he tried to pretend he had not, it quickly became apparent to his men that he was spent. So this was the great lover! They were inclined to jeer, but thought better of it.

'It's all that bloody wine,' the sergeant said sheepishly after he had climbed off. 'Right then, one at a time but make it quick, like I did. We don't want to get caught at it.'

In order of seniority each of the men screwed Sophia, mouthing obscenities she did not understand to heighten the animality and subjecting her to bites, scratches and other brutalities. They each took longer over it than the sergeant, who kept trying to hurry them on. When it came to the turn of the youngest soldier, who had begun to feel sick, he tried to demur.

'What about the Crusader's oath?' he asked nervously.

'That only applies to proper Christians,' the sergeant said scathingly. 'Greeks aren't proper Christians. How can they be? They don't believe in the Pope.'

The other soldiers murmured agreement.

'Come on then, boy,' the sergeant insisted. 'We're not having you opting out. That is unless you can't do it.'

Reluctantly the young man mounted Sophia's body, but it was a half-hearted affair and was soon over.

Philip had been powerless to do anything save try to close

his eyes as the men, who realized that Sophia was his woman if not his wife, taunted him. As she lay sobbing, exhausted and mentally shattered, he struggled to free himself to comfort her.

'What are you worried about?' the sergeant asked him, sensing some way of working off the frustration of his embarrassing failure in front of his men. 'She's not going to be any use to you anyway.'

He pulled out his dagger. 'Let down his breeches,' he ordered. 'That is if he has any under that chemise.'

The horror in Philip's eyes left no doubt that he knew what was about to happen as the sergeant grabbed his testicles roughly in his left hand.

'Don't complain, chum,' the sergeant said in a cordial tone, as Philip struggled and shouted in fear. 'We're doing you a favour. They say that if you have your ballocks cut off late in life you can fuck forever.'

He looked at the other soldiers and winked. 'On second thoughts, though, we can't have that, can we? So we'll give you the clean sweep, the lot off, Saracen style.'

Philip did not understand a word, but he knew what was meant as the sergeant gathered his penis into his hairy hand. As Sophia echoed Philip's screams he cut off the genitals with one curving sweep of the blade and held them up for inspection.

'A Saracen's ballocks, dried and carried in a bag round the neck, are a sure charm against the ague,' the sergeant said. 'But the ballocks of a Greek are good for nothing except making more Greeks.'

He hurled the flaccid tissues out into the arena contemptuously, and wiped his hand and knife on the nearest curtain.

'Get rid of him,' he ordered, nodding towards Philip, 'and don't get any of that blood on your uniforms. We don't want any questions. Push the bastard over the top. He must have seen us take that throne apart. And better throw her out, too. Two less Greeks is no bad thing. Treacherous bastards they are, especially these Byzantines.'

★   ★   ★

They had behaved no worse than the rest of the Crusaders who rampaged through homes and religious establishments, raping nuns and murdering monks. The troops seized everything they could lay their hands on—furs, tapestries and silks as well as gold, silver and precious stones. They sacked the churches, riding into Santa Sophia like Cossacks, smashing the altars for the marbles, tearing gold frames from ikons, pillaging chalices, crucifixes, censers, stoups, reliquaries and sacred vestments.

Some of the finest treasures of the ancient world disappeared in melting-pots, while irreplaceable copies of Greek manuscripts fed the fires below them. Even the huge Byzantine statue of the Holy Virgin, the cult figure of the city, was not spared. Along with a superb figure of Helen of Troy and a bronze Pegasus so big that it carried ten storks' nests on its back, it subsided in furnaces in the Street of the Bronzesmiths or elsewhere in the smoking capital.

In their obscene abandon, troops even went through the motions of installing a notorious whore on the throne of the Greek Patriarch, Byzantium's ecclesiastical ruler, where she danced and sang bawdy songs.

The behaviour of the men who so loudly professed a faith deriving from one who had preached tolerance and forgiveness, contrasted starkly with that of the infidel Saracens who, when they had been led into Jerusalem by Saladin, had violated no women and slaughtered no men for the sport of it. Saladin had taken no specific revenge even for the bloody massacre at Acre, when the sergeant and other soldiers of the Third Crusade had beheaded 2,700 Moslem prisoners while that paragon of knightly chivalry and Christian charity, Richard the Lion-Hearted, watched approvingly from a balcony.

Only the Venetians remained disciplined under the iron control of Dandolo, operating in bands to secure as many intact objects as possible for the State. A firm believer in the power of genuine holy relics and in the prestige they would bring to the Venetian churches, the Doge commanded his men to seize as many intact reliquaries as possible. They were so successful that he was able to select for his beloved Basilica of

St Mark alone, an arm of St George, part of the skull of John the Baptist and remains believed to be those of Saints Peter, Paul, Andrew, Matthew, James, Luke, Philip, Bartholomew and Thaddeus.

Of the ancient bronze statuary gracing the metropolis, only the four steeds of Lysippus survived unharmed, being carefully lowered under Dandolo's personal supervision after the fires had subsided and the sated troops were back under control. Dandolo felt that an old grievance had at least been partially requited as he watched live horses pull them away from the Hippodrome in carts for safe storage in a Venetian galley. So much so that he could not resist going down to the harbour to see them, if only dimly, winched on to the vessel.

'They will make a pretty souvenir of our work here, Vital,' he observed archly.

The remainder of the loot which could be recovered from the soldiers was collected in three churches designated as temporary warehouses for the share-out. After valuation, half was taken by Dandolo and half by the Crusaders. From their half, the Crusaders then paid Dandolo coin, precious stones and other goods to the value of 50,000 silver marks in final settlement of their debt. Coin and goods to the value of 100,000 marks were then divided among the Crusader troops, but the Venetian sailors and soldiers got little more than their wages. 'Give them more and they will only waste it,' was Dandolo's philosophy.

All the Venetian prizes belonged to the Republic, and the Council would be requiring detailed accounts of them all when the fleet returned home.

* * *

Baldwin of Flanders was elected the new Emperor of Constantinople after Dandolo had refused to compete for the title, while Montferrat became King of Salonica and married Margaret to make her his Queen. She had not mourned Isaac long, but The Giant was attractive and she seized the opportunity of remaining consort to a ruler. The alternative could have been a nunnery or worse, in a milieu where so many men gave credence to the description of St Jerome—'Woman is the gate of the devil, the path of wickedness, the sting of the serpent, in a word, a perilous object.'

All that Dandolo took for himself was a new title—Doge of Venice, of Dalmatia and of Croatia, Seigneur of Three-Quarters of the Empire of the East. It was Venice, not the Doge, that was acquisitive and as Dandolo remarked to his chief admiral, 'It is only fitting, Vital, that the Lion of St Mark should have the lion's share.'

In goods and cash Dandolo had made a tremendous profit for his country, but what he gained in trading power and influence was infinitely greater. Venice took three-eighths of the City of Constantinople as its own, plus those ports and parts of the Greek mainland and islands necessary to form a chain of bases through which the merchant fleet and warships could maintain a strong link with the East. Further, because Dandolo had supported Baldwin in the ballot for Emperor, realizing that he would be less dangerous to Venice than the ambitious and charismatic 'Giant', he was able to induce him to grant an important consolation favour to Montferrat, who then showed his appreciation by selling Venice the fertile island of Crete for only 10,000 marks.

Through brilliant opportunism Dandolo had eliminated Constantinople as a competitive trade centre and converted that important terminus of caravan routes into another Venetian port, extending the grain and spice monopoly, which he had preserved by keeping his bargain with the Sultan of Egypt, to include perfumes, gold brocade, emeralds and pearls. And by acquiring millions of new subjects, Venice, with a population of only about 100,000, had outstripped its most dangerous commercial rival, Genoa, and become the nearest thing there would ever be again to Ancient Rome—a small city-state with vast dominions.

*   *   *

It was one thing for the conquerors to declare the creation of a Latin Empire of the East, which they called Romania, and to parcel out wild territories, but quite another to hold them. In attempting to do this the chief characters in the saga paid in full for their greed. While trying to occupy Thrace, Emperor Baldwin I was defeated by a combined force of Greek rebels and Bulgars and was barbarously executed. Montferrat managed to secure his Kingdom of Thessalonica and briefly subdued much of Greece but, fighting bravely, he too was killed by Bulgarian troops, who cut off his splendid head and sent it to their king.

Dandolo, who could not resist leading his men on a similar mission, also failed but with superb generalship brought most of his force safely back to base. He returned to find that Rinaldo, who had been unable to accompany him because of a fever, was dead. His goldfinch too was gone, dead from starvation because nobody had cared for it during Rinaldo's illness. His kinsman, Vital, had departed for Venice, and Dandolo felt not only deserted but insufferably and irreversibly tired. After fighting his way back with implacable determination to survive, life suddenly seemed empty of purpose.

He had the satisfaction of knowing that he had accomplished all he could, but the rigours of a journey to Venice seemed insupportable and the plaudits of a triumph there pointless. The Four Horses and the other spoils, which were being ferried to Venice in red and gold galleys, would be evidence enough there of all he had achieved. The knowledge that he would never see Venice again saddened him, but he was more resigned than ever he believed he could have been, to laying his bones in a foreign land. After all, he consoled himself, Santa Sophia, Constantinople's great Church of the Holy Wisdom, where he had determined to be buried in a tomb of fitting magnificence, was, thanks to him, Venetian territory.

Though his horror of leaving life had evaporated, he remained prudent enough to take one major precaution. Persuasive to the end, he induced the Pope, a political realist, to lift the excommunication on himself and his fellow Venetians with an argument of blatant sophistry—'The attack on Zara was justified because the King of Hungary has no right to the privileges of a Crusader, as he has taken the Cross only as a pretext for plundering his neighbours.'

140

Dying in the Boucoleon Palace on 14 June 1205, he was buried with pomp and was spared even the suspicion that Santa Sophia would suffer the supreme indignity of being converted to a mosque, his own tomb being obliterated in the process so that all visible sign of his resting-place would be a plain stone slab inscribed 'Henricus Dandolo'. If any of his advisers had the foresight to realize that this would be an inevitable consequence of his rape of Constantinople, which showed the infidel Asians how easily the gateway to Europe could be prised open, they presumably lacked the courage to tell him.

*   *   *

The Latin Empire of the East lasted less than sixty years, throughout which Venice used the city as an art-quarry, as Rome had used Greece and Constantinople had used Rome. The city itself was reconquered by the Greeks, helped by the Genoese, in 1261; but Venice, through its naval supremacy, held on to most of her new possessions and enjoyed two centuries of peak prosperity and power. But the sack of the Byzantine city had irrevocably opened the way to its eventual capture by the Turks and their invasion of Europe. Instead of uniting the Greek and Latin Churches, it deepened the schism between them and created political animosities between Eastern and Western Europe that would stretch into the twentieth century and beyond.

So, throughout the slow decline of Venice, the Four Horses would also remind the world of the enormity and recklessness of the crimes which had been committed in the name of Christ.

*   *   *

Forewarned by a relay of carrier pigeons what to expect, the Venetians were in revelling mood when the first returning galleys were sighted by the look-out man on the Campanile. An erring priest, starving in his cage suspended from the bell-tower, was drawn up out of sight. The incinerated

141

remains of a friar-confessor, who had been burned alive at St Mark's Pillar for getting fifteen noble nuns pregnant in one year, were cleared away to allow the great welcoming crowd to collect on the Molo and in the Piazetta. Like the Ancient Romans from whom they claimed descent, they wanted to exult in the sight of the spoils of war and to honour the men who had borne them home in triumph.

There were mighty cheers as gold and silver objects were brought ashore in such profusion that the Treasury of St Mark's was stuffed like a pawnbroker's shop. Encrusted marbles, prised from the outside of Santa Sophia for the decoration of the thin veneer covering the rough bricks of St Mark's, raised Ohs! and Ahs! But no trophy received such acclamation as the Four Horses, which stood on the deck of the largest galley with much of their gilding intact. In spite of their aquatic environment, the Venetians still retained the Roman feel for the horse as the symbol of victory, though to ride 'in the Venetian style' was an Italian jibe for indifferent horsemanship.

The Horses were taken to the temporary safety of the Arsenal so that later, when the splendid Byzantine columns shipped back as ballast had been used to refashion the west façade of the Basilica, they could be winched up by living horse-power on to pedestals made from cut-down columns in the large lunette above the main entrance. They were not arranged in their original dynamic order, but strung out with those originally designed as the outer pair on the inside. This may have been because Dandolo was not there to give advice, or perhaps someone foresaw that, freed from signs of former restraint, the Horses would more eloquently express the liberty they quickly came to manifest.

As later Doges sat in state between them to watch the bread-and-entertainment spectacles in the square below, no emperor could have enjoyed a nobler seat. The Loggia dei Cavalli, as the niche became known, was the nearest thing to a triumphal arch that Venice, with its ingrained fear of personal adulation, would ever allow. Yet Dandolo's excessive plunder marked the beginning of a lethal shift away from the old ideals of service to the Republic to the accumulation of personal wealth, as had happened in Ancient Rome and in Constantinople; for many Venetian families carved out huge estates and even duchies for themselves in the Levant and grew enormously rich on the monopoly trade.

In the inexorable decline of the Republic, 'Four steeds divine, that strike the ground resounding with their feet, and from their nostrils snort ethereal flame' served to recall the days of glory, particularly to the foreign visitor, when ostentation was almost all that remained. Over the centuries they witnessed events of great splendour, of intense sensuality, of high political significance and of barbarous cruelty. Then, late in the eighteenth century, when the Piazza had become little more than an open-air theatre and the Horses seemed forever destined to be just tourist attractions, another extraordinary man burning with ambition that was to degenerate to greed plucked them back into the mainstream of history.

Plunder for Paris

'What horrors you've seen from the sword and the flame,
What flaunting of power in Liberty's name . . .'

Chapter Twelve

The two letters which the undersized young man with the large head, pale angular features and long dark hair folded and sealed with obvious irritation were headed 'Bonaparte, Général en Chef de L'Armée d'Italie'. He had recently dropped the Italian spelling of his name for a French version more fitting for a full general, particularly when he was only twenty-seven years old.

It was ten a.m. on the twenty-seventh of November in the chilly autumn of 1796, and in spite of the huge log fire, Napoleon shivered in the high-ceilinged room in Milan's magnificent Serbelloni Palace. He would always feel the cold, even in later life when he put on weight. That day the chill had crept into his bones because he was feverish, his skin faintly yellowed with the liver trouble that was to dog him to the grave. The succession of battles, which he knew could be won only if he directed them on the field, had exhausted him to the point of illness.

The first letter was addressed to his wife, Josephine, whom he had married only eight months previously and left after a 36-hour honeymoon for the battlefield. After four months of entreaty from her husband, she had torn herself away from her beloved Paris and slowly made her way to Milan but, as it always would, the urgent demands of war had overridden his need for her love and companionship. He had left her suddenly to achieve his most glorious victory to date, the Battle of Arcola, where he had galvanized his men into a final assault by seizing a tricolour and leading them into withering Austrian fire. It was such participation in his men's dangers and hardships that had earned him the title 'Little Corporal'.

Arcola had been a key triumph for his Army of Italy, which had been intended as no more than a diversionary force while the real fighting was to be accomplished by the main French

147

armies making a frontal attack on Vienna through Germany. Now, after proving his contention that the Austrians could be more easily defeated by attacking their rear, here he was back at his headquarters expecting to find Josephine waiting and she had gone to Genoa. He felt not only lonely and deprived but bitter and angry.

'I hurried eagerly into your rooms,' he had written in the spidery hand with the erratic spelling which betrayed his Corsican origin. 'I had left everything just to be able to hold you in my arms again. But you were not there. Who may this paragon be, this new lover who engrosses all your time? Josephine, be vigilant. One fine night the doors will be broken in and I shall be before you!'

It was so different from the passionate note he had dispatched from the Arcola battlefield—'Away from you the nights are long, insipid and sad. Close to you one regrets that it is not always night. I have not forgotten those little visits— you know, the little black forest! I give it a thousand kisses and wait impatiently for the moment when I shall be there. A kiss on your mouth, your eyes, your shoulder, your breast, everywhere, everywhere.'

He was indeed an ardent lover, almost frenzied when sexually aroused, and not to be resisted; not that Josephine ever tried. She was always accommodating in that respect.

Napoleon had sighed as he had pressed the seal on the folded paper. Those rumours about Josephine's flirtations, even infidelities . . . Were they only rumours? She was the first love of his life and he found it hard to believe they could really be true.

The second letter, which he had sealed with greater force and determination, was addressed to the Directory in Paris, the oligarchy of five who governed France after the Reign of Terror. Six months after his victory over the Austrians at the Bridge of Lodi, the Directory had instructed him to hand over command of the Army of Italy to the much older General Kellerman. But revelation had occurred at Lodi. The response to his fighting speech culminating in his battle cry 'Vive la République!' had shown him how words can induce men to give their lives for a leader they respect. Not words alone, of course. Words smartly followed by decisive action. Eloquence alone, the political windbags' pathetic belief that when they had said something they had done something, could so easily lead to disaster.

As he had sat upright in his saddle at Lodi watching his infantry charge into enfilading fire to overwhelm the enemy, the young man, who was to have nineteen horses killed under him, was convinced that he was such a leader set apart from other men. His ambition had suddenly expanded, for he saw that real power lay not with the politicians but with the man who controlled the French Army, and he knew he could be that man. So he had ignored the Directory's order to hand over his command and they had done nothing. Now 'the idiots' in Paris were ordering him to treat Venice as a neutral power. Venice, which was allowing defeated Austrian troops to retreat through its mainland territory taking their guns with them! Venice, the epitome of aristocratic rule, where only those whose family names were inscribed in a ludicrous Golden Book could ever hold office!

Napoleon, who would later create a whole new nobility including 31 dukes and 450 counts, detested aristocrats. What had the revolution been about? What was his army of Liberation doing in Italy if Venice was to be spared? Neutral indeed! He subscribed to the Revolutionary declaration, 'Those who are not with us are against us'. Neutrals were nothing and he had no time for them. He had no time for the Directory either.

Since the revelation at Lodi, the Imperial dream was already intruding into his waking thoughts. With total confidence in what he called his 'star' he had already conjured up a way of replacing the five Directors, but he had to keep them in office until he had made himself master of Europe. The way he was going, nothing could stop him. The key to supreme power in such a time of opportunity was to continue to conquer, as Julius Cæsar had shown; as Alexander the Great, the historic figure he most admired, had shown.

From his voracious reading of history—*The Glory of Alexander* was his favourite bedside book—he knew that he was the first since the great Macedonian to reach major command at twenty-six. And he had achieved it by similar methods. By

149

concentrating his forces on one objective at a time; by on-the-spot command mounted on a charger, sustaining discipline and morale by being seen directing the battle, sharing its dangers and showing concern for the wounded. And by making his decisions without consulting anybody, least of all politicians.

Like Alexander, he was determined to assume political command himself. Alexander the Great! Would he be known, centuries ahead, as Napoleon the Great?

In his fantasies he believed he was destined for greatness. Not destined by God. He had been christened Napoleon after a saint but he had no strong belief in God. In fact, he disliked Christianity because a God who dealt out retribution in the next world made soldiers afraid of death. And he had no faith in prayer. Men succeeded or failed by what fate had decreed. 'All that is to happen is written down,' he believed. '*Au destin*' was even engraved on the betrothal ring he had given to Josephine. But what men did for themselves was crucial. They had to provoke their destinies.

That he had the drive to convert his fantasies into reality he had no doubt. That his greatness would be permanent he could not be sure.

As he pressed his signet-ring hard into the soft wax on the letter to Paris, he was sealing not only the fate of the four-year-old French Republic but the fate of the thousand-year-old independent Republic of Venice.

'Ask Colonel Junot to come in,' he told the orderly, who took the letters away for immediate dispatch.

Andoche Junot had been a sergeant with Napoleon at the first triumph at Toulon and been commissioned for his conduct there. It had been Junot to whom Napoleon had written while briefly imprisoned as one of Robespierre's favourites, after the execution of the tyrant who had secured him such rapid promotion. Though two years younger than his prodigious commander, he had become first choice for personal confidences with the man who had unprecedented facility for generating loyalty but found few with whom he cared to be intimate. After a prestigious mission to Paris, where he carried the enemy flags captured by the Army of Italy to present

150

to the Directory, he had just been promoted to colonel's rank.

Junot marched in, smart in his hussar's uniform, clicked his booted heels and sat down.

'We must do something about Venice,' Napoleon said. He spoke with an accent still lingering from the Corsica he had left at the age of nine. 'I have just written to those fools in Paris. They soon shut up about observing neutrality when I showed them the Venetians could be squeezed into paying for the war. There's nothing they like more than loot. But they are still insisting I must not destroy their precious "Most Serene Republic". I have other ideas.'

Junot smiled. He knew the thinking behind those deep-set, grey eyes, both long-term and immediate. Bonaparte was already becoming bored with Italy. He wanted to conquer the heart of Europe, not just one of its legs. The dictatorship fantasy which was becoming evident to Junot would not materialize if the rival and senior general, Hoche, in charge of the Army of the Rhine, snatched the laurels. So he had made up his mind to reach a peace with Austria, a peace in which the Austrians would surrender Belgium, the Rhineland and perhaps other holdings to France, in exchange for Venice and some of its mainland territories. But the time for that peace was still months away. There was more fighting to be done to force the Austrians to the table. And the handiest source of money to finance it was Venice.

'The Venetians are going to pay for their so-called neutrality,' Napoleon declared, taking a pinch from his tortoiseshell snuff-box. 'I'm going to demand everything they have in cash and all the English money and stocks they hold.'

Junot whistled. He had been present when Napoleon had issued his Declaration to the People of Italy on taking up his command, 'The French Army is coming to break your chains. Your property, your religion, your customs shall not be touched.' He had also been there when Napoleon had first addressed his ragged and disgruntled troops—'Soldiers of the Army of Italy! You have had enough of misfortune and privations. I shall put an end to that. Over there, beyond the mountains, are stores, food, clothes, guns, horses and money

151

to reward us. Away with everything that keeps us from the enemy! Let us advance and thrust our bayonets into their bodies.'

The soldiers, while disciplined in action, had been so long without pay that they could only live through plunder, so they took their general at his word. Though he affected to disapprove of looting and was harsh on any caught seizing treasures for themselves, he was furious whenever anyone complained of their behaviour. And why should the troops have restrained themselves when they saw convoy after convoy of stolen goods setting out for Paris, destined not only for the Directory but for the homes of officers and even of commanders?

Napoleon had entered Milan to a hero's welcome under a rain of flowers, hailed as the deliverer from the Austrian yoke, but in short order he extorted two million livres to help defray the soldiers' arrears of pay. The Italian people were staggered by the young general's requirements not only for food, horses, forage and money but for paintings, precious stones, ornaments and other treasures, whether publicly owned or private.

As at Constantinople, where the invaders had promised to respect property if their demands were met, solemn assurances were no more than sandcastles to be swept aside in a rip-tide of greed. Junot was alone in knowing that the corruption of what had seemed a noble ideal had not been insidious. Immediately after the declaration to the Italian people, Napoleon had taken him aside and told him, 'We will take everything that is beautiful in Italy.' There was even a requirement from Paris to loot the Vatican treasures.

'Was this a further reason why Napoleon was so keen to annex Venice?' Junot wondered. The ancient city-state was stuffed with art treasures, many of them easily portable to France.

'I have just told the Directory that there is no government so cowardly and so treacherous as the Venetian, and none that hate the French so much. There is nothing to fear from them. They won't fight. They are just not made for liberty.'

'I'm sure that's true, sir,' Junot replied. 'I have never been to Venice, but from what I've read about the place the Venetians have been degenerate for years. All these thousands of women they call "courtesans"! Venice is the whorehouse of Europe and they live on the proceeds.'

Napoleon said nothing but looked at his subordinate with the penetrating gaze that made the roof of any recipient's mouth go dry. The mention of whores had been unfortunate.

'What rumours have you heard about my wife?' he asked gruffly, smoothing aside the hair hanging lankly on either side of his bulging forehead.

'None, sir. I know she went to Genoa as soon as she heard that you had triumphed at Arcola and were safe . . .'

'Don't beat about the bush, Junot. You know exactly what I mean. What rumours have you heard about my wife and Lieutenant Charles?'

'Oh that! I've heard no more, sir. I'm sure there's nothing in it.'

Junot looked at the marble-tiled floor in embarrassment. It was bad enough being present when Napoleon, who had several vulgar habits, took conjugal liberties with his wife, feeling her breasts and even lower. Being required to discuss her affairs when Napoleon even suspected him, Junot, of being one of her lovers was too much. Not that the suspicion was entirely groundless. Josephine had let the young aide know by look, gesture and teasing word that she was there for the taking.

'Charles is the man *now*, is he not?' Napoleon persisted. 'Didn't he travel with her from Paris when she came out to join me here in July? Didn't they stay together in the same inns on several occasions on the way?'

'But that proves nothing, sir. Lieutenant Charles was detailed to escort Madame Bonaparte from Paris to Milan. The coaches take at least ten days for the journey. They had to spend the nights somewhere.'

'But not together,' Napoleon snapped.

Junot smothered a sigh. He knew his commander's suspicions were well founded. Josephine's affair with the rather foppish Hippolyte Charles was widely known in Milan. She called him to breakfast with her in the Serbelloni Palace so regularly when her husband was away, that one of the coarser

153

French officers had observed, 'Well, of course, it has to be fed and it won't eat hay.'

The remark and its cause had quickly made their way to Paris, where the affair became essential gossip, especially among those looking for an opportunity to downgrade the jumped-up young general. But after his experience of some five months previously, Junot had no wish to fuel Napoleon's jealousy.

The Bonapartes had been staying together for a few days in Verona when the Austrians under Count Wurmser, the cavalry general, advanced on the city. Napoleon dispatched Josephine to Peschiera, about fifteen miles away on Lake Garda, sending Junot to escort her and her maid Louise to safety. As they were skirting the lake an Austrian gunboat fired on them, killing one of the escorting troops and two of the horses. Reacting quickly, Junot made Josephine and Louise abandon the coach and run along a ditch until they were out of range of the guns. Then he commandeered a cart and drove them to Castelnuova, where Napoleon was waiting. As her husband helped her from the cart and Junot recounted the episode Josephine, who cried easily at any time, broke down.

'Wurmser shall pay dearly for your tears,' Napoleon had predicted grimly.

He had been immensely grateful to Junot for the rescue, but within days was accusing him of flirting with his wayward wife and even worse. Junot could easily have told the truth—that it was the striking and statuesque Louise he had managed to seduce—but he knew that Napoleon, who at that stage of his life disapproved of promiscuity, spurning all his numerous opportunities, would be furious.

'If the maid, why not the mistress?' would have been the obvious question. So all he had done was to persist in a stubborn denial of any intimacy with anyone in the Commander-in-Chief's entourage. Besides, he liked Josephine and he also liked Hippolyte Charles.

After the Lake Garda incident, which was so widely publicized that Josephine became known as the 'Heroine of Peschiera', Napoleon sent her far from the firing line. But, as he later discovered, she had stopped, wilful as ever, at Breschia

154

where Lieutenant Charles had joined her for dinner, obviously by prearrangement.

Charles, then twenty-four, was younger than Napoleon and though no taller, his features conformed with his joyous extrovert nature, while those of the General were almost ugly in their sharpness. Josephine, who had told both Charles and her husband that she was twenty-eight when she was really thirty-three, was an ardent follower of fashion and admired the way her lover wore his clothes, in contrast to Bonaparte's carelessness about his appearance. He had a better figure for his gold-laced, hussar uniform and a better leg for a boot, Napoleon's being so short and spindly that 'Puss-in-Boots' had been cat-called at him when he had appeared in his first issue. Charles had charm and finesse in his sexual approaches while Napoleon, when he pleasured his wife in a fit of urgency by turning up her dress and dropping his breeches flap, smelled of gunpowder and horse-lather.

Josephine much preferred a nude engagement with prolonged preliminaries, followed by the mutual post-coital sleep with its warm suffusion of the skin. Usually, when her husband was sated he scurried away to some demanding task which had been only briefly set aside. But the decisive thing her lover could do for her which Napoleon could not was to make her laugh, particularly with his gift for appalling puns and double entendres. This proved overwhelmingly attractive after a few days in the company of the brooding Commander-in-Chief, for whom love could never compete for long with ambition, surrender in any form being unthinkable.

As Josephine expressed it to Charles, who passed it round to convulse others with laughter, 'Bonaparte is all do and no talk.' She had never yet called her husband anything but 'Bonaparte', while she addressed her lover as 'Hippolyte'.

'You were saying about Venice, sir,' Junot reminded the General, who was jerked out of his jealousy as the remark offered a different target for his tension.

'Ah, yes. Venice!'

He picked up a long document which had arrived from Lallemont, the French Ambassador in Venice—a résumé of the latest reports from agents of his Secret Service, who had penetrated his target as the Venetians had once penetrated Constantinople. The most productive of these 'spies', as he liked to call them, was Phillipe, the paramour of Josephine's maid, who would have married her had she ever become pregnant.

Phillipe was an Italian-speaking Frenchman, planted among Lallemont's diplomatic staff as an embassy servant. He spent most of his time sowing subversive rumours and collecting information over Turkish coffee—in the Caffe Sultana, Quadri, Venice Triumphant (also known as Florian's), the chess-rooms and other centres of intrigue around the Piazza San Marco.

'Citoyen Lallemont says that the Venetian rulers fear revolution more than they fear me. They are censoring books and plays and threatening to close down the coffee-houses. The nobles think a revolution would threaten their exalted position more than conquest by me.'

He stared at Junot, and his pale, thin lips curled into one of his rare smiles as he took another pinch of snuff.

'They could be wrong about that,' he said. 'But it's something we can play on. I'm instructing Lallemont to stoke up the revolution scare, though he says there's no fear of a spontaneous revolution. Except for a few thinkers the mass of the Venetians seem to like their stinking backwater the way it is—which of course suits our purpose.'

'Any information about their military strength?' asked Junot, who was to become such an able divisional commander that his mentor would one day make him a duke.

Napoleon picked up the document again. 'There's some very significant information about the condition of their navy. They've always owed their power to their navy but listen to this: "The navy is so obsolete that it is still using galleys rowed by convicts. Very few of the ships moored in the Arsenal are sea-worthy. Some have no sails, others no crews. Some are just rotting. The workmen have been using wood bought for ship-repair to heat their houses. The shipbuilding apprentices now buy their entry certificates to the Arsenal instead of earning them. There is gross overmanning".'

'Corruption at the core!' Junot observed. 'That's always a good sign in an enemy.'

'Yes indeed. Apparently the Venetians say that their last Doge took so long to die because his soul refused to leave his body without being paid first!'

Lallemont was not exaggerating. Corruption, which in the great days of Venice was unknown, if only because the laws against it were so terrifying, had become so rife that the election for the Dogeship itself depended on bribery. Even licences to beg at the doors of St Mark's had to be bought.

'I shouldn't think we've much to fear from the land defences either,' Junot said.

'No. Lallemont says they've been allowed to fall into total decay. The mainland army is commanded by a seventy-year-old general. Some companies consist only of the captain, who draws all the pay for his non-existent men. Half the guns are rusted. But they wouldn't fire them anyway. They've lost the will to defend themselves. That, my dear Junot, is what comes of putting material comforts and trivia before the needs of defence.'

There was contempt in his voice. Like Alexander before him, Bonaparte regarded the military profession as the noblest, and those who put commerce first as the Venetians had and as he believed the British, 'that nation of shopkeepers', also did, deserved all that was coming to them.

'It's unbelievable that people can be so short-sighted,' Junot said. 'They think they can be left in peace forever.'

'Yes, the Venetians haven't learned that you can't alter the time by stopping the clock. But they've had a good run. For two hundred and fifty years they've been prepared to be accused of cowardice rather than resort to war. Time always runs out for cowards.'

He dropped Lallemont's report on the table with a gesture of finality and remarked, 'The world is full of idiots, Junot, a dispensation of which we must make maximum use. We'll take Venice without firing a shot. You'll see.'

'When, sir?' Junot asked eagerly.

'When we've finally dealt with the Austrians. And with Wurmser in particular.'

157

At the utterance of Wurmser's name, Napoleon's gauntness was accentuated by the puckering of his rather small mouth. Junot fidgeted uneasily. He did not relish another tirade about Josephine. Of course, she had been selfish and stupid to take off for Genoa just because she had heard there were some fêtes there. But Napoleon ought to have known by now what she was like: she had been his mistress before he had married her and the mistress of Barras, the Director, and of General Hoche before that.

Junot appreciated that the jealousy of an ardent young man newly married was the most potent brand, but that morning Napoleon seemed more consumed with it than the situation warranted, for on the General's instructions he had already checked that Lieutenant Charles was not in Genoa but with his regiment. What Junot did not know was that earlier that morning while Napoleon was dressing he had picked up his travelling portrait of his wife and as he had stared at it, clenching the silver frame in his hands, the glass had shattered. He was superstitious enough to believe that this was a sure sign of her infidelity.

He could let her go, to lead her own life—or even divorce her. But that would be a defeat, and his basic need was to conquer. And he would conquer her even if it involved forgiving adultery. Forgiveness came easily to him, especially if conducive to the ambience which gave him greatest satisfaction, both professional and domestic—loyalty to his command.

There was nothing he had seen in the world that would not yield to unremitting endeavour, not even a stubborn, indifferent woman. He would follow his favourite maxim from Machiavelli, which he had learned to apply to obtuse military problems—'Never give up. Always wait for a change of fortune.'

That change could come when he had finished with the Austrians and might have more time to devote to Josephine. The key to it all was Venice.

⋆   ⋆   ⋆

It took Phillipe, the consort of Josephine's maid, two days to make the wintry journey to Napoleon's headquarters after Ambassador Lallemont had received the instruction in Venice to send him there. Lallemont had thought it unusual for the Commander-in-Chief to want a first-hand intelligence briefing from one of his agents. Everything Phillipe had reported had already been passed on to Army headquarters but the Ambassador, who was really responsible to the Directory of Five in Paris, had learned that it did not pay to ignore the 'requests' of the explosive little general. There was the future to think of and Citoyen Lallemont also knew where the power-base of post-revolutionary France really lay.

Phillipe, a dark, olive-skinned man in his thirties, of medium height, thin with straight, black hair tied in a short *queue*, a dark moustache and sideburns which gave him a conspiratorial look, had met Napoleon several times before. He had first rendered him meritorious service as a spy during the siege of his native Toulon, where Bonaparte had won his spurs and been drawn to the attention of Robespierre. Since then the association had led to the employment of his paramour, Louise, as lady's maid to Josephine, who liked her so much that she had become more like a companion, playing cards and often dining with her mistress. So he was well acquainted with much of the boudoir gossip and the General's idiosyncrasies. 'But why is he calling me all the way to Milan?' he wondered, as the poorly-sprung coach rattled over the rough roads towards the Lombard capital.

When Phillipe's arrival was announced, Napoleon was closeted with his divisional commanders, Augereau, Massena, Joubert and Rey. Surrounded by charts and pencilled sketches, they were working out the contingency plans to stop the Austrian army from relieving Mantua, which the French were besieging. He called a break and dismissed the generals, who were all so much older.

'You are doing very well in Venice,' Napoleon said affably, inviting the spy to be seated. 'The information you are providing is most valuable.'

'Thank you, General.'

159

'However, I want you to switch your talents to Paris for a while.'

'Paris? I can't see . . .'

'You will,' the General interrupted curtly. 'My wife will shortly be there for an extended stay. I want you to use your skills to do me a secret personal service.'

'How, sir?'

Napoleon stood up and paced the floor for a few moments, finding it difficult to mouth the words. Finally he looked at Phillipe squarely and said, 'I want you to watch my wife. Surreptitiously, of course. To find out who she is spending her time with. Particularly her nights. And who she might have been intimate with in the recent past. At Peschiera, for instance.'

Phillipe paled and shuffled his feet uneasily.

'It shouldn't be difficult,' Napoleon persisted. 'Louise must know everything that happens. Do your interrogation in bed. That's always the best place for intimacies—of any sort.'

Phillipe forced a dispirited smile. He wondered whether the General had somehow heard something which he believed to be a total secret—the nature of a particularly valuable interrogation source in Venice.

'You must understand that I don't want Louise or anybody else knowing why I have sent you to Paris,' the General continued. 'So far as she and my wife are concerned you are on extended leave as a reward for your efforts in Venice. Understand?'

'Yes, sir,' Phillipe replied without enthusiasm. He enjoyed the risks of spying as well as the rewards but not at that level.

'Don't despair, Phillipe,' Napoleon said, patting his hand. 'You can also do a professional intelligence job while you are there. I hear that the Royalists are getting back into positions of influence in Paris and hoping to recover their possessions. The last thing either of us wants is the return of the Bourbons after all we've been through together, eh?'

'But what about Ambassador Lallemont? I have work to do for him in Venice. Urgent work.'

Napoleon picked up his quill, wrote a short letter and sealed it.

160

'Give this to Citoyen Lallemont. He will give you indefinite leave of absence.'

Phillipe took the letter and rose from his chair.

'Right, off you go. Get to Paris as quickly as you can and then report to me personally as soon as you have any worthwhile evidence. The man to watch for particularly is a certain Lieutenant Charles. Hippolyte Charles. But he may not be the only one.'

'Could you suggest any other names, sir?' Phillipe asked.

Napoleon thought for a moment, then picked up another sheet of paper, tore off the heading, wrote briefly and handed it to Phillipe, who glanced at it cursorily. There were only two names. The first was that of Paul Barras, one of the Directors, who had been Josephine's lover before she met Napoleon and might be taking advantage of the ease of a repeat performance when it suited him. The second was 'Colonel Andoche Junot'.

Napoleon stood up to dismiss his agent before summoning back the generals. 'Do this for me and you will not regret it. Don't fail me,' he added rather menacingly. 'And be discreet—but then I don't have to tell you that. You are a professional.'

As Phillipe departed, Bonaparte unfastened one of the buttons of his tunic and slipped his hand inside to ease the area below his sternum, where the pain of his bouts of indigestion, touched off by anxiety, always seemed to be concentrated. It was a habit that was to become as much an historic hallmark as his general's hat.

Chapter Thirteen

Phillipe could hardly have felt more miserable on the journey back to Venice. He was fond of Louise but had a more delightful arrangement in Venice with a girl called Sofia, a servant in the Doge's Palace, whom he had met while both were masked during a carnival spree in the Piazza.

Sofia was quite different from Louise, both in appearance and nature. She too was dark, but in the fashion of most Venetian women, whatever their status, used the local recipe of centaury, gum arabic and soap solution, followed by bleaching in the sun, to give her hair, worn loose to the shoulders, the Titian red-gold tint. With her low-cut bodice and ankle-length skirt set off with a pretty apron and the readiest of saucy smiles, she was extremely fetching. Unlike Louise, she never scolded, was submissive, as Phillipe believed all women should be, and bubbled over with gossip she picked up inside the Doge's household.

Coupled with what Phillipe picked up from the gondoliers, who were told so much by the ladies' maids of the patrician families, it gave him considerable insight into the state of morale at the top despite the authorities' pathological concern with secrecy, which had not diminished down the centuries.

Sofia was a 'contact' in more ways than one. So much so that on one of the infrequent occasions they had thought it safe to meet, since all Venetians were encouraged to inform on each other as well as on foreigners, he had made her pregnant. In five months' time she would have his child, something that Louise had been unable to do for him, as Josephine had so far failed Napoleon. With luck he would have completed his unpleasant assignment in Paris long before then, but Sofia would fret, particularly if he had no chance to explain why he had left Venice so suddenly.

If Lallemont insisted on his immediate departure for the

French capital he might be reduced to leaving an explanatory note in their secret 'Letter-box'. There she deposited information she gleaned for him about the comings and goings in the Ducal Palace—in a niche in the pedestal supporting the rear legs of the second bronze horse from the right in the Loggia dei Cavalli. With the *confidenti*, the agents of Venice's secular Inquisition, both active and efficient, whatever the state of the forces might be, meetings could not safely be arranged at short notice. The Inquisitors could execute any citizen found guilty of treason, in total secrecy.

★　　★　　★

Citizeness Bonaparte, whom her husband called Josephine but was really called Rose, was delighted to be back in Paris. There had been a few occasions when she had enjoyed being with her husband at his public triumphs, like the splendid gala performance at La Scala in Milan on the seventh anniversary of the Fall of the Bastille, and she liked driving down the Corso with smart ponies while passers-by waved and curtsied. But camp-following, however grand, was not her style. And she was tired: Napoleon had hustled her from banquet to banquet to meet people whose names she could no more remember than the details of his battles. It was no great novelty for her to be a general's wife. After all, her first husband, Alexander, Viscomte de Beauharnais, had been Commander-in-Chief of the Army of the Rhine, apart from having presided over the Assembly.

Alexander had never insisted that she should join him on his campaign travels. Generals' wives did not do that, and those she knew thought she had been mad to agree to join Bonaparte in Italy.

It was so much more fun to be back in Paris, where she could not only bask in her husband's glory among people she cared about but usurp it. Every time he scored a success she was hailed publicly as 'Notre Dame des Victoires'.

In the reaction following the Terror, Paris was the gayest and most exciting city in the world, with a torrent of aggressive energy expressing itself in parties, dinners, opera performances, comedies and artistic, political and literary discussion. There were 'guillotine-balls', where men who had lost relatives to the sliding knife advertised that distinction by wearing their hair tied up behind, while the women sported a blood-red ribbon round the throat. Josephine, who loved to display her fashion-sense, exquisite figure and grace of movement on the ballroom floor, was certainly qualified to wear one. The Viscomte de Beauharnais had been guillotined, and she herself had been saved only by the timely overthrow and execution of Robespierre, the 'Incorruptible', whose humanity had been so corrupted by power over life and death.

Apart from the social whirl, she had such interesting friends in Paris, people in whom she could really confide. Like Thérèse Tallien, the scandalous but immensely amusing courtesan, with whom she had set the trend for wearing flimsy Grecian-style gowns which left so much bare. Like Paul Barras, who entertained lavishly, and of course Hippolyte Charles, her dashing hussar, when he was able to snatch some time away from the fighting.

'Isn't it marvellous to be back,' Josephine declared to Louise, as their coach rattled over the Parisian cobblestones. She wiped her eyes with the corner of her handkerchief. 'Do you remember how I cried when we had to leave for Milan? Well, now I'm crying because we're back. Isn't it silly?'

Unlike her mistress, who at that stage regarded her husband as rather a comic character in spite of his achievements, Louise was in love with Phillipe, though not immune to seduction, as Colonel Junot had so quickly proved. Before she appreciated the pleasures of coquetry through assisting Josephine in her amours, she had been a chaste convent girl whose religious fervour had not been affected by the Revolution. She still suffered some remorse from her occasional lapses, but it was a diminishing liability as she observed how her mistress, whom she so much admired, dismissed the sins of the flesh as 'trivialities'.

'Life is not only about taking pleasure, my dear,' Josephine assured her. 'It's about giving it too.'

As the coach turned into the home stretch, the Rue Chantereine, towards the impressive, pavilion-style house

Bonaparte had rented and would later purchase, Josephine was bubbling with excitement.

'I'm so looking forward to seeing the children,' she said.

'So am I, madame,' Louise responded with sincerity. 'We've been away from home far too long.'

The children were Josephine's by her former marriage, her son Eugène and her daughter Hortense. Though they were powerful reminders of her failure to conceive with Napoleon, who was already agitating for an heir, he treated them almost as his own.

In her heart Josephine wanted no more babies. She considered herself too old to start that again and, when consoling Louise for her failure to conceive with Phillipe, always stressed the unfairness of the length of pregnancy and the pain of labour compared with the brief masculine ecstasy responsible. Besides, the Tarot cards, which were so often laid out in Louise's presence, had predicted that she would never be pregnant again.

Josephine believed completely in the power of the cards to foretell the future. They had certainly never failed to foresee Napoleon's victories. When the Wheel of Fortune, card Number 10, showed up it was never inverted. Neither were Number 7, the Chariot, nor Number 19, The Sun—both sure portents of triumph and satisfaction.

Mistress and maid frequently played games, especially backgammon, which Josephine always won through superior skill, except when through her natural kindness she deliberately failed to take advantages. It was this warm-hearted, generous streak which endeared her to women and men alike.

In looks she could hardly have been described as beautiful, even while she looked excitedly out of the coach window as the driver, whom she had hired when she set out from Paris to Milan, pulled the horses to a stop. Her pale face with its large, deep-blue eyes had something of a perpetual look of surprise. Her hair, auburn-tinged and usually dressed in little curls on her forehead, was not memorable, though her eyelashes, both long and thick, were. She was but five feet tall, and when her small mouth opened to smile or speak she revealed several black teeth. Her voice was low-pitched for a woman, with a trace of Creole accent, but some men found that sexually stimulating as they did her whole outgiving attitude to intimate contact. Josephine had more than her share of the mysterious quality of charm and Napoleon was not alone in declaring, 'You set my blood on fire.'

*   *   *

For a whole week there had been no message from Phillipe. Every day, usually immediately after early morning mass in St Mark's, Sofia had slipped up to the Loggia dei Cavalli when she believed nobody was looking, to glance furtively in the crevice of the pedestal below the second bronze horse from the right, and there had been nothing.

What could have happened to Phillipe? She knew he had been called to see Bonaparte. His last note had told her that, but he had not expected to be away so long. With her belly declaring her condition more obviously each day she just had to be sure that she had not been deserted. Phillipe had always been so kind, so considerate, so generous with money.

'But do I really know him?' she asked herself. 'Might that story of the urgent call to General Bonaparte's headquarters just have been a ruse to let him get out of Venice without any fuss and rejoin that woman?'

Phillipe had made no secret of his long relationship with Louise, but after Sofia had conceived he had assured her that she was the woman with whom he would eventually spend his life.

After the seventh day of silence Sofia had made up her mind. In the eighteenth century, illicit relations and concubinage were common enough in Italy—*'Peccato di carne non e peccato'*—and pregnancy before marriage was no great disgrace, but the other servants in the Ducal Palace were already asking who the father was. It wouldn't be long before the Dogaressa herself might demand to know. Her uncertainty just had to be resolved. She would have to try to see Phillipe's boss, Ambassador Lallemont. Secretly, of course.

Sadly for Sofia it was no longer possible for her to do anything in secret. One of the vergers of St Mark's had been

166

informed of the girl's too frequent visits to the Loggia dei Cavalli, and a search had revealed Phillipe's note explaining how he had been ordered to Paris and might be away some weeks. In traditional Venetian manner the facts had been immediately reported to the secular Inquisition, which still retained its aura of terror, deliberately fostered over the centuries to maintain law and order.

The moment the Inquisitors had been alerted of Sofia's connection with a French secret agent, all the traditional wiles of Venetian reaction to treachery had been resurrected. Counter-spies were detailed to watch and follow her round the clock, recording every movement, every contact, with the relentless professionalism which, in the past, had resulted in violent death for so many offenders branded as traitors. Even glassmakers who had fled the Republic hoping to sell the treasured secrets of their craft in a distant land had been hunted down and killed.

Sofia had been an easy target. She had been seen going by gondola to the French Embassy hopefully disguised in a black hood and carnival mask, which was standard dress for six months of the year, and was seized and interrogated immediately on her return to the Ducal Palace. After token resistance before the terrifying Inquisitors, two in black robes, one in red, she had broken down within minutes and confessed everything.

'Yes, your Excellencies, I did tell him things I saw and heard in the Palace. But how could that hurt anybody? It was only gossip.'

'Yes, I do know about the old laws saying we mustn't be familiar with foreigners. But I thought they were finished. Out of date. That nobody takes any notice of them any more. Besides, when I first met Phillipe I thought he was an Italian . . .'

'Ah, but not Venetian!' an Inquisitor had interrupted. 'You must have known he was not Venetian.'

'Yes, your Excellency. I knew he was not Venetian.'

However helpless the Inquisitors might feel about the threat from young Bonaparte, they had no qualms about dealing savagely with a woman of the same age who was one of their

167

own subjects. Pregnant or not she was dispatched, after agreeing to her statement, to the Pozzi—the grim dungeons in the basement of the Ducal Palace. In a low, vaulted cell faintly lit by a narrow grating, with a trestle-board bed, she would compete with rats for the meagre ration of bread and soup. There she would stay until the hoped-for capture of Phillipe would enable the Inquisitors to decide on her final sentence.

★   ★   ★

Louise could not have been more surprised nor more pleased by Phillipe's arrival in Paris. Her mistress was delighted too for her sake and gave her as much free time as her essential duties, required by a round of social engagements, permitted. Josephine might be ridiculously superstitious but there was no suspicion in her nature. She tended to think the best of everyone, especially where affairs of the heart were concerned.

Neither did Louise suspect any ulterior motive in Phillipe's artfully interpolated attempts to secure the details of what had happened during the night-stops when Junot had escorted Josephine to and from Peschiera.

'What's she up to these days, that mistress of yours?' Phillipe asked with a yawn, as they lay contentedly in bed. 'I don't doubt there's a man on the scene somewhere.'

'What makes you say that?' Louise responded sharply. 'I know she had something of a reputation after her husband was guillotined by those brutes, but since she's been married to the General . . .'

'Oh, come off it, dear,' Phillipe interrupted. 'Her affair with this Lieutenant Charles is the talk of the Army. I even heard about it in Venice.'

'Then it's malicious gossip. He's just a friend, that's all.'

'Just a friend!' Phillipe laughed. 'Well, of course, there's friends and friends. Didn't she sleep with him on the way from Paris to Milan? That's what everybody thinks.'

'Well, they think wrong. But then they always do, don't they? If she'd slept with him I would have known, wouldn't I, and she didn't.'

'He's not the only officer there's talk about.'

'Oh! And who else's reputation are they trying to destroy?' Louise asked scathingly.

'It's that ADC to the General. That Colonel Junot.'

It was as well that in the darkness of the bedroom Phillipe could not see the blushing concern on Louise's features.

'But Colonel Junot is the General's best friend,' she countered.

Phillipe laughed. 'Surely you don't think that's going to stop a hot-blooded young man if he finds it's there on a plate, especially after a few glasses of wine.'

Louise did not reply. She doubted whether Phillipe would take that robust, understanding attitude if he ever discovered the truth.

For his part, Phillipe decided it was pointless to pursue the issue further at that time and rolled over, apparently to sleep but really to think who else might yield the information. He soon had an obvious lead—the coachman. Coachmen were always reliable contacts. There was little they missed, with their eyes or their ears.

*　　*　　*

'Was the coachman who drove you to Paris the same one that drove you out of Peschiera?' Phillipe asked Louise next morning.

'Yes, Jacques. Why do you want to know?'

'General Bonaparte asked me to find him and gave me some money for him. Not much, but a token of his appreciation for getting your mistress and you safely away from the Austrians. He decided he hadn't thanked him enough. He's a generous man, the General. Do you know where this Jacques is staying? I'd like to shake his hand anyway for saving *your* life.'

It did not take Phillipe long to track down the inn where the coachman was staying.

'General Bonaparte asked me to give you this,' he said, offering the coachman a small doeskin bag containing three gold coins.

169

'That's mighty civil of him, sir,' Jacques said, looking at the money tipped into his palm. 'It couldn't have come at a better time. Then money can never come at a better time, can it, friend? But tell me—who are you?'

'Oh, just a servant of General Bonaparte. He felt he hadn't thanked you enough for getting his wife out of Peschiera. I gather it was quite a caper.'

'You're damn right it was. We were nearly all killed. Let me buy you a drink and I'll tell you about it.'

Accustomed to patient listening, Phillipe filled his clay pipe while, over their glasses of wine, Jacques embellished the story to the point that he had been able to see the whites of the Austrians' eyes, so near had the Lake Garda gunboat been.

'If I hadn't whipped 'em up smartly we'd all have been blown to bits.'

'But didn't that Colonel Junot get Madame Bonaparte out of the carriage after the first shot? That's what the General told me.'

'Mm, yes, that's true enough,' Jacques replied diffidently. 'But I was left to drive the horses while they ducked down the ditch. There were two escort horses killed you know. If I hadn't whipped ours up smartly . . .'

'You were very brave, Jacques,' Phillipe conceded. 'And I drink your health. But that Colonel Junot! I believe he's quite a dog. With Citizeness Bonaparte, I mean.'

'Now look here, I won't hear anything about Madame Bonaparte. The gossips can say what they like. There never was anything between Colonel Junot and Madame. I can tell you that straight.'

Phillipe could see he was telling the truth, or at least the truth as he knew it, and was about to switch to Lieutenant Charles when Jacques conjured up a mischievous smile and confided, 'Now if you'd said *the maid* and Colonel Junot, that would have been different.'

'The maid? What maid?' Phillipe asked as casually as he could.

'Why Madame's maid, of course. Louise, the bossy one who thinks she's a lady herself. She was the one the Colonel fancied. And he got her—more than once. He's a little fellow isn't he? And you know what they say—"Big man big balls, little man all balls!" '

Phillipe flushed, but if Jacques noticed it he must have attributed it to the wine.

'How do you know that he got her, as you put it?'

'Caught 'em at it! In the back of my coach. One night when I was doing me round in the stable-yard. I opened the door to check inside, pushed me lamp in and there they were—at it. She had her skirt round her neck and he was in up to the hilt.'

Mistaking Phillipe's sharp intake of breath for erotic appreciation, Jacques went on, 'Oh, she was enjoying it all right. She had her legs wrapped round him as well as her arms. I got a right eyeful I can tell yer. Her stockings were held up with red garters which had something written on 'em. Of course I shut the door right away, but they'd seen the lamp. It was a different Louise when she saw me next morning, I can tell yer.'

Phillipe could stand no more. Outraged and infuriated, he stalked out of the tavern without so much as 'Goodbye'. It would have done him no good had he got around to asking questions about Hippolyte Charles. Lieutenant Charles always tipped Jacques handsomely, which Colonel Junot had failed to do.

The more Phillipe brooded on Louise's infidelity the more monstrous it seemed. There he was, doing a dangerous job in a foreign land and there was she, opening her legs at the first opportunity. In the back of a coach, by God!

That Jacques had been telling the truth he had no doubt. It had always been Louise's habit to wrap her long legs round Phillipe when he made love to her, beating his back with her heels in her orgasms. And those garters! They were the clincher. He remembered buying them for her from a pedlar in the Piazza and sending them to her in Milan. What was it the inscription had said, in French? *'N'eveillez pas le chat qui dort'*—'Let the sleeping pussy lie'? No. *'Qui ne risque rien, n'a rien'*— 'Nothing venture, nothing win.' Those were the ones. He had given the others, the saucier ones, to Sofia.

He felt totally betrayed. The fact that Sofia's pregnancy was the result of an urgent spurt standing in a dank and odorous

171

alley, suddenly selected because it was bereft of even the dim
glow of one of the numerous madonna shrines, was irrelevant.
He could scarcely restrain himself from storming back to
Madame Bonaparte's and confronting his common-law wife
there with her unforgivable wantonness, but his in-built dis-
cretion advised him to wait at least until she joined him that
evening.

With his sense of betrayal reinforced by impatience, his
natural preference for quiet and tactful interrogation was still
submerged in anger when they met. As Louise approached
him with a smile to embrace him he struck her hard across the
cheek.

'Whore!' he shouted. 'Whore!'

Louise was too shocked to defend herself. She broke down
in tears as Phillipe recounted the coachman's charge, and
though she admitted nothing her failure to deny it was
enough.

'I'll kill him,' Phillipe said quietly. 'I'll kill him.'

From the set of his face and her knowledge that he had
assassinated before in line of duty, Louise could see that he
meant it.

'What good will it do you to kill Colonel Junot?' she asked.
'They will shoot you.'

'I'll take that chance. It wouldn't matter to you anyway.'

'That's a lie and you know it,' Louise said, drying her tears
and recovering her composure. Secretly she had been rather
proud of being taken by Junot, a friend of the General's and
obviously destined for high rank. Why should she deny it? She
wasn't Phillipe's wife!

'What happened at Peschiera was nothing,' she insisted. 'I
was carried away. It meant nothing. We had just been thrown
together, that's all. And both had too much wine. It's only you
that I love. I've never done it with anybody else.'

'Are you suggesting he raped you?' Phillipe asked sarcastically, remembering Jacques' account of how much she seemed
to be enjoying it.

'I did try to resist him but he was determined.'

'I'll kill him,' Phillipe repeated. 'You'll see. As for you, I've
finished with you. When I walk out of this room you will

never see me again. But you are not to say anything to your mistress about all this. That I have been questioning you about Peschiera. Understand?'

Louise nodded, twisted her handkerchief in her trembling hands and looked at him imploringly.

'Don't leave me, Phillipe. Please don't leave me.'

Momentarily he was tempted to say something that was not harsh, but found it impossible.

'I can't live with a whore,' he said grimly, as he strode out of her life.

Chapter Fourteen

It took the discerning Josephine no more than a glance to see that something had made Louise desperately unhappy as she came into the bedroom to lay out her clothes.

When she asked how she had come by the swelling bruise on her cheek, Louise poured out most of what had happened but denied even the smallest intimacy with Junot. The mistress would have been greatly displeased to discover that the gallant Colonel had preferred her maid's charms to her own.

'You poor dear,' Josephine said consolingly, putting her arms round her. 'You know how it is with all these men, one law for them and a different one for us. They can do whatever they like, but if they even suspect us of straying we can be finished. If that's the way Phillipe feels, you are well rid of the brute. Striking you like that!'

While sincere in her concern for her maid, Josephine sensed the real reason why Phillipe had been sent all the way from Venice to question the coachman. Knowing her husband's priorities and the needs of war it seemed doubtful that he would have sacrificed the services of one of his best agents, when the Italian situation was rising towards its climax, without some pressing personal motive.

*   *   *

After making a few desultory checks on Barras, which showed that the demands of his new mistress, the exquisite and avaricious Thérèse Tallien, left him neither time nor energy for any other, Phillipe decided to return to Italy and seek out Napoleon at his headquarters, wherever they might be. His show-down with Louise had made it impossible to discover anything useful about Hippolyte Charles, who was not in Paris, but he would not be returning without evidence.

174

As his anger had subsided and his native cunning resumed command, Phillipe found it unnecessary to do anything as dangerous as killing Colonel Junot. He would destroy him by reporting to Bonaparte that his suspicions in that direction had been fully justified. He was highly skilled at concocting persuasive disinformation. For Louise in the back of that coach, read Josephine—with all the spicy details—and Citizeness Bonaparte, Junot and the coachman could deny it as best they could!

*　　*　　*

Fortunately for Junot, and perhaps for Josephine, Phillipe never reached the General. While night-stopping at Breschia, three armed agents of the Venetian Secret Service, who had followed him all the way from Paris, forced entry into his bedroom, bound and gagged him and bundled him into a waiting coach. He was taken to Venice, and in front of the Inquisitors was confronted with Sofia.

'I admit nothing except to being a personal emissary of General Bonaparte, Commander-in-Chief of the Army of Italy. I am a citizen of France and should any harm come to me or to my friend, be sure that you will pay for it.'

'We are addressed as "Your Excellencies",' the red-robed Inquisitor said haughtily.

'Not by me, you're not,' Phillipe replied. 'In my world, which will soon be yours, the only label you're entitled to is "Citizen".'

Satisfied by their agents that nobody had witnessed the capture of Phillipe and that his disappearance could not be traced to them, the Inquisitors made no further response beyond announcing, 'You are guilty of gross treachery to the Venetian Republic of which you have been a guest. Take him away!'

Denying him any knowledge of his fate was part of the punishment. Any time his cell-door creaked open it could be to admit the State Strangler.

Over the weeks he was repeatedly awakened to be grilled about Bonaparte's intentions towards Venice and the French intelligence effort inside the city, especially concerning the names of any other Venetians assisting it. But his spirit and resolution held out. The Inquisitors would have liked the assistance of the rack or the spiked boot but physical torture was no longer legal, even for them. Sofia, who had been so sapped by her experience that she did nothing but answer in a monotone 'Yes' or 'No' to the Inquisitors' further questions, was sent back to her cell in the Pozzi. Phillipe, meanwhile, was consigned to the Piombi, the windowless prison under the lead roof of the Palace, where the cells were larger but freezing in winter and stifling in summer.

★   ★   ★

Three months later Phillipe was given his first news of the outside world.

'You have a son,' his goaler said, as he stooped in under the low door bearing his prisoner's food. 'I haven't seen him but I am told that mother and child are doing well.'

'Where are they?' Phillipe asked, mustering what interest he could from the depression of his solitary confinement. 'My son wasn't born in prison, I hope.'

'Certainly not,' the gaoler, a friend of Sofia when she had been on the palace staff, replied huffily. 'What do you think we are, Frenchman? Barbarians? As soon as it was clear her time had come she was put in the care of the nuns of the Convent of San Zaccaria. She had her baby there. You can be sure that the nuns will be looking after them. They are all ladies at San Zaccaria. From good patrician homes! The Abbess is a Dandolo!'

Phillipe's only response was a dejected snort. He had not needed the gaoler to regale him with tales of a notorious predecessor in his cell, one Giacomo Casanova, to have no high opinion of the ladies of San Zaccaria. The place seemed to be little better than a high-grade whore-house. The young nuns were able to get out whenever they pleased, to go masked to carnival celebrations or to the gambling dens. They certainly had their share of illegitimate children, some of them sired by the priests, though during carnival months any man could get into the convent if masked, as Casanova had proved.

176

'Sorry there's nothing better to wet the baby's head,' the gaoler said, half jokingly, half sarcastically, as he filled the water bowl.

'What will happen to them?'

'Well, of course, Sofia will have to come back to prison. She's a traitor, isn't she? Thanks to you. She can't be set free just because she's pupped a Frenchman's bastard. You couldn't expect that, could you?'

'I suppose not,' Phillipe replied without feeling. 'What about the boy? What will happen to him?'

'Oh, he'll be all right. The Mother Superior will see to that. He'll be reared in some orphanage. Don't ever ask me which, because I won't know and I wouldn't be allowed to tell you if I did.'

As he took away the prisoner's metal plate to refill it, the gaoler noticed in the dim candlelight that the previous day's food was still on it almost untouched.

'What's this? Not hungry?'

'Not for that muck. Anyway food doesn't seem to have much taste in the dark.'

'There's one other thing I can tell you,' the gaoler said as he moved to lock up the cell. 'Your son has been baptized in the True Faith. They've called him Alessandro. The Mother Superior thought you should know but don't tell anyone I told you.'

Phillipe had not lost all hope that Venice would soon be taken by the French and that he and Sofia would be released and make a life together. Having little else to think about he felt his reponsibility for her keenly. But the next news he had of her from the gaoler demolished that dream. In a fit of depression at the loss of her baby, Sofia had hanged herself with her stockings.

'The Inquisitors will die for it,' Phillipe assured himself. 'Every blasted one of them.'

*　　　*　　　*

Josephine was not one to let bitterness bloat through festering introspection. Louise had retailed more about Phillipe's

177

inquiries after talking to Jacques herself, though still without admitting her intimacy with Junot, and had ensured that the coachman gave no clues in that direction. So Napoleon found himself challenged in the next letter he received from his wife:

'You must have told Phillipe of your suspicions, so you not only degraded me but yourself as well. It was undignified for a man of your position. Besides, there is nothing that Phillipe could have discovered about me. As for the suggestion that there has ever been anything between myself and Colonel Junot, the idea is preposterous. He has never done anything but carry out your orders with grace and respect. Your behaviour seems an odd way of rewarding him for saving my life at Peschiera.'

Napoleon felt no remorse on reading the letter; only anger that Phillipe had bungled the job. He would have him recalled immediately for a full explanation. As for degrading himself, well, as he put it in another context, 'If I want a particular man I'm prepared to kiss his arse.'

In later days Josephine was to degrade herself by paying serving women to spy on the affairs of Napoleon when he too had discovered the stimulant pleasures of promiscuity, after his success in winning his wife's love had diluted his interest in her.

*　　*　　*

As the weeks passed and there was no news of Phillipe, beyond Josephine's assurance that he had left Paris, Napoleon assumed that the spy simply lacked the courage to face him after his failure and had gone into hiding somewhere. That was the explanation he offered to Ambassador Lallemont in writing, though giving no clue to the nature of Phillipe's mission.

Chapter Fifteen

'The time has come, Junot,' Napoleon announced early in the spring of 1797. 'I want you to go to Venice and confront this "Serenissima", as this pantomime government calls itself: confront them with their perfidy. Understand? Their perfidy! Read them this letter and show them this document.'

He handed Junot an unsealed letter and a piece of paper purporting to be a secret directive from the Venetians, ordering their subjects on the mainland to attack the French wherever possible.

'Show them the document to *prove* that we know they have breached their neutrality. Read from it but do not let it into their possession. I must have it back.'

Junot nodded. Like Napoleon, he knew the document to be a forgery.

'Keep your accusation short and don't put up with any of their fancy courtesy and farcical ceremony. That's just part of their delaying tactics. Tell the Doge and his Council that what I say in this letter is what I require—immediately. I want these people frightened out of their wits.'

As Junot marched out Napoleon called to him, 'This "Queen of the Adriatic" is like an old whore who has nothing coming in but insists on keeping up the appearances. Treat her as such.'

Junot thought that the General's attitude seemed unusually tough—brutally outspoken and tactless though he always was. The lust for domination that was to become insatiable, and the willingness to use terror as a weapon, were clearly showing in these demands he was being sent to make. But if those were the orders he would carry them out to the letter. And not without some enjoyment. Some of the arrogance of power had already rubbed off on to him.

★　　★　　★

179

Travelling with the speed Bonaparte always demanded and displayed himself, Junot arrived in Venice on Easter Saturday, on which, in the Venetian calendar, the first Mass of the Resurrection celebrations was traditionally held. It was one of the very few days when no business of any kind was transacted in the merchant city, but as soon as Junot reported to the French Embassy, Lallemont informed the Ducal Palace that the Doge must summon his Council immediately. He brushed aside the religious objection by quoting St Mark, 'The sabbath was made for man, not man for the sabbath.'

Doge Ludovico Manin, a weak and dispirited character, the antithesis of Dandolo and others who had occupied his position, had been half expecting some ultimatum. From their beginnings as refugees from the wreck of Ancient Rome, the Venetians feared any Cæsar and made sure that no man could attain a tyrannical position in their State. In Bonaparte they saw such a Cæsar, and had already been frightened by Lallemont's repeated demands for explanations about assaults on French troops in the mainland Venetian territories. So, Easter Saturday or not, the Council, or as many as could be mustered at such short notice, were summoned to the Ducal Palace.

The sun was shining in a mother-of-pearl sky as Lallemont conducted Junot across St Mark's Square, pointing out the many buildings of note. While impressed by the palaces on the Grand Canal, the young colonel was appalled by the general dirtiness, with the great Piazza fouled by the smell of fish and poultry stalls, by beggars swarming, rattling their bowls and exposing their deformities, by prostitutes and pedlars of obscene novelties and literature.

'This whole place is crazy,' Lallemont told him. 'And all the people in it, though delightfully so. They say Nero fiddled while Rome burned but here the whole population is fiddling away, which really isn't surprising when the Government's motto is like Nero's—keep them frivolous and they won't cause trouble!'

'Are they both blind and deaf?' Junot asked.

'Not really. They just live in a dream world. The French Army is just across the water, yet if you'd come here a few weeks earlier you'd have seen this piazza plunged in merrymaking for days and nights on end. This tiny circle of sea has saved them so many times in the past they assume it will again.'

'Well, they are overdue for a rude awakening,' Junot said, reassured that his mission should not be too difficult.

Lallemont nodded, rather sadly. 'Meanwhile, nothing must interfere with the fun. Can you believe it? When the last Doge died eight years ago his death was kept secret for ten days because it was a particularly hectic week of the Carnival and the authorities did not want to put a damper on the festivities!'

Junot shook his head incredulously. Like his master, he despised play-abouts. Nor did he admire the style of the Basilica as they approached it closely enough to see the sly-looking saints in its glittering mosaics. It all seemed oriental and out of place in Europe.

'It may be very old but to me it's a mess,' he remarked. 'These bits and pieces stuck all over it. I think the whole thing's in bad taste.'

'Perhaps, but on a majestic scale,' Lallemont countered, not wishing to disagree entirely with General Bonaparte's emissary, whom he found brash to the point of boorishness.

'Now *they* are different,' Junot said, pointing to the four bronze horses over the main door.

'Yes, they're very special. They were looted, like almost everything else here, but for centuries the Venetians have regarded them as the symbol of their own power. Their enemies used to claim they would "bit and bridle the horses" when they meant they would take Venice. But nobody has ever done it.'

'Somebody may well do it now,' Junot remarked, knowing the extent to which Napoleon was sending art treasures to the Louvre. 'They are wasted up there anyway. They look as though they are on a perch. They should be on a triumphal arch in a more important place where people can really see them.'

The Ambassador, who deplored what had already been done to the city with which he had fallen in love, did not comment as they turned into the Ducal Palace through the Porta della Carta.

*   *   *

181

The Grand Council—the Doge and his Cabinet—which the Venetians called the Collegio, met in the most magnificent hall of the palace beneath the carved and gilded ceiling, painted by Veronese to show the Queen of the Adriatic kneeling before Christ, with Mars and Neptune as the pillars of the Republic.

As Junot strode in from the sumptuous ante-room, waving aside the Master of Ceremonies with theatrical contempt and more than a little nervous of the imminent encounter, he remembered Bonaparte's remarks about the state of the guns and warships. Mars and Neptune were of little use to Venice now, but to stem the ebb of his youthful courage he whispered to himself the resounding command of Danton, the guillotined revolutionary, *'De l'audace et encore de l'audace et toujours de l'audace!'*

Until that moment, the long succession of ambassadors, Papal Nuncios and noblemen had approached the Doge and his Councillors with respect and even awe as they looked up at them in splendour on the dais. Junot marched in, booted and spurred, sabre clanking and with his hat on, and sat himself on the right hand of the timid Doge in the seat reserved for the Nuncio. Ignoring the Doge's courteous greeting he pulled Bonaparte's letter from his belt and began to read it in a loud voice, rubbing in the insult by speaking in French. The onus of translation therefore fell on the Doge, though Lallemont was bilingual.

'Everywhere the villagers have armed themselves and cry "Death to the French". Do you think that although I find myself in the centre of Germany I cannot cause the first people of the universe to be respected? The blood of my comrades will be avenged. If you do not at once disperse the hostile peasants, war is declared.'

After allowing a few moments for the message to penetrate, Junot continued, 'I also have here one of your documents which has fallen into our hands, a document proving that you are actively inducing your subjects to fall upon the French . . .'

'We have issued no such document,' the Doge assured Junot after looking at his senior colleagues, who were shaking their

182

heads emphatically. 'Let me see it. There must be some mistake . . .'

Junot ignored him and continued to recite the accusations about atrocities against honest French soldiers risking their lives to do the whole Italian people a magnificent service by liberating them.

'But Colonel, we Venetians do not need liberating,' the Doge protested. 'We were a republic for many centuries before France ever thought of the idea. We are the longest-lived republic the world has ever known.'

'You are not General Bonaparte's idea of a republic.'

'But it is we Venetians who have kept the whole concept of a Senate alive, ever since Ancient Rome.'

'Yes, and restricted its membership to the upper crust and a very thin crust at that. Ordinary Venetians have no political rights.'

The Doge was genuinely surprised at this objection.

'But the people are very happy that way. Stop some of them and ask them. They much prefer order and security to what you call liberty.'

Junot was beginning to feel uncomfortable. 'Whatever you may say, Venice is not governed by the people,' he reiterated.

'What state ever can be, Colonel? One must face realities in government. In France you have a Directory of only five men representing the people. Here . . .'

'I am not here to argue,' Junot snapped. 'Simply to deliver General Bonaparte's accusations and his demand to know what you intend to do about them.'

The Doge sighed resignedly. 'We can do no more than assure General Bonaparte that whatever may occur on the mainland is not on instructions from Venice. These things happen on both sides in war—spontaneously when people are provoked and tempers flare. We are doing all we can to observe strict neutrality . . .'

'Strict neutrality!' Junot scoffed. 'Was it neutrality when your representative in Verona allowed the town and fortress of Peschiera to fall into the hands of the Austrians? Was it neutrality when you let the Pretender to the Throne of France, the Comte de Lille, as he calls himself, set up a full court with

183

foreign envoys in a palace in Verona? Was it neutrality . . .'

Neither the Doge nor his Councillors had any answers to the recital. They knew they were guilty of bending neutrality, at which they had become past-masters over many centuries. It had been the only way they could survive. And they lacked the courage to point out that Bonaparte had consistently violated their neutrality when it suited him. As they sat there terrified by this young man's tirade and what it foreshadowed, they did not even regret their failure to take the advice of the British Ambassador that they should formally ally themselves with Austria. They had chosen inaction and still they could not see the folly of it.

After so many years of compromise, trading-off and wheeler-dealing the Venetians had no friends, and even some of Napoleon's enemies would not be unhappy to see them humbled. At that moment, Bonaparte was already negotiating a secret agreement with the Austrians through which Venice and most of its mainland territories would be ceded to Vienna. Doges like Enrico Dandolo would have been the first to hear of such a move.

After Junot had marched out as arrogantly as he had entered, returning to the French legation to await an answer, the Venetian leaders discussed what they should do. Their deliberations concluded with agreement that 'The Venetian Government apologizes most humbly for any illegal acts which might have been committed against the forces of France by its subjects.'

Junot was well satisfied when Lallemont passed him the statement which had been rushed over to the embassy.

'I want these people frightened out of their wits,' Bonaparte had ordered. That, literally, was what he had achieved.

★　　　★　　　★

Events, some accidental, some planned, moved swiftly in favour or Bonaparte, who had been looking for an excuse for decisive action. On that same night, in Verona, a scuffle between French troops and Slavonian soldiers keen to fight in defence of Venetian territory, led to the death of several

184

Frenchmen. Napoleon responded by sending a French ship called *The Liberator of Italy* to enter the Lido port on the following Wednesday, knowing it would be against the strict Easter laws of the Republic. As he had hoped, the Venetian commander in charge of the port opened fire, killing five of the *Liberator*'s crew including the captain.

Again the Doge and his Councillors reacted with nothing but cowardice. Instead of protesting against the illegal entry of the French vessel, they dispatched two envoys to Graz, where Napoleon had moved, to make a humiliating explanation.

Enraged at the news, Napoleon turned on them, storming: 'For this I will be an Attila to Venice. Your government must go at once. Understand? I will have no more of your Senators, no more of your Inquisitors and your detestable prisons where people rot for years at their whim. It is I who will make the law. Me!'

* * *

Reporting the details of his successful mission to Napoleon at the latest temporary headquarters at Graz, Junot briefly described the new prize of Venice, which the General had never visited. Bonaparte listened somewhat impatiently until the aide kindled his interest by saying about the Four Horses of St Mark's, 'They claim they were made for Alexander the Great.'

'You mean they actually belonged to Alexander himself?' Napoleon asked incredulously. 'That he might have touched them . . .'

'That's what they say.'

'Are they lifelike, Junot? You know my views about art. You can't have real art without craftsmanship. It has to be accurate, true to life. I mean do these horses look as though they would be steady under fire?'

'They look magnificent, sir.'

'Then there's only one place for them, isn't there?' Napoleon said.

'I agree, General. It struck me when I first saw them that they ought to be on a triumphal arch.'

185

Bonaparte's hero complex about Ancient Rome, nourished by his avid historical reading, had engendered a strong appeal for the Roman arch as a symbol of military genius, an attraction fortified by his love and respect for the horse. He knew just where such an arch for the Four Horses should be built.

The French Crusaders at Constantinople had not wanted the Horses of Lysippus, except to melt them down for coin, but this Corsican masquerading as a Frenchman did. He was beginning to want everything. He was behaving like a Gallic Cæsar or a medieval Doge in his rape of foreign art treasures to take back to his capital. But he would not admit to any personal greed for glory or yearning for immortality.

'My intention is to make Paris the most beautiful capital in the world. Whatever is needed for that will be secured. So we'll ship those horses to Paris. Of course, Junot, these baubles mean nothing to me, as you well know, but they'll help to satisfy the Directory's appetite for *La Gloire*.'

'If the fools are still there,' he added in thought. By the rules, he could not become a Director until he was forty, but he was not made for rules and with the Army behind him nobody could withstand him, not even in Paris.

'Consul' would be a good title for a start. It had a Roman ring to it. No! 'First Consul' would be better. That was it. First Consul. And then King? No. That would recall the detested Bourbons, who had held his beloved Corsica in tyrannical subjection. There was a much grander title—also redolent of Rome.

*　　*　　*

As Bonaparte was to admit later, he had already convinced himself that public law really consisted in the right of the stronger. He immediately ordered his generals to cut off all communications between Venice and its mainland territories, instructing General Baranguay d'Hilliers to move his forces to Mestre, the little settlement nearest the city.

With maximum insolence d'Hilliers, after seeing his troops in position, moved into the Palazzo Dandolo, soon to be renamed the Daniele Hotel following its purchase by an entrepreneur called Dal Niel.

Instead of ordering the General to move, the Doge sent an emissary to whom d'Hilliers curtly replied, 'I have no idea of General Bonaparte's intentions. I simply carry out his orders and I shall do that whatever they may be.'

The Doge then tried his luck with Ambassador Lallemont, who responded in writing, more diplomatically. 'I am sure the Republic of Venice will be preserved—with certain alterations in its form of government, of course.'

Slightly reassured, envoys were dispatched to entreat with Napoleon directly but he refused to see them.

'Send them away,' he told his aide grimly. 'Tell them that they and their Senate are dripping with French blood.'

In utter confusion the Doge summoned an emergency conference in his private apartment that night. Those present met in the splendid Sala Grimani with Carpaccio's winged lion looking at them. To enter it each visitor had to pass through the Sala dello Scudo, the Room of the Shield—decorated with painted maps of those areas associated with Venice's glorious past. They received no leadership from the Doge in their deliberations to decide 'how best to communicate to the Great Council our unhappy condition'. His contribution was to walk up and down with the despairing cry, 'This night we are not even safe in our beds!' For far too long the people of Venice had relied on their noble families to solve their problems for them. Effete and gutless, the nobility let them down.

With no move from the Venetian government, Bonaparte declared war on the Republic and immediately ordered the destruction of the emblem of St Mark in every Venetian city on the mainland. Only one man, Angelo Giustiniani, one of the deputies who had been sent to plead with Napoleon, showed any of the courage and dash of his forebears. Confronting the fearsome little commander with the gaunt, parchment face, he told him that the captain of the French warship had been killed entirely as a result of his own rashness, and that the atrocities of the French troops were responsible for the attacks on them.

Looking at him with adamant eyes Napoleon said, 'I disagree with what you say but you are a brave man to dare to say it.'

Giustiniani then unbuckled his sword and threw it down shouting, 'I surrender myself as a hostage for Venice. If you must have blood, shoot me and spare my country.'

Bonaparte was even more impressed. 'You are a good citizen and I shall not only spare you but when I seize the property of the nobility yours shall be left untouched.'

'General, I am not so vile as to think about my own advantage when my country is in mortal danger. I care to receive neither my life nor my property as a favour from you.'

Napoleon bowed, bent down and handed back the belt and sword, then ushered the visitor out silently but with courtesy.

*   *   *

On the following day, 2 May, French troops were on the shore of the lagoon. The Venetians summoned enough initiative to obtain an armistice but though there were eleven thousand Slavonian soldiers at hand eager to fight, few of the Councillors favoured any defence of the city. There was no leader of spirit: no Enrico Dandolo. After a spate of lamentation the morally bankrupt Government decided that the city must be surrendered, in the hope that the French troops would then be speedily withdrawn for action elsewhere.

Like Constantinople before her, the great city-state, unique in never having been invaded much less occupied, was defeating itself. Napoleon had the will to win. The rulers of Venice did not even have the will to survive.

*   *   *

The Venetian people, gathering in the Square of St Mark, as they had always done during crises and triumphs, were enraged when they learned how they had been betrayed. Not since their last hours in the Hippodrome had the Four Horses witnessed such fury in a mob. Shouting *'Viva San Marco! Viva la Repubblica!'* they hoisted the banner of St Mark, and marched off to threaten the homes of those patricians they believed to be responsible for calling in the French.

188

On Friday 12 May the members of the Great Council arrived by gondola and horse to meet in the Great Hall of the Palace. Only five hundred and thirty-seven patricians attended, because so many had fled the city or barricaded themselves in their palazzi, but they set about sealing the suicide of the State, although a quorum of six hundred was minimal by law. Surrounded by wall-paintings of episodes of the Fourth Crusade, with the exploits of Enrico Dandolo facing the waterfront from which he had set sail, they went through the motions of expressing their great admiration for the French and agreed to the release of all political prisoners.

With the crowd outside still clamouring for offensive action, the Doge rose on the dais, pale and trembling. 'We have no alternative but to accept the demands of General Bonaparte,' he announced. 'Resistance would be impossible. General Bonaparte has in fact been quite magnanimous in his suggestions for reforms, which give us all hope of a better future. I therefore propose to you that the old form of our government now be abolished in favour of a democracy.'

Mollified perhaps by the Doge's assurance that Napoleon had promised to leave the city's possessions and their own intact, the patricians remained silent until a few musket volleys fired by Slavonian soldiers as a farewell salute induced some of the more frightened to cry, 'Let us vote!'

Only twenty votes were cast against this total abdication as the brilliant State, ruled by an unbroken succession of one hundred and twenty Doges for more than a thousand years, ended in a craven whimper.

Infected by the panic around him, the Doge rushed to his private apartments, stripping off the insignia of his ancient office as he ran. He ordered his servant to pull down the ducal hangings from the wall in case the French might be offended. Weeping like a woman, he removed his linen skull-cap and gave it to the valet muttering, 'Take it. I shall not need it any more.'

When the crowd outside heard what had happened they turned on the traitors who had emerged from the palace without their wigs and gowns, hoping to escape detection. Impotent against the enemy but brutal against their own,

189

patricians mounted cannon on the Rialto Bridge and, firing indiscriminately, killed several of the citizens who were still demanding that they should fight. The patricians had already agreed to 'request' the French to send in four thousand troops to protect them and keep order in the city. For this service, which he had no intention of continuing for more than a few months, Napoleon exacted six million francs in cash plus paintings, manuscripts and other treasures belonging to the Venetian people.

On the night of 14 May, Venetian sailors in forty Venetian longboats ferried General d'Hilliers and his soldiers across the lagoon into the city. The Doge shut himself away in the Pesaro Palace after refusing to head the provisional municipality which, while ordering the closure of the Venetian prisons as bestial and uncivilized, brought in all manner of new capital offences, especially against any who should criticize by word or deed the French 'liberators'.

The events so sickened Ambassador Lallemont that he wrote to his Foreign Secretary, 'I shall not disguise from you how much our conduct towards these people has increased their already existing hatred of all we are and all we stand for.'

It was a dispatch he would quickly regret.

*   *   *

Among the few who emerged into the daylight from the Pozzi when Napoleon insisted on the release of all political prisoners was Phillipe. He had been transferred there after Sofia's death, and though the Inquisitors would have preferred to silence him by secret execution they were too busy saving their own skins.

Even the gaoler, who equated the French with the guillotine, made himself scarce after racing round the few occupied cells, flinging open the doors and crying, 'You can go—courtesy of General Bonaparte!'

Scruffily bearded and with his clothes in poor condition, Phillipe quickly realized that at that moment St Mark's Square might be no safe place for a French civilian. So after a quick upward glance at the Four Horses, which in a way had been responsible for Sofia's death, his own imprisonment and the loss of his child, he sidled his way through the Venetian crowd and French troops to his old embassy, to pour out his story to the compassionate Lallemont. But the Ambassador had gone, recalled on the order of Bonaparte and eventually to be dismissed, and as yet there was no replacement.

The remaining officials welcomed Phillipe when they heard his story, but sympathy was scant. Nobody was interested in his clamour for revenge against the Inquisitors. No further excuse was needed for action against any Venetian officials, and the French were far too busy coping with the stream of instructions arriving from Paris and Bonaparte's headquarters.

The little General with the big demands was requiring the suppression of all the *scuole*, the ancient guild schools, in the name of liberty. The embassy officials were doing all they dared to explain that this would complicate the administration of the city, throwing thousands of widows and old and sick people on to charity because these excellent brotherhoods looked after their own. But Bonaparte had not been moved.

'There'll be some hardship at the individual level,' he had conceded. 'But there always is. The principle is what matters. Get on with it.'

Further, the envoys knew that Phillipe had been a spy and spies were expendable. Wasn't that all part of their peculiar game? Spies were always unpopular with diplomats. They had their uses, of course, but they were apt to cause trouble— just at the wrong moment.

'You must provide transport for me to report to the Commander-in-Chief,' Phillipe urged the senior envoy.

'Write him a letter and I will see that it is delivered,' the envoy replied. Having achieved control of an embassy, even if only temporarily, he resented the demand.

'I warn you. This is a most important matter. A highly personal matter. I must talk with the General in confidence. You may rue it if you delay me.'

The Envoy was as immovable as Bonaparte was being over the guild schools. All he would undertake was to deliver a note recording Phillipe's emergence from prison and his desire to speak with the General.

Napoleon read it along with a stack of diplomatic messages and military dispatches. He was irritated even to be reminded of the mission on which he had sent the former spy. He had forgiven Josephine her infidelities to that date, and there was no longer any link with Phillipe through Louise. He had not relished domestic contact with a lady's maid who aided and abetted his wife's lovers. So Louise had been dismissed on his orders.

No, Phillipe had bungled the job and Napoleon had no time for bunglers. Once a spy's cover had been broken he was unreliable for further service in that capacity and, since spies were so devious and prone to double-dealing, it would not be safe to employ him in any other.

He dictated a brief instruction, ironically to Junot, who was regularly employed by Napoleon as a scribe because of his beautiful handwriting. 'Send this man back to Paris as soon as convenient and make arrangements for him to be paid off there.'

Shocked and embittered by this treatment after all his suffering in Bonaparte's service, Phillipe went in search of his baby son, Alessandro. Just to see him would be some joyous recompense for the grim months of confinement. If he could get possession of him and take him back to France he might even be able to induce Louise to adopt him. He had been thinking a lot about Louise. She was a warm-hearted woman and it didn't look as though she could have children of her own. Alessandro was proof that her barrenness was not his fault. True, he had told her she would never see him again but prison had taught him that 'never' was a long time.

His inquiries at the Benedictine Convent of San Zaccaria were completely fruitless. The abbess behaved like the Dandolo she was and refused to have anything to do with any Frenchman, whatever his business. She and her sister Brides of Christ were in sufficient fear of being raped by Frenchmen without admitting one of their number voluntarily. Besides, so far as she was concerned, Alessandro was a Venetian and would be brought up as one in a Venetian orphanage, unless one of her visiting friends or relatives took a fancy to him.

As Phillipe was turned away from the convent entrance he

spat in disgust of all mankind on the pavement. Hoisting his cloak round his shoulders, hunched more by dejection than by weakness, he summoned a fleeting smile as he noted a particularly phallic pillar standing between the convent door and the adjacent church. It reminded him of the bawdy stories he had heard about the inmates, abbess and all. Venice was a rum place, all right. And the more you saw of it the rummer it became. Best then to get out of it and go home. He was a soldier of fortune and if his fortune was due for a change, surely the mainland of society would offer more scope than a stagnant backwater.

So Phillipe found himself accompanying the next consignment of loot to Paris, where he was summarily dismissed from government service.

⋆　　⋆　　⋆

On 16 May two notices appeared in the Piazza San Marco. One formally announced that the Great Council had voluntarily yielded its authority to a Provisional Government, though in fact the real power lay with a five-man Committee of Public Safety, modelled on the French Committee of which Robespierre had been head. The other lauded the Great Council for being so wise and far-sighted, a compliment to which the Councillors responded by ordering the St Mark's authorities to stage a *Te Deum* Mass—'We praise Thee, O God'—for the splendid new system.

No foreign country mourned the take-over. At her death old Venice paid the penalty of being a loner. She did not have a single friend, a situation not lost on Napoleon who, in the context of personal as well as political relationships, held that 'Only the dead have no need of friends.'

Chapter Sixteen

In June 1797 Napoleon was reunited with his wife in Milan for the wedding of his sixteen-year-old sister, Pauline, to General Leclerc, one of his divisional commanders. Pauline, whose outstanding beauty was to be preserved in marble by Canova, so disliked Josephine, as did the rest of the Bonapartes, that she did her best to fan her brother's jealousy by insisting that his wife was still being unfaithful with Hippolyte Charles. But Napoleon, who at that stage was determined to secure the domestic harmony he needed so badly to offset his professional problems, responded by promoting Charles to captain, while Junot, who was again acting aide-de-camp while recovering from recent battle wounds, was encouraged to entertain Josephine to alleviate her boredom. Left alone with her one afternoon he tried to interest her in his visit to Venice while they were playing vingt-et-un.

To her, Venice was just another Italian city which had fallen to her husband's cupidity for conquest, which seemed insatiable, but as Junot described it her heart warmed to its romantic reputation.

'The palaces along the canal would fascinate you,' he said. 'One of them is supposed to have belonged to Desdemona and there are all sorts of tales about a rogue called Casanova, but the whole place is so out-of-this-world that it's hard to separate legend from fact.'

'I find romantic legend far more interesting, but Bonaparte only has time for hard fact. He says that being romantic is taking a view of people that you know isn't true just because it's more gratifying than reality.'

'I shouldn't believe everything he says,' Junot cautioned. 'He says he's not interested in treasures. "Baubles" he calls them. But he keeps shipping them back. There are some "baubles" in Venice you might like.'

'Such as?'

'Well, for a start, there are four splendid bronze horses in front of the cathedral.'

'Bronze horses!' Josephine laughed. 'Whatever would I want with them? They're more to Bonaparte's taste. He's always going on about how "progress has only been achieved through the sweat of horses". Horses are the last thing I want, dear Andoche. I'm sick of the smell of horses.'

'Oh, they'd be very appropriate on an arch specially set up for a queen to drive through,' Junot said, taking her hand.

'But Andoche, dear,' she responded with an affectionate squeeze, 'I'm only the wife of a general.'

'Not *a* general. *The* General. And he has a lot further to go yet. All things are possible for him. Indeed, I don't think he will ever see where the possible leaves off. That's his danger.'

Junot had a clearer idea than Josephine of Bonaparte's ambitions, both for himself and his rapacious family, who were all greedy for kingdoms to govern. He knew that Napoleon was determined to get rid of the Directory and who else was there to replace it?

'But France has finished with queens, Andoche. Surely, Marie Antoinette was the last.'

'Oh, the pendulum of history never stops swinging and it could swing back quicker than we think. Perhaps it's only the Bourbons we've got rid of.'

Josephine frowned, though even then there were few wrinkles on her marble-like brow. 'I'm sure I wouldn't like to be a queen anyway. I've often thought about it, you know.'

Junot gave her a puzzled look.

'When I was ten years old and living in Martinique, a native woman prophesied that one day I would be Queen of France. I remember telling my parents about it and how they laughed.'

'Maybe they shouldn't have laughed.'

'Perhaps not, but like most prophecies there was a sting to it. The woman said I would not die Queen of France. Let's see what the Tarot cards say.'

She went to the window on the eastern side of the room and picked up the wooden card-box, always kept there to absorb 'the light of inspiration'. Removing the square of purple silk in which the cards were wrapped, she smoothed it out on the table then shuffled the brightly coloured pack reverentially and laid out a seven-card spread on the silk. Josephine threw a startled look at Junot and indicated the cards. The spread contained cards Numbers 3 and 4, the Empress and the Emperor, and both were the right way up.

'The Tarot says you could be right, Andoche. It has never been wrong yet about Bonaparte. He believes in it as firmly as I do. As he says, if fate has determined his career—and he's sure of that—then why shouldn't the cards be able to reveal it?'

'Why not indeed,' Junot replied. He had no faith in cards or any other form of divination but he knew that Napoleon did, or at least pretended to. Had he not met Josephine when he was reading ladies' palms at a ball? He certainly missed no opportunity to assure his soldiers that fortune was on his side.

'Their belief in my invincibility is worth an extra army in the field,' he had said.

Junot appreciated the advantage but also foresaw the dangers if the General came to believe he was invincible.

'Oh dear!' Josephine sighed as she swept up the cards. 'As a king, Bonaparte would be unbearable. He's too serious as it is and he'd work himself to death.'

Junot agreed. 'He's a realist in dealing with people but he refuses to come to terms with time. I'm afraid that one day he won't have time to see some terrible mistake.'

'It's no use talking to him, Andoche. He was in dreadful pain the other day and when I told him that rest was the best cure, what do you think he said?'

'I can guess—"*Work* is the best cure, for anything." '

'Absolutely right. "I can't interrupt my programme just because I've got the bellyache," he said. He's wrong, of course. It's the overwork that's causing the pain. But you daren't tell him he's mistaken . . .'

Josephine was convinced that her husband would get whatever he wanted provided he didn't drive himself to death before he achieved it. And her fate would be entirely governed by his. She had a special reason to fear becoming a queen. It would make an heir essential and in that she was still failing,

196

either with Napoleon, Charles or anyone else. And as Queen of France her freedom would be sharply curtailed.

Regrettably for Junot, he happened to be sitting a little too close to Josephine when Napoleon walked into the room unannounced and in a bad humour. Creeping up behind his aide he seized his hair so savagely that a half-healed scalp wound tore open, drenching the General's hand and Junot's face with blood.

'I'm sorry, Junot,' Napoleon apologized as Josephine called for towels and cold water. 'It was only a joke. I'd forgotten about your head wound.'

'That was absolutely uncalled for,' Josephine remonstrated, after Junot had left with his head bandaged. 'You are getting so irritable. You simply must take a rest . . .'

'Rubbish. I'll be resting long enough in that little box. What were you and Junot talking about? Me, I suppose?'

'Not at all. Andoche was telling me about Venice. It sounds a most romantic place.'

'Romantic!' Napoleon scoffed. 'That's all you women ever think about. Romantics are a nuisance to themselves and everybody else. Look at Romeo in Shakespeare's play! He spoiled everything for everybody, including himself. It's not love that makes the world go round. It's order and stability.'

Josephine heaved an exaggerated sigh. 'Oh, there you go again. You just seem to want an argument these days. I simply remarked that Venice sounded a romantic place. Andoche was telling me about those wonderful horses.'

'Ah, I believe they're very fine. Stolen, of course, like everything else in that degenerate city. If you want them you can have them.'

'If *I* want them?'

'Yes. I'm going to take them anyway. But if you want them I'll see they are put in a special place.'

Josephine smiled incredulously. 'What sort of place?'

'You'll see,' Napoleon said darkly. 'And when you do, perhaps you'll finally forgive me for sending Phillipe to spy on you.'

'You are a strange man. I've completely dismissed all that

from my mind. Oh dear, I don't suppose I will ever really know you.'

'Does anyone ever know anybody?' Napoleon commented, as he turned and left the room as abruptly as he had entered it.

When Enrico Dandolo removed the Horses from Constantinople he had no clear idea where they would be installed in Venice, and for some years they had languished outside the gates of the Arsenal. Napoleon knew exactly where he wanted them and why.

*   *   *

Josephine was concerned about Napoleon's peculiar animosity towards Venice. He seemed determined to destroy the ancient republic purely in the interests of his 'star'. To her this seemed just another excuse to make war, which he had come to enjoy so much that he was to fight sixty battles, many of them against the same enemy over and over again. She was not impressed by his dictum, 'History shows that red-blooded people want their leaders to be fighting men,' and was deeply concerned about the mounting casualties, French as well as enemy, for which her husband's appetite for triumph was responsible. Nor did she approve of his conviction that the French were some kind of master-race—*'le premier peuple de L'Univers'*—as he had described them in his harsh letter to the Doge. To her, a Creole from an island with a large black population, people were just people whatever their nationality.

Josephine was also worried, as were Junot and some of the divisional commanders, by Bonaparte's increasing ferocity and ruthlessness when he was baulked. It was probably part of his Corsican inheritance, she believed, but if he did become King it might make him a tyrant.

*   *   *

On Sunday 4 June 1797 a 'National Festival' took place in San Marco Square to celebrate the change of government. The Piazza was decorated with the new red, white and green colours of the 'democracy' and in the centre stood a Tree of

Liberty. This was topped by the red cap symbol of the French Revolution and flanked by statues representing Equality and Fraternity. The rousing sound of 'La Marseillaise' was welcome to the ears of the French and the few genuine revolutionaries in the crowd, but to the Venetians, as to the rest of Europe, it conjured up the savagery of the Reign of Terror.

A procession wound twice round the Piazza, a sad reminder to the inhabitants of the pageants of the past, then entered the Basilica where the *Te Deum* was sung in thanksgiving. Members of the new government and of the occupation forces, headed by General d'Hilliers, then marched back to the Tree of Liberty, where the insignia of the old 'tyranny', the Doge's regalia and a copy of the Golden Book, were burned on a symbolic pyre. The Countess Querini-Benzoni, a friend of Byron, danced around the tree, sporting the flimsy Athenian garb popularized by Josephine, and the celebrations continued throughout the night with general dancing, fireworks and a gala performance at the Fenice Theatre.

Equality and Fraternity were mythical concepts from the start. As for Liberty, Napoleon had already betrayed that principle, through which he had fleetingly appeared as a champion of human rights to minds as perceptive as Beethoven's. After convincing the Directory that if Austria could be bought off, war against the most dangerous enemy, England, could then be seriously planned, he signed the Treaty of Campo Formio on 17 October, trading Venice and some of her mainland territories to Austria for the Rhineland, Belgium and certain islands.

*   *   *

Before the French quit the city so that Austrian occupation troops could move in, Venice was required to pay further sums of money she could not possibly find. So Bonaparte ordered his generals to seize what portable valuables they could. They took pictures, cameos—including the famous Zeus cameo discovered in the ruins of Ephesus—gold and silver vessels from churches and the entire contents of the

Arsenal, even stripping the gilding and ornaments from the last Bucentaur and converting it to a gunboat. They pulled down the Winged Lion from the Column of St Mark and then set about the more difficult task of taking down the Four Horses of Lysippus.

The former ambassador, Lallemont, compounded his disloyalty in Bonaparte's mind by recording in Paris, 'We tricked our way into their capital and provinces and are handing them over to a new master, having robbed them shamefully.'

*　　*　　*

The Piazza was full of French troops on the foggy day in December 1797 when the windlasses were erected to lower each mighty Horse on to a wooden-wheeled car specially constructed for the task. Each needed six live horses to pull it to the barge that would ferry the foursome to the cargo ship destined for Marseilles. For six centuries they had been so much a part of the fabric of the Piazza that they had been scarcely noticed except by visitors, as had been the case in Corinth, Rome and Constantinople, but the anger of those few Venetians watching the rape of their remnant of glory was intense. Bonaparte was flagrantly breaching his assurances, and the few who even thought about it felt that time had expiated the greed of their forefathers, through which they had acquired the Horses.

When the Loggia dei Cavalli was empty and the French troops had departed, the Venetians placed nothing on the pedestals there. They left them standing spare—to await their rightful tenants' return.

*　　*　　*

Along with crates of other loot the Horses were off-loaded on to barges at Marseilles, then laboriously drawn by towpath horses up the Rhone and through canals to the Seine, where they were finally moored near the Jardin des Plantes. A series of processions modelled on the former triumphs of Ancient Rome were organized so that the distinguished and

200

influential, as well as the common horde, could see what the brilliant General Bonaparte was sending them. It was not by chance that the destination for the cavalcade including the Four Horses was the parade ground called the Field of Mars.

On 17 July 1798 the outsize cart carrying the statues four abreast and pulled by eight strong horses, followed a cage containing a large lion. Napoleon had not considered it fitting in that day and age to parade the deposed Doge in chains but the lion, clipped of its wings, could be taken as his symbol.

Each item of plunder was cheered by the crowd as it moved, escorted by troops, to the Altar of the Revolution, which was set high on a dais for the final ceremony. None raised a louder cry than the Four Horses as the spectators read the banner above them proclaiming '*La Grèce les céda, Rome les a perdus. Leur sort changea deux fois. Il ne changera plus.*' Their capture by Venice was not mentioned.

As the crowd sang 'La Marseillaise', '*Le jour de gloire*' had undoubtedly arrived.

*   *   *

Napoleon did not witness the procession for he was far from Paris, but at his suggestion the Four Horses were positioned separately on temporary plinths at the courtyard entrance to the former Royal Palace of the Tuileries, where he was confident he would soon be installed. He intended that eventually they would surmount an Arch of Triumph to commemorate the victories of the armies he had led, but he did not yet have the authority to command the building of such a structure. Nor did he think it politically wise at that juncture to request it. Indeed it was more prudent to let people believe that he was indifferent to such baubles. He remembered, from his reading of ancient Roman history, what had happened so quickly to the arch of the presumptuous Nero.

As in battle, so in politics, timing was everything. He would wait until he could inaugurate the arch by driving through it, at least as First Consul or maybe something grander.

*   *   *

201

The keys of the city of Venice were handed ceremoniously to the Austrians on 17 January 1798. To express their resentment of Napoleon's betrayal of the Republic, the Venetian Committee of Five stood between the Columns of St Mark and St Theodore to perform the distasteful ritual, dressed in deep mourning.

The Austrians were appalled to learn how much treasure Bonaparte had stolen and were particularly incensed by the removal of the Four Horses, but their condolences were not well received. Those who had lived under their own rule, however strict, for a thousand years had no welcome for the representatives of any foreign emperor. Nevertheless, on Austrian insistence, a *Te Deum* was sung in St Mark's Basilica praising God for the arrival of the Austrian army of occupation.

Chapter Seventeen

By a simple coup which took only two days to complete, Napoleon, who had become known throughout France as 'The Saviour', assumed command of the government at the age of thirty. With the majority of the generals backing him, he persuaded three of the five Directors to resign. This left France without a legally constituted government, and after only minor resistance, easily dispelled by a bayonet charge, Napoleon was sworn in as First Consul. Although he had agreed to have two others below him he was virtually dictator of France, with unlimited power.

Both Alexander the Great and Julius Cæsar had been born near the pinnacle of power. He had hoisted himself to their position from the ground.

The new Constitution was ratified by a national referendum and in February 1800, Napoleon and Josephine moved into the Tuileries Palace, where he was determined to live but which, out of deference to his hate for the Bourbons, he renamed 'The Seat of Government'.

As their coach passed between the Four Horses, Napoleon pointed them out and remarked, 'There they are, just as I promised. They've taken two thousand years to get here.'

Josephine did not have the temerity to voice her thought, 'I wonder how long they'll stay'. Instead she said, 'They are very beautiful and much bigger than I expected. I wonder how long it took to make them.'

'Months I suppose. You see, my dear, the sculptor, the writer or the builder can do so little in one day but a fighting man can change the world.'

'Yes, but their works last longer,' Josephine said as their coach came to a halt.

Napoleon frowned. He knew enough of history to know she was right about the past, but was becoming sufficiently self-deluded by the consciousness of his enormous power and opportunities to believe that in his case permanence might be possible. After all, revolution, as he was exploiting it, was something entirely new. As a commander-cum-statesman he would be unique. At least since Alexander the Great. Of that he was utterly convinced.

Josephine's thoughts were on a less optimistic plane as they mounted the palace steps between two rows of guards. She was afraid of having to live in rooms from which Marie Antoinette had so recently been dragged to her terrible death. But her fears were temporarily assuaged when the First Consul, who was prepared to enjoy every minute of his astonishing fulfilment, crowned the day with, 'Come little Creole, come and sleep in your master's bed.'

*   *   *

A little more than two years later, Napoleon was created Consul for Life, making him dictator in perpetuity with the privilege of naming his successor. In that time he had had his hair close-cropped, his face, figure and legs had padded out and he had become more caring of his appearance, establishing the image which was to make him the most recognizable figure next to Christ.

It was but a step to becoming Emperor, which occurred in 1804. The title Emperor of the Republic, which the Senate conferred on him, was to be hereditary, so Josephine's failure to produce a son for him suddenly seemed more ominous. She had expressed her fear openly in a letter to him, deploring his decision to make himself Emperor and warning him that he would be despised as an upstart by existing monarchs and could become a target for assassination. Her chief anxiety was allayed when on 1 December of that same year Napoleon remarried her in a secret religious ceremony to confirm their civil marriage.

'Surely this will make divorce impossible forever?' Josephine asked her close friends, earnest for reassurance.

They all agreed with her—whatever they thought in private.

Next day a great triumphal procession wound its way from

the Tuileries to Notre Dame. Like Nero before him, Napoleon wore a circlet of laurel leaves, but his were of gold. Seizing the Imperial crown from the hands of the Pope, who had been summoned to the presence, Bonaparte placed it on his own head, being unwilling to appear indebted either to God or his Vicar. Then he crowned Josephine, an act which convinced her that her position must be secure. The Pope did not relish this usurpation of his sacred authority but, as a virtual political prisoner, there was nothing he could do as he watched the proceedings sourly, save to assure himself that for some inscrutable reason it must be how God wanted it.

The ceremony was the centre-piece of a golden day which cost the French Exchequer eight and half million francs, most of it going on a nation-wide bun-fight, with bread, meat and wine being distributed free. Like so many predecessors in absolute power, except for the Bourbons, Napoleon appreciated that he could not continue without the support of the masses, the despicable *canaille* he had once dispersed with a 'whiff of grapeshot'.

He took care to provide the bread as well as the entertainment because, as he expressed it, 'I fear a revolt caused by lack of bread more than a great battle.' He also took care to keep himself appraised of the dangers of rebellion, increasing his army of informers to such an extent that Talleyrand, his Foreign Minister, referred to him as 'a regular little Nero'.

*   *   *

After his elevation Napoleon's marriage settled down into a loving and peaceful relationship, which he desperately needed as he flung himself into the task of governing. This he did in such detail that he wrote in his own hand a new Civil Code of Law, his most lasting accomplishment. Fearful of the effects on his health and deeply concerned about his stomach spasms, which were becoming more frequent and more painful, Josephine remonstrated to the point of nagging.

'You just can't do it all yourself,' she told him as he even took on the task of replanning Paris, creating new boulevards, building new bridges, all named to immortalize his triumphs.

'I can and I must,' was the response of the man who was to write, 'All my life I have sacrificed everything—comfort, self-interest, happiness—to my destiny'.

Though he indulged in sexual affairs, more than compensating for his lack of success with women when young, he made frequent use of the secret staircase which connected his quarters with the Empress's boudoir. He would walk down there in a dressing-gown with a silk handkerchief tied round his head, and his servant would light the way before him, holding high a silver candlestick. When Josephine was honoured with such a visit she made sure that the whole household knew next day.

The Emperor also honoured his private pledge to her in a public way, by ordering the erection of a Triumphal Arch as near to the Tuileries Palace as possible. With his architects he decided on a copy of the splendid Arch of Septimius Severus still standing in the Forum of Rome, where it had been set up to commemorate the victories of that aggressive emperor whose speed and determination Bonaparte so much admired. The Place du Carrousel, the location chosen for it, was a small square where the guillotine had claimed its first political victims. For proportion's sake the Arc de Triomphe du Carrousel had to be a two-thirds replica, but Napoleon consoled himself by commanding the erection of a second Arc de Triomphe which was to be the biggest in the world, though it would not be completed until after his death.

Whatever destiny might do to him, some unread headstone, the only defiance of time most men achieved, was not for him. The whole of central Paris would be a memorial.

The Arc du Carrousel symbolized not only the victories of his armies, particularly those of 1805, but his personal triumph over his jealousy concerning Josephine. She had confessed her previous infidelities, and though under Napoleon's new Civil Code adultery was restored as a crime for women while remaining a péccadillo for men, he had forgiven her. She had no option but to condone the Emperor's indiscretions, a situation which made for tranquillity if not for bliss. Their relationship had matured into sincere mutual affection and concern by the time Napoleon took his Empress to see the completed arch topped by the Four Horses of Lysippus. He was even resigned to having no successor of his own loins.

The Horses had been reharnessed to a chariot designed to hold a bronze of the Emperor complete with robes and sceptre, but in a moment of politic modesty he had rejected this.

'I am not one for whom statues should be made,' he declared. 'Let the victory chariot remain, but empty.' And so it did remain, giving rise to the malicious pun, *'le char attend le charlatan'*.

'You didn't think it would happen, did you?' Napoleon asked his wife as their coach approached the arch.

'I didn't think what would happen?'

'This,' the Emperor said, pointing to the arch, then indicating the crowds. 'Everything.'

'On the contrary, my dear,' the Empress replied, touching his hand. 'I always knew you would get whatever you wanted. You always will.'

Napoleon sat back in mute agreement, but Josephine was not convinced that all she had said was true. She still believed her husband had made a political blunder in becoming Emperor. She was deeply distressed he should be gratified by reports that he was so feared throughout Europe that mothers were frightening their children with 'Boney will get you', if they misbehaved. As she had quoted to Thérèse Tallien, who had been barred from the Palace, 'He has become a monster unto many.'

Worse still, the cards were predicting bad fortune—for both of them. Sitting up in bed that morning she had consulted the Tarot pack. The first card she had drawn, Number 16, showed a thunderbolt shattering the battlements of a tower and hurling a man and a woman to the ground. The third card had been the seven of hearts—a sure sign of disappointment and betrayal.

*　　*　　*

Josephine's luck was the first to fail. The more grandiose and despotic Napoleon became, the more he confused his own destiny with that of all mankind, the further he drifted from her, circumscribing her life with increasingly strict rules of conduct. During his Polish campaign he fell in love with Marie Walewska, a Polish countess who eventually bore him a son. Although he continued to profess to Josephine that she was the only true love of his life, he slowly began to weaken against the campaign of the politicians and his own family, who urged him to divorce and marry someone who could produce a legitimate heir. The Bonapartes, who had acquired wealth and rank far beyond their worth, were terrified that they and their children might lose all if the dynasty foundered.

Reacting to the pressures, the Emperor had good reason to recall a previous observation to Junot—'Relations with one's own relations are the most difficult of all. Friends are so much better. First, you can choose them and second, you can discard them if they become a nuisance.'

To Napoleon's genuine distress—it was his wife's fertility not his love which had died—the divorce was set in motion in December 1809. On the bleak day that Josephine quit the Tuileries Palace to live on her own at Malmaison, retaining the title of Empress, courtiers and servants were weeping as she descended the great staircase. She was driven away, heavily veiled, in a rainstorm, to spend the remainder of her short life looking back in sadness and looking ahead in fear.

*   *   *

Napoleon's political marriage to Marie Louise of Austria was quickly blessed with a son, who was named King of Rome at his birth: Napoleon had accepted an invitation to become King of Italy in 1805 and been crowned in Milan with Josephine beside him. But fortune which, perhaps, had favoured Napoleon too much when he was young, turned her face away from both him and his heir, fulfilling Junot's prediction to Josephine that 'Nobody's luck lasts forever.'

It was ironic that Bonaparte's military defeat and the ruin of his reputation for invincibility should be caused by a man named after his idol, Alexander—the baby-faced Alexander who was Czar of All the Russias. Alexander Romanov, who had the largest territory in the world, was not only unprepared to yield an inch of it willingly but was greedy for more. As he remarked after the final defeat of the French at Waterloo, 'Napoleon or Alexander! The world is not big enough to hold us both.'

*　　*　　*

Before Napoleon became King of Italy he had defeated the Austrians again in battle, and they had been forced to yield their recent acquisition of Venice back to him for inclusion in his new Italic Kingdom. But after Napleon's final fall following the anticlimax of Waterloo, the Austrians had re-entered Venice and its former territories. To curry favour with the sullen Venetians, the Austrians demanded the return of the looted art treasures from Paris, particularly the Four Horses and the Winged Lion which, for the Venetians, had become symbols of revenge and liberation from French tyranny.

So on 29 September 1815, only three months after Waterloo, French crowds looked on angrily as the Horses were lowered from the Arc du Carrousel. Though they had been in Paris only eighteen years, the French regarded their removal as a breach of solemn treaties which, in fact, Napoleon had enforced at bayonet point. This resentment extended to all the other art treasures plundered from Italy, including even the Vatican jewels which the Pope had been forced to 'present' to the Louvre.

Within the week the Four Horses, intact save for the small, ornamental mask depending from each collar which had been wrenched off by souvenir hunters, had finished their fretting by the sluggish Seine and were on the way back to Venice and the lively sea. Parisians who had never seen them or rarely looked up if they were passing through the Place du Carrousel, went to stare at the void they had left.

*　　*　　*

It was a somewhat different Piazza the Horses surveyed when they had been hoisted back on to their old plinths. After Napoleon visited the Piazza, which he called 'the best drawing-room in Europe' in November 1807, he ordered that the buildings at the western end, including an ancient church, should be demolished and replaced by a Napoleonic wing in the neo-classical style, 'to add a ballroom'. The wing was to be topped by an effigy of the great 'liberator' himself, but Europe was liberated from him before the sculpture was ready, though the building itself was completed.

Such was the hope of softening Venetian hearts through the Horses' return that the Austrian emperor himself, Francis I, arrived for the re-installation celebration. The statues, freed of their French harness, had been dragged from the Molo by blue-uniformed Austrian troops on 13 December 1815—eighteen years to the day since their removal. But the Austrian court, its sycophants and soldiers, had the ceremony to themselves because the Venetians boycotted it. When the Emperor showed himself on the dais with bands playing and cannons firing, there were few residents to cheer—an insult which made Francis regret that he had not indulged his original impulse of carting the Horses direct from Paris to Vienna.

The Venetians paid for their pride with harsh, repressive rule which leaned particularly hard on the intellectuals, and the Four Horses did not fully resume their symbolic status for them until March 1848, when in a revolt against their continued slavery they drove the Austrians from the city. While the heroism of the revolutionary leaders expiated the cowardice of 1797, the new Republic was forced to yield to the Austrian guns yet again after only a few months of freedom. Not until the final defeat of Austria in 1866 were the chains of occupation broken, when liberated Venice, in a truly democratic referendum, voted almost to a man to join the Italian nation.

*   *   *

Bonaparte's association with the Four Horses, which had reflected his love affair with power so faithfully, had suffered its final indignity in 1828 when the space on the Arc du Carrousel they had once occupied was filled by a bronze chariot group in the classical style, celebrating the restoration of the Bourbon kings, divine right and all.

210

He was not alive to hear of it. He had died on the dull island of St Helena seven years earlier, knowing that he would never be 'Napoleon the Great'. Alexander had left a well-ordered empire, so secure that some of his companions and their descendants were to rule it for 150 years. Napoleon had left France weaker than when he had assumed command and surrounded by more powerful enemies. The Russia he had ravaged was stronger. Prussia had been presented with the natural leadership of a German federation with fearful consequences. England was undisputed mistress of the seas. Napoleon's only hope of immortality lay in the chance that, with the passing of the years, legend would extol his virtues and discount his defects, and that his undoubted military genius would attract other men driven by hunger for power to study his methods.

In the desolate days of painful retrospection he became only too aware of the truth concerning another association which had ended disastrously. Speaking of Josephine, who had predeceased him by seven years, he recorded wistfully, 'She was the most alluring, most glamorous creature I have ever known. She was the woman I loved above all.'

*　　*　　*

For more than one hundred and sixty years the Horses remained undisturbed in Venice, save for temporary removal for restoration or for transfer to less vulnerable places during the two World Wars. But the tide of terror, surging ceaselessly somewhere or other, could not pass them by indefinitely.

EPISODE 6

Vengeance in Venice

'While musing away in your fine, vaulted den,
Give us now your answer—What motivates men?'

Chapter Eighteen

In the Loggia dei Cavalli, the Four Horses were closer to destruction than they had ever been since the flames licked near them in the Hippodrome in Constantinople. Venice's enemies had so often threatened to 'bit and bridle' them, but nobody had imagined it would ever be accomplished with strings of high explosive.

So far there had been little verbal contact between the hostages and their captors, though crammed so closely in the confines of the alcove. While outwardly calm, the terrorists were gripped by tension as forcibly as their captives. Santos disclosed his by his silence, the set of his jaw and by chain-smoking cigarettes. The Arabs and the German youth fidgeted, needlessly checking their guns, retying their shoelaces and peering out into the Piazza. Suddenly, almost explosively, the German girl—who had been identified as Freya Bilderberg, a member of the Baader-Meinhof organization wanted for at least two murders—channelled her excess adrenalin into strident animosity towards Ruth. Dangling the gold medallion she had confiscated, she expressed her detestation of the Star of David embossed on its front, for she despised all Jews, not just Israelis.

'What's this writing on the back?' she inquired with distaste. 'Hebrew isn't it?'

Ruth nodded reluctantly.

'Then what does it mean, arrogant bitch?'

Ruth did not reply until prompted by Paul, who feared the girl might swing the heavy object across his wife's face.

'It means "Bone of my bones and flesh of my flesh".'

'How touching! Let's hope your bones and your flesh don't end up scattered out there in the Piazza!'

Remembering Ma'alot, Ruth shuddered. She knew that the terrorists would not hesitate to shoot them one by one and throw their bodies over the balcony if there was any undue delay in achieving their demands—Freya looked as though she might even enjoy it—and having heard the requirement about the release of Israeli prisoners, delay or blank refusal seemed inevitable.

Sensing Ruth's resentment as she pocketed the medallion and chain, Freya snapped, 'All right, you'll get it back if your Zionist friends do what they are told. We are revolutionaries, not criminals.'

Ruth was relieved that, so far, Freya had not tried to bait Paul, for she sensed that emotionally he was least fitted of all of them to withstand a prolonged ordeal. He was sitting with his head down and his hands clasped, staring at the floor, and Ruth longed to reach out and stroke the crinkly hair at the nape of his neck.

If it came to the point where the hostages were to be shot one by one to tighten the squeeze on Jerusalem, she might well be first because she was an Israeli and she feared that witnessing her murder could shatter Paul if he managed to survive. Might it be kinder if he went first? She did her best to dismiss such morbid thoughts. She desperately wanted Paul to live; yes, even at the price of capitulation by her people. It was, after all, an exceptional situation, with the Cardinal who was so gentle, and clearly rather splendid, to consider.

Raising his head, Paul forced an encouraging smile and felt for his pipe. He had been forbidden to light it because he was so near the gelignite, but just sucking it gave him some nervous relief.

'So Kliney-boy needs his titty-bottle!' Freya sneered, to which Paul responded by sheepishly putting the pipe back in his pocket. He could not help wondering how the redoubtable Yigael would have behaved in such a situation and feared that might be in Ruth's mind too.

The Arabs were speaking quietly to each other while the two German youths tried to strike up a philosophical conversation with Talamini. Having served as Papal Nuncio in Bonn he spoke their language, but he was busy communicating in a more important direction as he clasped his rosary, the flaccid lips of his rather large mouth moving noiselessly.

216

'Worry beads?' Freya asked. 'You've less to worry about than these two,' she said indicating Ruth and Paul. 'You've had your life. They've got far more to lose.'

'The same goes for you, so can it,' Santos ordered peremptorily.

He rather admired the Cardinal's composure, and the girl's remarks were irritating as he re-checked out his notes—a task on which all of their lives could depend.

★   ★   ★

Travelling supersonically to London, Samuel Kline arrived at Venice's Marco Polo Airport, where Luigi was waiting, soon after eight p.m. While his hair was silver, save where eroded by the family trait of frontal baldness, he had retained his youthful figure, and his handsome square-jawed face was surprisingly creaseless for a man of fifty-five, though drawn by the strain of the past few hours.

They embraced affectionately and the American could not wait to ask, 'How are they? Have you any news?'

'They're standing up magnificently, Sam, though there's no change, I'm afraid. But I'm sure they'll be released soon. The Press and the radio are insisting that the guerrillas' demands must be met, and the Government is determined that there will be no shooting heroics in Venice. Too much is at stake. Not just lives—irreplaceable art.'

Sam shook his head sadly. 'I just can't see the Israelis releasing those prisoners. The fact that Ruth is General Yacob's daughter makes it even more difficult. People would say the Government was giving in only because one of its own Ministers had a special interest. I'm almost in the same spot, Luigi. Time and again when other people's sons have been held hostage I've urged no surrender. How can I take part in surrender now when my own son is a captive?'

Kline did his best to pretend that his tears were caused by the breeze as their private water-taxi skimmed across the lagoon between the weed-encrusted tripod piles and bollards. Normally he would have been peering in rapture at the expanding skyline of the city, one of the few for him where familiarity

217

intensified enchantment. Instead he stared at the white wake of the boat in silence until Luigi asked, 'Have you heard what the developers are calling the lagoon these days? Good building water!'

The American forced a smile at this effort to cheer him up. 'Like we say in the States, you can't stop progress! But you must admit, Luigi, that if the first developers had not taken the same view Venice would never have been built.'

'I suppose not,' Luigi conceded. 'But this modern lot are so greedy they'll make the city into a suburb of an industrial slum if we don't stop them. Talking about money—have you any ideas for raising the ransom?'

'Raising it is the least of my worries. I arranged it as soon as I heard the figure in London. My agent met me there at the airport and I imagine the Banca d'Italia here is already collecting a million dollars in used notes. As I told you, my problem is handing it over without betraying everything I stand for.'

'If I forget thee O Jerusalem . . .' Luigi thought, recalling the quotation on Sam's desk. 'Couldn't you say that the money has been provided by your friends?' he ventured.

'The only friends I have who could put up such a sum are Jewish themselves. Anyway, who'd believe it?'

'What you need is someone who is well known, isn't Jewish and obviously can spare the money, to come out and say he's provided it, even if it isn't true.'

'Regrettably, I don't know any such person. Anyway the first thing I'm going to do is offer myself in exchange for Paul. I've had my life. He has the best of his in front of him.'

'They won't accept that, Sam. Making you grovel in front of the television cameras is part of the act. They've already refused any replacement for the Cardinal.'

'Well, it's sure worth a try.'

Luigi shrugged resignedly. 'OK, I'll see if they will listen.'

'Is that island named after the George who killed the dragon?' Sam asked.

'The very same, but I'm afraid his achievement is as legendary as he is. He is supposed to personify the triumph of chivalry over cruelty!'

Sam made a wry grimace. 'That sure is ironic considering

218

my daughter-in-law's plight at this very moment. She's such a splendid girl. Just what Paul needed. I've always been so afraid he'd be a pushover for some gold-digger.'

Luigi looked away as Sam wiped the corners of his eyes. It was true enough. No gallant knight was coming to Ruth's rescue.

In the glow of the sunset the reflections of the brick and marble edifices of the Island of San Giorgio turned to wavering streamers of red and gold, while the gondolas, swaying gently among the coppices of thin, unbarked mooring-poles looked more like black scorpions than ever.

'That's what I like about Venice,' Sam remarked. 'You get everything twice—two cities for the price of one!'

As the boathooks were thrust out from the landing stage of the Danieli Hotel, Kline looked at the mother-of-pearl sky and sighed. The screaming swifts were hawking insects as they had done ever since men had dared to erect the tall towers which served them as nesting sites on what amounted to enormous rafts of wood. It seemed the world's least likely site for violence and tragedy.

Since Kline was to be one of the major characters in the dramatic resolution of the terrorist situation, arrangements had been made by the Chief of Police for him to stay in the Danieli. He was no stranger there. The hotel, with its patrician atmosphere, marbled inner courtyard, sumptuous furnishings and stupendous panoramic view across the lagoon, had been his favourite on his numerous visits to the 'Queen of the Adriatic'.

With so many dignitaries insisting on being involved in the desicion-making, Fanti had set up one large operations room with separate desks and telephones. When Kline and Luigi entered, Fanti was sitting at his desk with a surprisingly pretty girl he had hired as his secretary. She was efficient and also fulfilled his other essential requirement of having long legs. He had a wide choice of candidates for the job, for he still had strong attraction for young girls.

Kline's attention was immediately gripped by the large colour television screen near Fanti's desk. There he could clearly see the terrorists, two of whom were leaning nonchal-

219

antly on the balcony with their guns at the ready, and the heads of Paul and Ruth who were sitting on chairs as though tied to them.

'What the hell are they up to?' Fanti asked, as he spotted the four Arabs kneeling on the floor of the Loggia with their backs to the balcony. 'Good God, they're praying!'

He looked in astonishment at Kline, who had eyes only for his son and daughter-in-law and was murmuring, 'I just can't believe it. I just can't believe it.'

'We'll get them out—somehow,' Fanti assured him, as he led the American over to another desk where Mayor Pizza was already installed. Pizza, still wearing his little black hat, was in the process of padding his huge frame still further from a plate of cream cakes he had ordered from the hotel kitchen, licking his fat fingers as each calorie-laden mouthful disappeared. He too was reassuring as he shook Kline's hand.

'My Council has met and we have drawn up the housing guarantee they are demanding,' he said enthusiastically.

Fanti smiled. He didn't imagine that when all was resolved the piece of paper would count for much. Pizza was a lawyer, and being also trained in Marxist-Leninist philosophy should have no conscience difficulties in repudiating the promise, if only on the grounds that it had been extracted under duress.

The ecclesiastical representative, who was the Chaplain originally captured with the Cardinal and then released with Luigi, gripped Kline's hand and held it warmly in both of his. 'We must trust in God, my son, and do all we can through prayer.'

Kline's final introduction was to the Defence Ministry official from Rome who had been flown in to check Fanti's arrangements and report back on any deficiencies.

Rome's first reaction on hearing of the Palestinian strike had been, 'It would be bloody Venice, wouldn't it?'

There was little love lost between the two cities. There never had been. The Venetians who regarded themselves as direct descendants of the Ancient Romans did not even consider themselves to be Italians.

*   *   *

Samuel Kline had not been the only distinguished Jew on the plane from London to Venice. Sitting next to him had been Gideon Arad, one of the most senior officers of Mossad, the Israeli Intelligence Service. Arad was normally based in Paris, the Mossad's European centre, but had been switched to London as soon as his headquarters in Tel Aviv learned that Kline would be transitting through London. General Yacob had made immediate contact with Sam as soon as the plight of their children became known, so Tel Aviv was informed about his movements and intentions.

Aware that the Italian authorities would be resolutely averse to any Israeli intervention in Venice or anywhere else on their soil, Arad needed to make a surreptitious assessment of the situation in the Piazza San Marco. During their conversations at London Airport and on the plane, Kline had agreed to keep him fully informed of any developments he heard about in the Danieli, and an accredited member of the Israeli Embassy staff who had flown in from Rome was detailed to act as courier between them.

With Fanti's approval, small Israeli and American film units had been allowed to join the Italian television crews in the Piazza after representations from the two embassies in Rome, because of the intense domestic interest both in Israel and the United States. The Israelis had ensured that one of the technicians in their camera crew was a Mossad agent instructed to report everything he could see and hear direct to Arad at his hotel, the unobtrusive Regina. This was conveniently sited near the Piazza and had three exits—one on to the Grand Canal by gondola or speedboat, the other through a neighbouring hotel and a third through a narrow alley offering the quickest route to the Piazza.

Film and stills were flown back to Tel Aviv that evening so that the commando unit which had staged the successful raid on Entebbe Airport could make a detailed model of the Loggia and possible access to it. Arad's report, which accompanied the photographs, was anything but optimistic. Italy was not Uganda and, diplomatic problems apart, there seemed to be no way that Israeli troops could storm the Loggia without killing the hostages. And if the Four Horses and the front of

221

the Basilica were demolished in any action, the artistic loss would remain as a permanent memorial to what the world would regard as an unforgivable infringement of national sovereignty.

The section of Arad's information concerning the identities of the terrorists, particularly the leader, greatly intensified the problem.

*   *   *

The Ministerial Security Committee of the Israeli Cabinet, meeting in emergency session in a room of the Knesset in Jerusalem, had no option but to accept General Yacob's offer to bar himself from taking part, as he was too intimately involved to give objective judgment. In his absence his political opponents were quick to point out that only two Jewish lives were at stake in Venice, compared with more than a hundred at Entebbe. Nevertheless, it was appreciated that because Ruth and Paul were who they were, the propaganda impact was severe. At the start of the meeting a majority was in favour of an outright refusal to hand over any of their terrorist prisoners because that was a propaganda defeat which could have political consequences in Israel, where public morale needed boosting, not depressing.

This inflexible stand began to be eroded when the Foreign Secretary, who was exceptionally eloquent and persuasive, emphasized the intense pressure being exerted on behalf of the Italian State and the Vatican by the US State Department and the White House. Israel was once again in delicate negotiations with the US for further supplies of sophisticated armaments, an issue the American President did not favour so automatically as his predecessors. Further, the President, who had a reputation for being a deeply religious man, would achieve international acclaim if later it could be leaked that he had been largely responsible for the Cardinal's release.

The arguments could have continued through the night but were quickly settled when a copy of Gideon Arad's first report was rushed into the Prime Minister's hands. Its contents were decisive.

*   *   *

Arad, who had none of the physical features popularly associated with Jewishness and could easily have been mistaken for Northern Italian with his round face, small nose and pale complexion, had been half expepecting the visitor who knocked on his bedroom door. He had deliberately taken no steps to conceal his identity, which could only have raised suspicions, but feigned surprise when a senior official of Italian Intelligence entered the room. They had met before in connection with previous terrorist incidents in Rome, so there was no requirement for diplomatic fencing.

'I'll come straight to the point, Gideon,' the Italian said after he had settled himself in a chair. 'I do hope there's nothing violent afoot.'

'Violent?' Arad echoed in mock astonishment. 'What could we possibly do that's violent here?'

'You shook us all so much with Entebbe that we wouldn't be surprised if you burrowed up through the Piazza! It was a great operation and I only wish that in similar circumstances we would have the guts to do the same. But it was a serious infringement of national sovereignty. If anything like that was attempted here . . .'

'What could we possibly do?' Arad asked, extending his arms. 'I know the set-up round those Horses. There's no way we could kill the terrorists without killing the hostages, and we certainly couldn't risk harming the Cardinal.'

'You've sized it up then? the Italian asked anxiously.

'Purely as an academic exercise.'

'I hope that's really how it is, Gideon. I'm not alone in suspecting you might try to pull something.'

Arad bowed. 'Considering the impossible scenario, that's a compliment. But let me ask *you* something. Have you any rescue plans yourselves?'

'Are you joking?' the Italian replied bitterly. 'You know how soft our politicians are. And not just ours. The Germans, the British, the Scandinavians are no better. They don't even take the Russians seriously in spite of all they are doing to destroy our way of life. So how can you expect them to get tough with a few Palestinians? And you know how it is when money talks. A shoot-out is bad for business. It frightens off

223

the tourists and brings reprisals. These blasted guerrillas seem to grow out of the ground like your namesake's soldiers in the Bible.'

'We prefer to call them terrorists. And we think that being tough with them is best for business. We are dependent on tourism too, you know. Softness never pays with people like this Santos.'

'But from what you say, Gideon, it looks like you're taking a soft line this time. That's what makes me suspicious.'

'If we have to take a soft line it is only because irresistible pressures have been put on us by others to do so. Left to our own devices the hostages would have to take their chance—whoever they might be. After all, it's your problem really, not ours.'

'That's what I hoped you'd say,' the Italian said with relief as he prepared to leave. 'Come down to the bar and I'll buy you a drink on it.'

'No,' Arad said, ringing the bell. 'Be my guest.'

★   ★   ★

Fanti was instinctively opposed to any approach by Kline to Santos suggesting a father and son exchange.

'It will give the terrorists another opportunity for TV propaganda and I'd rather leave them quiet. They'll turn you down and simply use the occasion to insult you.'

'Let me take that chance,' Kline pleaded. 'At least it will let my son and daughter-in-law know that I'm here, near them.'

Fanti gave way, not out of sympathy, moved as he was by the appeal. He needed an excuse to give somebody else a close look at Santos—the French agent who had seen him twice before and had arrived from Paris. He could take him into the Piazza with Kline and Luigi, posing as one of his own plain-clothes policemen.

★   ★   ★

When Luigi announced Kline's proposal at close range over a loud-hailer, Santos rejected it with outward scorn though

224

not without some private admiration for the old man's courage.

'I thought I had made it clear that we are not prepared to make any changes in our demands or in the time by which they must be satisfied. I hope, for your son's sake, that you have the million dollars when next you parade here—at four p.m. tomorrow. And your Israeli friends had better see reason this time. If they do not, you and the world will have to hold them responsible for what will undoubtedly happen.'

The Police Chief's advice had been right. The encounter had made compelling television—a drama of mounting tension set on the world's most magnificent open-air stage with lighting effects supplied by searchlights beaming from the Campanile and the clock-tower.

Turning away to return to the Danieli, Kline looked up again at the Horses and waved encouragingly, a greeting to which only Ruth responded because Paul was sobbing so profusely.

'Luigi, I never thought those noble beasts would cause me and mine so much distress,' he said as he wiped his eyes.

'Come to think of it, Sam, they've never brought much luck to anyone.'

Fanti was far more interested in the comments of the Frenchman. 'With that moustache, the peaked cap and the possibility of plastic surgery, I can't be absolutely sure but you'd be wise to work on the principle that it is Santos. That Czech VZ52 automatic is Santos's favourite weapon and the machine-pistols those Arabs are carrying are Czech Skorpions, which also fit Santos's European cell. Try and get his finger-prints. When they lower that plastic water-container for a refill, see if you can switch it. I've got his prints with me.'

★   ★   ★

Cardinal Talamini did what he could to comfort Paul, who was deeply embarrassed by the way he had broken down in front of strangers who had no way of knowing how close he and his father were, particularly since his mother had died. His gentle concern irritated Freya who sneered, 'I can't understand

225

why you should care about Jews when they were the ones who crucified Christ.'

'My dear child, we Christians crucify Him every day. You are doing it now. So are the rest of you . . .'

'Break it up,' Santos said curtly, disapproving of over-close contact between his captives. He nodded to Freya who pulled Ruth away with unnecessary force.

'Try to be a little more compassionate,' the Cardinal remonstrated. 'There's enough cruelty in the world as it is.'

Freya, a Bavarian who had been baptized a Catholic, scowled fiercely but was too overawed by the backlog of deference to priests to argue with His Eminence.

Turning his attention to Santos, the Cardinal inquired, 'Does the suffering you inflict on others never cause you distress?'

The terrorist leader, who was making more notes, was ready with his answer. 'What we have to do to a few people for a short time is aimed at ending suffering for millions who have been deprived of their basic human rights for years—their homes, their land, their way of life. Have you seen the conditions in the refugee camps—the shanties, the poverty, the squalor?'

The Cardinal shook his head.

'Then you are in no position to criticize. That's the trouble with clerics as exalted as you. You don't see what's really going on. We do. So don't preach to us.'

Talamini, who was by no means so remote from the facts, almost asked him why the Arab rulers, who had so much money and so much empty land, had not rehoused the refugees. But he knew he would not get the truthful answer— that they had been left to suffer as publicly as possible to serve the politicians' purpose of drawing attention to a running sore which could be blamed on Israel. So instead he eyed his captor with benevolent sadness, believing that he understood what motivated him—a poisonous brew of ideals, ideology and compulsive lust for the unique excitement of total, if only temporary, power over others.

Watching Santos sitting in a corner cross-legged on the floor checking his notes, the Cardinal marvelled at the consistency with which short men compensated for their lack of inches by aggressiveness. It was true at all levels of life, in his experience. Even the most fearsome Popes, like Martin V, Alexander Borgia and Julius II, had been of small stature.

★ ★ ★

As soon as Arad got rid of his Italian visitor, he left by the small alley-way to join the old friend he had telephoned immediately on arrival at Venice Airport. As he passed the Church of San Moise on his way to Harry's Bar, hard by the San Marco landing-stage on the Grand Canal, he noted that a middle-aged couple, whom he had seen booking in at the Regina, had followed him out and that the man was still carrying his camera-case and other paraphernalia of the photographic addict.

Frank Bozzoni was waiting at a downstairs table in Harry's Bar, and hailed Arad noisily as he pushed through the swing doors.

'Gideon, you old son of a bitch, I haven't seen you since Tel Aviv!'

Bozzoni was a highly successful American writer, and spent about three months of the year in the small Palazzetto Falier, on the Grand Canal, which he had bought with the money made from his first hit novel, *Bianca Cappella*. This had been based on the true story of a rich Venetian girl who shocked everyone by running away with a bank clerk, ditching him to end up Grand Duchess of Tuscany. He had discovered the fruitful formula of sex and violence, and his succeeding novels were such sure-fire sellers that he was able to arrange million-dollar package deals for all rights, including films.

Harry's Bar was one of the few places in Venice which welcomed Bozzoni, who had been a circus performer, actor and boxer, among other things, before achieving literary success, and rarely missed an opportunity to display his modest talents in any of these directions. His eccentric exhibitionism and his habit of picking fights had led to his being barred in most other bars and restaurants.

Arad had helped him during a sojourn in Israel when Boz-

227

zoni had been researching a novel which was suitably pro-Israeli and anti-Arab to merit Mossad assistance. The time had come for Bozzoni to reciprocate the favour.

'What will you have to drink?' Bozzoni asked, thrusting out his neatly trimmed, pointed beard. 'Their specialties are a "Bellini"— champagne and peach juice— a "Roger", called after the bar-tender Ruggiero—that's gin, peach juice, orange and lime—and a great new concoction. Tell him about it,' he urged the waiter.

'It's navy grog, lime and cold Coke. They are all four-letter words so we call it a "Bozzoni".'

The American hooted with laughter and slapped Arad on the thigh. 'Can you beat it? Oh boy, there are no flies on the Venetians when it comes to making money! Mine has to be a "Bozzoni". I'm stuck with it.'

'Rum is a very suitable drink for someone as piratical as you. I'll settle for a dry martini.'

Arad noticed that the camera-laden couple had also entered the bar and settled two tables away. He was not surprised when the largest camera-case was placed carefully on the square table at the corner, pointing towards him.

'You can do us a great service, Frank,' the Israeli said in almost a whisper. 'And do yourself one at the same time.'

'Name it, my friend. Name it.'

Arad then explained Sam Kline's predicament over the ransom money. 'What I am asking is that you volunteer to put up the million dollars publicly. I have a guarantee from Mr Kline in my pocket that he will repay it either immediately or later, as you prefer.'

Bozzoni looked interested so Arad continued, 'The money is already organized and will be available at the Banca d'Italia in the morning. But you will have to go through the motions of making a telex transfer from wherever your main funds are located.'

'Los Angeles, my friend! LA! I pay my taxes.'

Arad nodded appreciatively. 'That will ensure that nobody at the bank knows there's been an arrangement. The publicity will be good for you and you will be helping poor old Kline.'

228

'Good for me! You can say that again. You couldn't buy that kind of publicity. Show me the guarantee.'

Arad passed him the paper.

'OK, you have yourself a deal,' Bozzoni said, pocketing the document. He looked at the wooden clock behind the bar, where the bar-tender was joking with a group of middle-aged American women. 'It's still only late afternoon in LA. If I get on the telephone right away I can fix the transfer to arrive here first thing in the morning. When should I make the announcement?'

'Tonight. The sooner the better. We don't want these terrorists getting trigger-happy.'

'You're giving in then? Completely?'

'What else can we do, Frank? With the Cardinal in line to be next Pope and the Basilica in danger of destruction they have us over a barrel. I have to hand it to that Santos. He's a real pro . . .'

'It is Santos then?'

'It certainly looks that way, Frank.'

'Have you heard anything from Jerusalem?'

'No, but I expect an announcement before the night is out. It's tragic because it will offset so much that we achieved at Entebbe, but you can't win 'em all.'

'Do you know what I'd do, Gideon?'

'Tell me.'

The American cleared a space on the table and placed his glass in the centre.

'Right. There's the Basilica. I'd bring those prisoners over like Santos says and line them up right there.'

He dipped his finger in his glass and drew a wet line in front of it. 'Then I'd say, "Right, Mr bloody Santos, this time you've used your own balls for bait. We are all going to sit this one out until you surrender, and the moment you harm one of the hostages we'll shoot two of your comrades. And if you press that plunger we'll shoot them all." And I'd mean it!'

Arad gave him a patronizing smile. 'The Italians would never allow us to bring arms into the Piazza.'

'OK. Then line 'em up at Tel Aviv Airport and shoot 'em there.'

229

'That would be illegal under Israeli law.'

Banging his fist on the table Bozzoni cried, 'To hell with the law! What notice do these bastards take of the law? You didn't worry about the law at Entebbe.'

'That didn't break *Israeli* law,' Arad said mischievously. 'No, Frank, Venice isn't Entebbe. Your idea's OK for one of your novels but it's not realistic.'

Bozzoni looked disappointed. 'You mean that the million bucks will just be handed over to these bandits?'

'I'm afraid so. The Algerians may go through the motions of taking it away from Santos and company when they arrive at Dar El Beida but they'll give it all back to them.'

'Christ, Gideon, and I used to think that, next to God, I was the greatest perpetrator of sick jokes! Have the Algerians agreed to have them?'

'What else can they do with Cardinal Talamini aboard? They're anxious to improve their world image so they'll say they are accepting the terrorists with "extreme reluctance" as a service to humanity! But you know what we think about them. They are Arabs and they hate us.'

Bozzoni called for the bill. 'Pity there's not time for another one . . .'

'There's just one other thing, Frank. When you've fixed everything, telephone the Police Chief and tell him you are volunteering to put up the money. He'll tell Kline. They are both at the Danieli. It'll look more spontaneous that way.'

'I'll do that, Gideon. I'll do that right away. I've got my boat outside. Can I give you a lift?'

'No thanks, I'm going back to my hotel. I'm expecting a few calls.'

The American paid the bill and the two men left, followed soon after by the middle-aged couple.

Arad walked the small distance to the mooring where the *Bianca Cappella* was waiting.

'Great boat you have there, Frank,' he remarked.

'The gondoliers don't think so, do you fellers?' Bozzoni said, addressing the gondoliers moored there.

The author had a bad reputation not only with the gondoliers but with the vaporetti skippers for the way he drove his speedboat about the canals and the lagoons. Repeated complaints had been lodged with the police but, like reports about his rowdy parties at the Palazzetto Falier and his brawls in restaurants, they were usually stifled. So little was ever done about his misdemeanours that it was assumed that Fanti must be well supplied with 'hospitality' in various forms, not excluding some of the girls in the Bozzoni entourage, to which the Police Chief's current secretary belonged.

'Can I peek inside for a minute?' Arad asked.

'Sure! Welcome aboard!'

When they were alone in the cabin the Israeli made a further financial proposition which he had not been prepared even to whisper in Harry's Bar. This too was accepted.

Arad waved farewell, and as he returned up the narrow street he noticed that the middle-aged couple were looking in a shop window displaying garish Venetian glassware. He passed seemingly without perceiving them.

The couple then scurried to the temporary headquarters of the Italian Intelligence officer who had called on Arad.

With a triumphant flourish the woman produced a tape cassette and handed it over. 'I think we got it all.'

'Good, let's listen to it.'

The directional microphone hidden in the camera-case had done an excellent job.

'Well, that seems clear enough,' the officer said with some relief. 'It looks as though all we have to watch now is the airport. To make sure there are no fireworks there.'

The two agents nodded.

'Right, take a rest then. I don't think friend Arad will be doing much more tonight but sitting by the telephone. And we have that tapped.'

But he was by no means at ease as he sat back in his chair and lit another cigarette from the butt of his last one. The Israelis could still be up to something. He just couldn't see them accepting a political defeat so easily. As Arad had said, it was difficult to see what they could possibly do, but after Entebbe . . . An old stager in the Intelligence game, he knew that no agency, however resourceful, could win all the time. A run of successes always engendered arrogance, and he was

231

certain that one day, somewhere, the Israelis would attempt some impossible venture that would fail with appalling consequences.

Within the hour Bozzoni had telephoned Fanti with what the Police Chief regarded as remarkable news for Sam Kline.

'Your problem's solved, Mr Kline,' Fanti announced heartily. 'An American friend of mine is offering to put up the entire ransom.'

'Who is it?'

'A writer called Frank Bozzoni. He lives here part of the year and your luck's in because he's here right now.'

Luigi, who had disapproved of Bozzoni ever since he had heard him boasting in front of his daughter that he had christened her 'Venetia' because she had been conceived in a gondola, was astonished.

'You mean he's prepared to put up a million dollars out of his own pocket?'

'That's what he says and I'm sure he means it.'

Kline smiled broadly for the first time since he had left New York. 'That's marvellous. Of course, I'll pay him back later . . .'

'No. He won't hear of that. He wants it known that he put up the money and he doesn't want any anti-climax exposures later.'

'What's his motive, sheer publicity?' Luigi asked.

'I didn't ask him,' Fanti replied with some irritation. 'But, gentlemen, let's not look such a gift horse in the mouth.'

Luigi's astonishment was shared by Mayor Pizza, who had joined them in the operations room and had to be told of the development. He shook his great head decisively. 'I think we should try elsewhere. I don't like that Bozzoni and I don't trust him. It could just be a stunt. He might let us down at the last minute.'

'Mr Bozzoni has instructed the Banca d'Italia to have the money ready first thing in the morning and to deliver it to us here,' Fanti insisted.

Pizza still seemed unimpressed. He had never accepted the Police Chief's jocular explanation of his lifestyle, that all one needed to live like a millionaire was the hospitality of enough millionaires who happened to like you.

'Gentlemen, we must accept Mr Bozzoni's offer without further delay,' Fanti repeated. 'The instructions from Rome are to do all we can here to encourage the Israeli Government to accept the peaceful terms the terrorists are offering.'

The Mayor was as anxious as anybody to prevent any violence. It was unfortunate that Santos was a Marxist because, with the Italian Communist Party so near to achieving national power through democratic election, it was extremely sensitive to being associated with anything smacking of force. But Pizza had a personal detestation of Bozzoni, and was highly suspicious of the Police Chief's connection with his sudden intrusion into the scenario.

'I don't see why this villain should be given the opportunity to appear as a philanthropist,' Pizza argued. 'He'll probably recover the whole million dollars as publicity expenses. Can't the Church put up the money? After all, the Basilica and the Horses are Church property.'

'Oh God, another political point,' Fanti thought, as Pizza looked at the Chaplain with an expectant smile that did little to offset his hang-dog look. 'The fat old bastard avoids embarrassing the Church in public because that's the Party line at the moment, but won't miss a chance in private.'

He produced his silver toothpick and began to dig industriously at his strong white teeth, a sure sign that his temper was fraying. But the Jesuit's pale face was devoid of emotion as he answered quietly, 'The Church is in the same position as Mr Kline. We couldn't possibly do business with terrorists. In any case, the Church does not have that kind of money available . . .'

A trace of a disbelieving smile flitted across the Mayor's features but he hid it by wiping his bulbous nose, while Luigi decided the time had come to intervene.

'Gentlemen, I dislike Mr Bozzoni as much as the Mayor does, but Mr Kline's son and daughter-in-law are in the clutches of dangerous fanatics. While we talk trivialities they are suffering agonies of anxiety. I propose we accept Mr Bozzoni's generous offer with heartfelt thanks and urge him to announce it forthwith.'

'Please,' Kline added with a pitiable gesture of supplication.

233

Pizza, whose objections had never been much more than polemics, without which life for him had become pointless, agreed with a further show of reluctance.

The Police Chief's annoyance had intensified the scent of aromatic deodorant from his body, and though Kline, who was sitting between him and the Mayor, found it preferable to Pizza's garlic odour, he welcomed the opportunity to stand away from both.

'I couldn't be more grateful to Mr Bozzoni, whatever anyone says about him,' he said, as Fanti telephoned the American author prior to going round to see him. 'I can only trust that it will encourage the Israeli Government to collaborate.'

The Jesuit raised his bony hands. 'Let us be like Abraham who, against all hope, believed in hope,' he said.

'Old humbug,' Pizza thought, as Kline smilingly appreciated the biblical reference. That was the trouble with these clerics. They could always dredge up some quotation from the Holy Book to suit their purpose. Kline was a humbug too, he decided. All that brave talk about never giving in to blackmail and here he was, not only fiddling a way round his personal problem but wanting the Israelis to capitulate!

*   *   *

Bozzoni's announcement that he was putting up the million dollars, ably exploited by his publicity machine in New York, surprised those who knew him but did not fuss Santos so long as it remained clear that it was Kline who would suffer the ignominy of handing it over. The statement issued by the Israeli Prime Minister's office round about midnight, Italian time, caused international astonishment and delighted Santos:

'In view of the widespread concern for Cardinal Talamini, who is not well enough to endure a lengthy ordeal, in the interests of the other hostages, and with our well-known concern for irreplaceable ancient monuments, the Government of Israel has decided with the greatest reluctance to accept the conditions demanded by the gunmen.

'On the firm understanding that all hostages will be released unharmed, the ten named prisoners will be taken to

234

Ben Gurion Airport and flown by El Al aircraft to Venice for hand-over to the Italian authorities. As stipulated, General Isaiah Yacob will accompany the prisoners and will be present when they are handed over to the gunmen in the Piazza San Marco.

'We will make one stipulation—that two armed Italian guards travel in the helicopter from Venice Airport to the Piazza to prevent any personal assault on General Yacob by the prisoners.'

After giving this condition careful thought, Santos accepted it. The last thing he wanted was any fighting on the helicopter which was to be their means of escape. But he insisted that once the machine had landed in the Piazza, the Italian guards should leave and walk to the far end of the square.

There were some, including Santos, who suspected that, as with the negotiations over Entebbe, this statement could be a cover for some secret Israeli ingenuity, but such expectations were to be extinguished early next morning when all the prisoners duly appeared under heavy guard at Ben Gurion Airport.

★　　★　　★

Hundreds of Israelis, including relatives and friends of those whom the prisoners had killed or maimed, screamed their objections to their release and vowed vengeance on the Government, especially at the sight of Okamoto, the Japanese who had murdered so many helpless civilians in the very airport from which he was now to be transported. There were boos and catcalls for Tabbucci, the Greek Catholic Archbishop, dressed in his black cassock and head-dress set off with a gold chain and crucifix. A Christian Arab, who had changed his name from Tabushi to improve his Catholic image, he had abused his ecclesiastical privilege to smuggle in weapons and explosives used indiscriminately to kill tourists and Jews. His beard was slightly greyer and he had put on a little weight but he walked with dignity, aloof from the Palestinians who received their share of noisy condemnation.

The Prime Minister, who deemed it politically wise to

235

brave the insults at the airport, was briefly interviewed by newsmen and for television, soon to be broadcast world-wide.

'I find it as hateful as any of you to see these murderers go free, perhaps to kill again, but the diplomatic pressures brought to bear on us from almost every quarter have been unprecedented. When all the facts become known, if ever they do, you will appreciate that we have been given no alternative. The entire Cabinet has approved the action.'

He refused to be drawn on specific details, fending off questions about telegrams from the Pope and telephone calls from the White House, but the Press were not discouraged from assuming that without this surrender the supply of vital new weapons for the defence of Israel could be prejudiced.

Speaking on Yacob's behalf, the Prime Minister offered the General's apologies for failing to be present for questioning.

'I think that, knowing General Yacob, you will understand that this situation is worse for him than for any of us. Frankly, he is too distressed to talk to you and will need all his emotional resources to deal with the appalling situation he faces shortly in Venice. He asked me to tell you that he had no part in our decision and he requests your sympathy and your prayers.'

With considerable courage the Prime Minister then chose to push his way on foot through the clamouring crowd, and photographs of him comforting the wailing mother of one of the terrorists' child victims were flashed round the world.

General Yacob, identifiable by his bald head and the stump of his right arm, which had been shot away in the Yom Kippur War, was driven straight to the blue and white Boeing 707 of El Al Israel Airlines crewed up for take-off. Its Star of David insignia, high on the tailplane, was clearly visible in the Mediterranean sunshine. He looked hunched as he climbed the steps, but turned at the top to recover his military bearing and wave wearily to the crowd.

The ten prisoners were then off-loaded from a security van under armed guard and were paraded for close-up photographs. Interviews were forbidden because the Prime Minister was having no pro-Palestinian propaganda on Israeli soil. The fullest use of the photographs would be made outside by gloating Palestinian leaders, but there was nothing he could do about that. Some of the prisoners, like the little Japanese, remained sullen and impassive. Others were grinning and giving V-signs and clenched-fist salutes as they were marched to the plane and boarded it. An Israeli armed guard travelled with them, but on-the insistence of the Italian authorities these were not even to step on to Italian soil.

*   *   *

Watching the whole departure on the portable television set later that morning, Santos could not refrain from shaking his colleagues' hands in joyful self-congratulation, and the clapping and cheers as they watched the 707 take off from Ben-Gurion Airport drowned the wails of the spectators there. They were succeeding where every Palestinian attempt before had failed. It was complete capitulation.

Santos was elated but not surprised. He had never failed in any previous enterprise, however risky it had seemed before he had applied his blend of determination, ice-cool courage, firm leadership and meticulous attention to detail. Knowing the time of departure he calculated the time of arrival at Venice and made a note of it.

The mounting exhilaration of a violent operation followed by the almost orgastic relief of tension when it was successfully resolved, was a major motive for Santos, and none that he had ever staged before had carried such potential recompense in these respects. He was already savouring the climactic moment when the freed men would be handed over to him. He had never worked with any of them and neither had any of his comrades, most of whom were so young that those being released had been captured before they had joined the Movement. But by listening to Damascus he had official PFLP confirmation that all ten who had left Israel in the El Al plane had been positively identified as those demanded.

Though the list had been supplied to Santos by his Arab superiors, Okamoto's release would give him great personal satisfaction. Here was a man like himself, prepared to create

237

near-suicidal situations in a cause in which he needed no personal involvement beyond the burning conviction that it was just. Okamoto's last mission on behalf of the PFLP had been to shatter morale and damage the Israeli tourist trade by killing and maiming the maximum number of people at Ben Gurion Airport, into which it was virtually impossible to smuggle a knife, much less a machine-gun. He and his two 'Red Army' comrades had not only notched up more than a hundred casualties with machine-gun fire but Okamoto had survived!

In spite of the murderous record of the freed terrorists, and Okamoto's in particular, most of the world's press and radio commentators applauded the Israeli decision, which led Santos to ask the Cardinal, 'Doesn't it strike you as strange that while the world's imagination is always fired by the threat of sudden destruction, it is prepared to shut its eyes to a far bigger catastrophe so long as it is only happening slowly?'

Talamini agreed but he was not thinking about the plight of the Palestinian refugees. The contrast in his mind was nearer home—between the Four Horses immediately threatened by their burden of high explosives and the entire city of Venice menaced by the sea.

* * *

It had been Ruth's turn to weep as she had watched her father mount the airplane steps, an event which Freya had pointed out with malicious satisfaction.

'So poppa's on his way!' she had taunted. 'You didn't think he'd give in so easily did you?'

Chapter Nineteen

Ruth could only sniff helplessly. She knew how much the surrender was going to hurt her father. To be the central figure of
such ignominy would probably end his political career. Whatever the Prime Minister said about the General's absence when
the decision was taken, it was inevitable that people would
believe that the recovery of his only daughter had been his
private priority. They would say that in pursuit of his personal
interest he had forgotten Jerusalem. Through unstinting service to the State of Israel, Yacob had no right hand to forget its
cunning, but details like that were quickly forgotten by a fickle
and emotional electorate. In being thankful, if only for Paul's
sake, that her country had decided to sacrifice its principles,
Ruth was aware that she was forgetting Jerusalem herself but
consoled herself that there had been nothing she could have
done.

Paul did his best to comfort her but he had sunk into deeper
depression exacerbated by lack of sleep, for like the other
hostages he refused the amphetamine pills the terrorists
offered and were using themselves. Unlike Ruth he did not
have the consolation of prayer. There had never been any
question of his deserting the faith. His conversion of Saul to
Paul had marked no religious change, but he was not a regular
attender at the synagogue. His blank passiveness disturbed
Santos, who had promised to hand back three fit hostages and
was determined to keep his word.

'Cheer up!' he said briskly. 'You'll soon be in Algiers. Let's
celebrate with a little music. We still have some hours to kill.'

He indicated the cassette player which Freya switched
on, turning up the volume. The verse of the Four Horses
song, rendered rather raucously by a film actress who had
been convinced that she could also sing, seemed particularly
apposite:

While musing away in your fine, vaulted den,
Give us now your answer—What motivates men?
Observing the pageants of rulers and Popes,
Spurred on by ambition, by fears and by hopes,
Some sure to succeed, others destined to fail,
Does reason or primitive instinct prevail?
What force dominates all the love and the hate?
Which is it? The drive to destroy or create?

*   *   *

After the bronze blacksmiths on the clock-tower had hammered eleven strokes on their bell anvil, Santos picked up his loud-hailer and cried, 'We want to talk to Professor Scarpaccia.'

The senior policeman in charge on the Piazza used a field telephone to contact Luigi at the Danieli, and he and Fanti were quickly round. They were accompanied by the senior official from Rome, who took the opportunity of a close-up appreciation of the situation.

'We need food and water for the hostages,' Santos announced. 'It's not for us. We have enough for ourselves so don't bother to drug it. We shan't be touching it.'

'Understood,' Luigi signalled. As they turned away, Santos shouted as an afterthought, 'Don't bring any pork!'

The onlookers thought it remarkable that in an atmosphere of such suspense he could make an attempt at humour, but if he was not relaxed after seeing the scene at Ben Gurion Airport, he was putting on a very convincing act. He reached into one of the hold-alls and produced a bottle of wine and several plastic cups.

'Like a drink?' he asked his captives affably. 'There's plenty. They never touch it,' he added, pointing to the Arabs. 'They are very holy.'

'There is nothing wrong with that,' the Cardinal observed, accepting a cup and urging Ruth and Paul to join him. 'It will do you good,' he assured them.

Ruth accepted with a wan smile, hoping it would help to raise her husband's spirits. 'My father, whom you'll be meeting soon, says the best thing about our religion is that it enjoins us to drink wine.'

'So does mine—for a few of us,' the Cardinal quipped. 'I drink to the health of all of us. The continuing health!'

Santos raised his cup. Ruth lifted hers to Paul and to the Cardinal with the Hebrew toast, 'Le hayim!'

'Le hayim!' Paul responded, grateful for the chance to moisten his throat which was arid through anxiety.

'Does that mean "Good health"?' Santos asked suspiciously.

'It literally means "To life".'

'Well, I'll certainly drink to that,' the terrorist said. 'Le hayim!'

He was sitting on the edge of the balcony, completely assured that nobody would shoot him, and raising his glass at the television cameras he induced his captives to do the same, with some gun-prodding from the Germans. The Cardinal took the opportunity to bless the cameramen and others in the Piazza, to which they responded with clapping and shouts of 'Evviva il Cardinale!'

'You see our hostages are being well treated,' Santos shouted. 'We are not savages.'

Those viewers who knew the terrorist's record of cold-blooded killings were unimpressed.

*   *   *

Before nine o'clock that morning the million dollars in used notes, packed in two suitcases as demanded, had been delivered under police escort to the Hotel Danieli from the Palazzo Manin, where the deplorable last Doge had lived and which had become the headquarters of the Banca d'Italia. After inspecting it, Fanti announced that the ransom and the housing guarantee were ready so that the terrorists could be completely assured on two of their demands. The armed guard, which had been mounted on the operations room from the beginning as well as on the front of the hotel, was reinforced. Fanti was taking no chances that any home-bred criminals might take advantage of such an enormous sum so handily packed for lifting.

241

With feigned reluctance, the Algerian Government had announced its agreement that the terrorists would be allowed to land at Algiers and had undertaken to oversee the release of the hostages. At its invitation representatives of the Vatican and the US State Department, which would also be acting for Israel, were on the way there.

All seemed set for a smooth and peaceful solution but the Police Chief was understandably apprehensive. He could hardly wait to see the terrorists and their hostages safely off Italian soil with the Four Horses and the Basilica intact. Further developments would be none of his concern. He had slept reasonably well considering that he had spent most of the night in the same bed as his delightful secretary, who was proving to be satisfactory in every way, and at nine-thirty had set off for the airport to inspect the arrangements there. The El Al plane was due to arrive soon after midday and there would be need to feed its occupants. He wanted to ensure that this would be done aboard the aircraft, since he did not want the freed prisoners disembarked until the moment they were to transfer to the helicopter in the afternoon. Eight terrorists in the Loggia were enough. He had been told that the big Augusta-Sikorsky helicopter which would ferry the prisoners to the Piazza had arrived, and he wanted to inspect it and to talk to the pilot about exactly where he would land and how he would take off. He had learned from harsh experience that it never paid to leave such details to others.

Fanti also wanted to make sure that his strict instructions that no reporters or cameramen were to be allowed anywhere near the Israeli plane or the helicopter were carried out. Television cameras were to be allowed to operate but only at a distance. Security was going to be difficult enough without problems which would be caused by the overzealous media.

*   *   *

Another interested person had preceded the Police Chief to the airport—Gideon Arad, who had been tailed there by an Italian Intelligence agent. As Arad settled in the airport lounge to read the newspapers, the agent felt he could report to headquarters with some confidence.

'I'd say he's definitely waiting for the El Al plane to arrive. He's checked out of his hotel and he's got his bag with him. If there is going to be any Israeli action it could be here, though there's no other sign of it.'

His chief at the other end of the telephone, who had great respect for Arad, was puzzled. It was true that he did not really know how many armed Israeli guards would be flying in with the prisoners, though the Italian Government had been assured there would be only four. But it was difficult to see what any number could possibly accomplish at the airport before the hostages had been released in the Piazza, and by that time the El Al plane was scheduled to have left Venice, complete with the guards. Further, an Italian Army detachment was already deployed at the airfield with quite a show of force—armoured cars, some even fitted with light anti-aircraft guns.

'I think you must be right,' he admitted.

'Is he to be allowed to talk to General Yacob or the Israeli guards?'

'Absolutely not. He's here as a private visitor and that's how he's going to be treated. If he wants to return to Israel by the El Al plane after it's all over I can see no objection to that.'

Chapter Twenty

If the Italian security men and police were increasingly apprehensive as the hours clanged by, their tautness was fractional compared with the mounting tension in the Loggia dei Cavalli. Most of the terrorists had taken to chewing gum they had brought for the purpose. So had Ruth and Paul. Only Santos and the Cardinal, who had politely refused the Arab's advice, 'Take some, it helps,' seemed imperturbable. They had their different fears but the basic reason for their composure was the same—neither was really afraid to die, the Catholic because he was certain that the consequence would be a better life, the Marxist because he was equally convinced it would be oblivion.

Even in the few hours they had all been confined together, an unconscious rapport had begun to build up between the terrorists and their captives, deriving from the common peril of their predicament. Like most humans, whatever their race or character, they were displaying, albeit unconsciously, the unique adaptability to hostile circumstances which had enabled the species to lord it over the earth and even the moon.

Only Freya remained uncompromisingly remote. The primitive sanitation arrangements, in a corner of a small room between the Loggia and the steps leading down into the Basilica, required that Ruth and Freya should sometimes be alone together. Paul had often joked that in his experience it only required two girl strangers to go to the lavatory together for them to emerge firm friends, but there was no breakdown of barriers with Freya, who kept pointing her gun at her captive as though itching for an excuse to use it.

*   *   *

The television cameras at Venice Aiport picked up the El Al airliner as it circled to land, and nobody watched it more

244

closely than Santos. His first remark as he looked at his watch was 'Twelve-fifty. Bang on time. Three hours—just what I expected a 707 to take from Tel Aviv. They haven't dawdled on the way.'

The plane taxied off the runway to a remote part of the field, well away from the parking area of the scheduled civil flights. No photographers were allowed near it but, with their zoom lenses, the television cameramen recorded the exciting moments as the steps were trundled up and the doors opened, after eight armed Italian carabinieri had been stationed around the plane.

Fanti, who was driven out in a police car, was soon aboard with an airport official and an aide carrying a revolver. Everything seemed normal. The papers and the internal inspection showed a regular El Al crew plus four Israeli armed guards, the ten listed prisoners and General Yacob. The airline had already supplied packed lunches for all the passengers, so after stationing two of his carabinieri aboard, Fanti allowed the crew to leave on the understanding that they remained within the airport, while the rest were required to stay aboard until further notice. He personally warned the guard around the plane that nobody was to be allowed to leave it, and then returned to the Danieli, where he found that Santos required his presence in the Piazza to receive further instructions.

*   *   *

'This is how events will now be managed,' Santos announced from his notes:

'At 2.45 p.m. the Mayor, Samuel Kline, Professor Scarpaccia and the Chief of Police will line up facing me between the three flagpoles. They will have with them the housing guarantee, the ransom money and two unarmed men to carry the suitcases.

'At 2.55 the main door of the Basilica below us must be unlocked from outside by one unarmed man.

'At 3 p.m. as the clock strikes, the Mayor will march forward alone and hand over the guarantee to me in the doorway of the Basilica. If this is satisfactory he will then retire to the line from which he came.

'At my command Kline and the two porters will then bring the suitcases to the door of the Basilica. The porters will then return to the line but Kline will remain. Should the money be counterfeit, Kline will also be taken hostage. If it is correct he will also return to the line.

'Any attempt to interfere with these proceedings will result in the execution of all the hostages, including Kline.

'Once these proceedings have been concluded, all those in the line will then march to the far end of the Piazza and remain there.

'At 3.30 precisely, the helicopter with the ten freedom fighters aboard and General Yacob, but nobody else, except the crew and two Italian guards, to which I have agreed, will leave Venice Airport for this Piazza. It will land on a cross which the police must mark at the point nearest to us where the pilot says it is safe to land and take off. Yacob will be the first to leave the helicopter. He will stand facing me just in front of the flagstaff on my right. The two Italian guards will then disembark and march to the end of the Piazza. The freedom fighters will then disembark one by one and line up on General Yacob's right, facing me.

'The Italian helicopter crew will remain aboard throughout but the engines will be switched off.

'When all this has been accomplished to my satisfaction, further orders will be issued. Meanwhile, the Italian airplane to take my party to Algiers must be ready for take-off at Venice Airport.

'I repeat that any attempt to interfere will result in disaster for the hostages, this building and these Horses you seem to prize so much. The Cardinal has told us he is not afraid to die. Neither am I.'

*　　*　　*

Nobody disbelieved Santos, least of all Pizza, who was terrified at the prospect of meeting him alone at close quarters. He wondered whether he too might be snatched as an addi-

246

tional hostage. Like many vocal left-wing politicians, he was a bit short on physical courage. He claimed to have been a partisan but had been too fat for active service, though it was rumoured that he had been very active in sending others on suicidal missions. However, there was no way out if he was to survive politically. He was coming up for re-election soon.

Pizza's arrival on the Piazza accompanied by Fanti was greeted with some merriment by the Arabs. Even Santos could not forbear a smile.

'He's fatter than you, Cardinal,' he exclaimed affably, to which Talamini conceded good-naturedly, 'Perhaps we have both lived too well.'

The Mayor was quickly joined in the line by Samuel Kline and Luigi. At the sight of her father-in-law Ruth stood up, but was sharply dragged down again by Freya with Santos's approval.

'I warn you that during this hand-over none of you may move or shout. It could be very dangerous—for all of us.'

He motioned to one of the Arab explosives experts to bring the detonating mechanism into full view on the balcony and to keep his hand near the plunger.

Promptly at 2.55, a policeman holding aloft the key of the central bronze doors of the Basilica walked forward and opened one of them, the massive bolts having previously been withdrawn from the inside. Then, as the hour of three sounded, Pizza marched forward towards the door. Before he reached it Santos stopped him and commanded him to read the guarantee aloud.

'Take your time,' he said laconically. 'The revolution isn't going to be delayed just because you are out of your office!'

With tremulous fingers, Pizza put on his spectacles, took the document from his inside pocket and announced, 'On the understanding that no harm befalls the Basilica of St Mark, the Four Bronze Horses or any other of its monuments, we the Council of the City of Venice undertake to allot an additional thousand million lire for the improvement of housing in the poorer districts, particularly in Canareggio and Castello in the coming financial year.'

Santos had little doubt that the two districts must house

247

many of Pizza's political supporters but that was no concern of his; however, he could not resist remarking, 'I see you make no mention of our hostages. You are only interested in your precious Horses. Lumps of metal matter but human life does not and you call yourself a Communist!'

'The hostages are not my problem,' Pizza snapped, in his gravelly voice.

'No, but you will be our problem if you fail to honour this guarantee. Some of my comrades will be back looking for you. And you are hardly a difficult target to find.'

Many of the onlookers laughed, as much to relieve their own tension as at the Mayor's discomfort, while Fanti observed to Luigi out of the side of his mouth, 'The factions of Communism hate each other more than they hate Fascists.'

Santos ordered Pizza to approach the door; then, with the Arabs and Germans pointing their guns at the heads of the hostages in full view of the cameras, he slipped down the back stairs to the open door. The television viewers could just see Pizza hand over the document in the dark doorway; then he waddled back to his place in the line.

After regaining the Loggia, Santos raised the loud-hailer to announce, 'I am now going to give this guarantee to the Cardinal who, I suspect, represents the interests of the people of Venice more truly than the gentleman who has just delivered it.'

Handing the paper to Talamini he added quietly, 'You may not like the way this has been obtained but if the poor benefit . . .'

'I think you are trying to say, as I often say myself, that God moves in mysterious ways,' the Cardinal said as he slipped the guarantee into the pocket of his cassock.

'I hope you will shame the Mayor into honouring it.'

'If God spares me,' the Cardinal replied.

The terrorist gave him a half-amused look, as though saying that if His Eminence was to be spared it would be through his favour, not God's.

'Right, Samuel Kline and porters forward!' Santos commanded.

Kline moved carefully in step with the two men carrying the

heavy suitcases. Paul found it near impossible to remain silent, but the fear in Ruth's eyes subdued him.

'Stay there,' Santos ordered the three men when they reached the point where Pizza had read out his guarantee. 'Now open the suitcases.'

This was done to expose the neatly bundled notes.

'Mr Kline, I want you to inspect that money and give me an assurance that it is genuine. You are a banker, you should know.'

Kline removed sample bundles from each case and examined them. 'So far as I can judge, these notes are genuine.'

'And is it all there? One million dollars?'

'So far as I can judge, it is.'

'Right, Mr Kline, you who said it would be over your dead body if you ever did a deal with freedom-fighters: which do you prefer, to hand that million dollars over to me or see your son shot? Answer loud and clear so that the whole world can hear you.'

There was absolute silence in the square as Kline responded haltingly, 'I prefer to hand over the money.'

'If that is so, bring those cases over one by one and deposit them in the doorway.'

Kline did so and his public humiliation could hardly have been sweeter to the terrorists or more bitter to his relatives.

'Well done, Mr Kline!' Santos said sarcastically. 'Now you can return to your place.'

The timing had been perfect. Within a few minutes the prisoners were to be transferred from the airliner to the helicopter, and the TV interest switched to the cameras at the airport.

At 3.15, under the supervision of Fanti's deputy, the door of the airliner opened and General Yacob emerged and came down the steps. On touching the ground he was frisked by one of the carabinieri guards, managing a smile to say, 'I'm afraid it's a long time since I wore a gun.'

Two of the Israeli guards then appeared and, remaining at the top of the steps, frisked each of their prisoners as they emerged with their hands on their heads. The prisoners were then marched smartly by the carabinieri to the waiting helicopter, which took off immediately they had embarked.

Within minutes the noise of the engines could be heard in the Piazza, and as the big machine hovered down to land on the large cross painted at the required point Santos remarked, 'Ah, an Augusta-Sikorsky 61A. That's plenty big enough to carry us all. So far, so good.'

The rotor blades came to a gradual stop and the door opened to release General Yacob, who walked with military dignity to the appointed place in front of the designated flagstaff. The Archbishop followed, then the eight Arabs to line up on Yacob's right as instructed at the airport by Fanti, with the little Japanese appearing last to stand nearest to the central flagstaff.

The Archbishop, impressive with his full beard and becoming garb, caught the Cardinal's eyes and bowed his head, while Santos could not resist a welcoming wave to the Japanese, who returned it with the nearest thing to a smile he could manage. Santos was well satisfied as he scanned the line. Except for the Archbishop who was impassive, as though still resenting that he should ever have been locked up with such men, the prisoners looked happy while Yacob, whose face was very familiar, looked sick with disgust.

'Come on, let's go,' Santos announced.

While the hostages, whose hands had been tied behind them, were directed down the stairway to the main door of the Basilica, the Arab who had been holding the plunger remained on the balcony, but once his colleague was in sight outside he gingerly lowered it on its long lead into the other man's hands. The lead was then pulled down gently until there was enough to reach the helicopter.

At Santos's command, one of the Arabs walked towards the helicopter and entered it to inspect the interior for hidden troops or booby traps. He soon emerged to given an OK signal and remained, gun in hand, by the door of the machine.

Freya, who was holding a length of nylon cord, then moved over to the General and tied his single hand tightly round his waist. There was murmuring from Fanti and others at this move but there was nothing they could do.

The suitcases with the ransom were then carried aboard the

machine one at a time and stowed there. Then the plunger linked with the Four Horses was taken inside the helicopter, causing Luigi and others to fear that at the last minute the terrorists might carry out a vengeful destruction of the front of the Basilica.

The three hostages were herded nearer the clock-tower and told to face General Yacob. Santos was determined that Ruth was going to witness her father's shame.

As she turned to face him, Yacob thrust out the stump of his right arm and shouted at her in Hebrew, 'Remember the left-handed Jew and the very fat man!'

'Silence,' Santos commanded angrily. Then turning to one of the Arabs who understood Hebrew he asked, 'What did he say?'

The Arab looked puzzled. 'Something about a left-handed Jew and a very fat man. I suppose he's complaining about being tied up. The fat man might be the Cardinal . . .'

Santos nodded. The General, Ruth and Paul were all securely tied and under the barrels of several guns. There was nothing they could do and all the Palestinians in the line-up, who must have learned some Hebrew during their years in Israeli prisons, seemed unconcerned.

'Right, General. Now you can talk. I take it you do speak English?'

'Of course.'

'Then repeat this after me, every word of it. Unless you do so you will be shot here and now.' Recalling the occasions when Israeli commandos disguised as mechanics had entered hijacked planes, Santos brandished his automatic and declared, 'I owe it to my dead comrades to execute you, but we who work for the Arab cause keep our bargains.'

He handed the loud-hailer to Yacob so that what he was required to say would be picked up strongly by the television and radio microphones. Then producing a paper from his breast pocket he read phrase by phrase:

'I, General Isaiah Yacob, formerly of the Israeli Army and now of the Israeli Government, admit that these ten brave men who have been branded as terrorists are freedom

251

fighters for the just cause of the liberation of Palestine from Zionist aggression.

'I further admit that they have been monstrously treated as criminals when they should have been treated as prisoners-of-war. I apologize for the Zionist crimes against these heroes, and now deliver them back personally to the Movement for the Liberation of Palestine in the knowledge that they are free to fight again for the restoration of the oppressed peoples of Palestine to their homeland, which will inevitably occur.'

Unable to watch her proud father so terribly degraded, Ruth closed her eyes. At that moment, her pulse quickened as her subconscious mind, which had been searching her memory-store for the meaning of his strange outcry, suddenly expelled what she believed to be the answer. It centred around a story they had read together more than once about the Kingdom of Moab, where her Biblical namesake, the great-grandmother of King David, had been born. She whispered its significance in Paul's ear and was silenced by a painful jab in the small of the back by an Arab gun-barrel.

His abject admission concluded, Yacob stood in silence, his chin thrust out, his lips compressed in what semblance of defiance he could muster while his tormentors smiled in satisfaction. Then, as though unable to contain their joy a moment longer, the Palestinians and the Japanese erupted into noisy self-congratulation, and flinging their arms in the air they surged forwards to embrace the men who had released them.

Santos alone was concerned by this unexpected intrusion into his meticulous timetable, but seeing the Arab guards with the guns still pointed at the hostages, he could not resist the grateful grasp of the Japanese he so admired. Disconcerted by the tightness of the embrace, he was moving to free himself when from the Archbishop, who had remained aloof from the rejoicing, there came a staccato cry in Hebrew, 'Ehud! Ehud!' which, though Santos could not comprehend it, sounded like a command. He was appalled to see Yacob fling himself down, commando-style, to be followed by Ruth and then Paul, who grounded the Cardinal with a shoulder-charge. As he tore his gun-hand free he saw the hostage guards, who had raised their weapons in bewilderment, being mown down by the Archbishop, who had produced a Usi sub-machine gun from his cassock.

Within seconds, five of the other terrorists, the three Germans and the two remaining Arabs, were writhing on the ground, for the embraces had been fatal for them all. As the freed prisoners had smiled their gratitude, each had drawn a long-bladed knife from a sheath taped to his chest and plunged it into the belly of his partner in the sinister salutation. Leaving it embedded there in the viscera, each had finished off his victim with a light ·22 pistol.

Santos had been severely wounded by the Japanese, but after shooting his assailant in the head was loping, holding his groin, towards the waterfront, the only possible escape route. As he passed the corner of the Basilica he caught sight of two carabinieri who had been stationed there and were raising their guns at him. One of them, who was Filippo, fell wounded as Santos beat him to the trigger; but as the terrorist staggered on, the other Italian shot him through the lungs and he fell to convulse and die in a pool of blood between the Pillars of St Theodore and St Mark.

* * *

Save for the gunfire, the killings had been accomplished almost in silence. Death had come so unexpectedly that even Freya had succumbed without a scream, while the police and television crews had been rooted in mute astonishment by the suddenness of it all. Then, in an instant, all was noise and confusion as the police, reporters and others rushed forward.

Obeying previous instructions, the prisoners, except for the Japanese who was dead, were pulling out their knives from the bodies and throwing them together with their guns in a heap on the ground. After ensuring that both Arab guards were dead, the man in the Archbishop's garb cut the bonds of the General and the hostages, and helped them up. Then he too dropped his knife on to the pile where he had already deposited his Usi, and put up his hands to be followed by the rest in this gesture of surrender.

Ruth was quickly in the tight embrace of her father, who longed to whisper some information which had so sweetened the outcome for him and would, he was sure, stir his daughter's soul, but he had been sworn to total secrecy.

As Sam Kline hurried to greet his son, Paul was retching violently at the sight of so many twitching corpses.

Though relieved to be free, the Cardinal was appalled at the bloodshed and nauseated by the pumping of bullets into helpless wounded. None of the terrorist's victims was alive to comfort and there was no way he could offer last rites to Muslim Arabs, but he sensed that Santos and perhaps the Germans had been baptized Catholics. He knelt and prayed briefly by their bodies before his attention was drawn to the wounded Filippo near the Porta della Carta. He hurried over and, seeing the injury inflicted by Santos's heavy calibre pistol, administered extreme unction before being led away by his chaplain, his head bowed in sorrow, his hands clasped round his pectoral cross and his lips muttering in Latin.

The Jesuit thanked God forthrightly for answering his prayers. The Cardinal too thanked his Maker for his protective hand, though with less fulsome enthusiasm. The dead terrorists may have threatened his life but they were human beings for whom he felt kinship and some respect, engendered through the dangers they had shared. In his view nobody, innocent or guilty, should die in such a horrible way. The longer he lived the more mysterious did God's ways appear. But they were not to be questioned. As the Crusaders would have dismissed the horror—*Deus lo vult!*

Fanti's first concern had been to secure speedboat ambulances to rush Filippo to hospital and get the bodies to the mortuary, but Luigi had a more urgent priority. After closing the helicopter door so that nobody could touch the plunger, he raced into the Basilica, scrambled up the forty-two marble steps leading from the portico to the Loggia, and pulled out the detonators from the gelignite round the Four Horses. He stayed collapsed on his elbows on the balcony for a few moments to recover his breath, then signalled the all-clear to

254

the police. He had not run so fast since he had been shot at by Nazis on Mount Maiella in the Abruzzi partisan campaign more than thirty years previously.

★   ★   ★

Nobody could really understand what had happened until General Yacob explained Operation Ehud, which he and others had worked out in Jerusalem, with Gideon Arad playing a crucial role in Venice.

The real prisoners had indeed been embarked in an El Al airliner, but the bald-headed man seen going up the aircraft steps had not been Yacob but an Israeli actor. The plane had flown low over a secret military airfield north of Jerusalem, where an identical El Al 707 had taken off to replace it while the first was landing. Inside the second plane were Yacob and ten commandos chosen to look as alike the prisoners as possible. The man in the Archbishop's garb was the colonel in charge of the operation. The Jewish faith embraced all races, and the Japanese commando who had given his life was the grandson of a Japanese Californian who had married an American Jewess, and whose own son, born in the faith which goes through the female line, had emigrated to Israel.

The code-name of the operation and General Yacob's cry had special significance, as Ruth had guessed. As recorded in the Book of Judges, a left-handed Israelite called Ehud freed the tribe of Benjamin from oppression by gaining access to the very fat King of Moab by a trick. Claiming to have a secret message and holding out his right hand in a gesture of peace, Ehud had reached with his left for the long dagger strapped beneath his robe to his right thigh and plunged it into the Moabite's belly.

As Luigi listened to the almost incredible details he was greatly disquieted by the risk Yacob had deliberately taken with his own daughter's life, but when he mentioned it to Samuel Kline, the American had such scant sympathy with his criticism that he wondered whether he had also known in advance of the danger to his son and accepted it.

255

'My friend, in no way should those villains have been allowed to get away with it,' Kline responded. 'True, the lives of our own children were at risk, but those monsters would have killed many more Jews and others just as innocent as Ruth and Paul.'

Knowing how emotional Kline could be, Luigi wondered how he would have behaved had the 'Archbishop' not managed to shoot the hostage guards in time. There must be something about the Jews that he didn't understand, he concluded. Something arising perhaps out of their uncompromising religion or out of their centuries of persecution. He shrugged as he decided that perhaps to understand them fully you had to be one.

*　　*　　*

The Venetian authorities, led by Mayor Pizza, and the Italian Government in Rome were incensed at the way they had been deceived, their sovereignty infringed and the Cardinal's life and Church property endangered, and called for the most searching inquiry into the conduct of Operation Ehud.

The Israeli Ambassador, who had left Rome by road earlier that day, allegedly on a visit to Florence, was quickly on the scene. From then on, Yacob refused to give any further information on the grounds that it had become a matter for high diplomacy, save for commenting, 'We are prepared to be judged by the world, which would be a safer place if others dealt with the threat of violence as we do.'

Cables between Rome and Jerusalem were sizzling, and so were the communications between Jerusalem and Washington. Arab countries backed by the Soviet satellites and some African states were demanding United Nations condemnation of what they were calling the 'San Marco Massacre', claiming that it had not been motivated by need to rescue the hostages but by Jewish revenge against the previous operations of Santos and his comrades. The Venice kidnapping had offered a chance to kill Santos, and the Zionists were so merciless that they had allowed neither respect for territory nor thought for innocent lives to stand in their way. Some pro-Arab western newspapers elaborated the theme of treachery, likening the commandos' stratagem to the kiss of Judas.

Italy was accused of complicity, the comparison with Kenya's part in the Entebbe operation being quickly drawn; and the suggestion that the Israelis would never have dared stage such a raid on a NATO country without the approval of the US, where the Jewish vote was a powerful domestic factor, was most unwelcome in Washington.

To rebut such charges, an Israeli spokesman in Jerusalem issued a statement which was explanatory but in no way apologetic:

'Responsibility for all the events in Venice lies firmly with the Palestine Liberation Organization, which planned and executed a heinous crime against the Italian State. The Government of Israel became involved only because of the demand that murderers and other dangerous criminals legally held in its prisons should be released.

'After careful study of the situation, it was decided that as it is against the policy of the Israeli Government to yield to terrorist blackmail, the lives of the hostages and property in Piazza San Marco were at grave risk. What was done offered the only way of resolving the issue.

'The fact that one Israeli soldier was killed and an Italian member of the carabinieri injured by the same terrorist is deeply regretted, but many more lives would have been at stake had the Palestinian gang been bought off once again.

'No member of the Italian Government and no other Italian official had prior knowledge of the operation. It should be obvious that for reasons of secrecy alone, information about the operation had to be restricted totally to those few Israelis involved in it.'

The statement was helpful but there were those in Italy who agreed with the Arabs that certain aspects of the way Police Chief Fanti had handled the affair merited deeper exploration. The most vocal among them was Mayor Pizza who, speaking from his headquarters in the Palazzo Farsetti—once the home of Enrico Dandolo—wanted to know why Fanti had left it to the Israeli guards to frisk the men brought in by the El Al plane. Had the carabinieri done it their weapons would have been found! He also wondered why the Police Chief had been so adamant about preventing any close photography of the freed prisoners when they arrived at Venice Airport. Had pictures been taken the deception might have been spotted.

Pizza's reason why Fanti should have deliberately organized things that way was the simple one—bribery. He knew that Fanti had seen his friend Bozzoni. Could the American writer have been the go-between with the Israelis? That would account for his strange intrusion into the situation. Just how much had Bozzoni known? If he had been told that the terrorists were not going to be allowed to escape, his rush to pay the ransom was much more understandable. And, come to think of it, how much had Samuel Kline known? He, the Mayor, seemed to be the only one who had been kept in the dark. Until such doubts were resolved—and Pizza sensed they never would be—there could be no question of implementing the housing guarantee extracted by the terrorists. After all, a thousand million lire of public money was involved!

The Mayor's suspicions were shared by Italian intelligence chiefs, who had the further information that Bozzoni had been in long discussion with Gideon Arad. His doubts were quickly fed to the left-wing newspapers which used any weapon to attack the Government, and the intelligence officials, anxious to protect themselves, made their information known in Rome.

Fanti issued his denials forcibly and even amusingly through a Press conference, blandly suggesting that it seemed that Mayor Pizza was sorry that the terrorists had not escaped because they were Marxists. Rebutting the charge that Pizza had been deprived of information, he told the reporters that it was a subject on which the Mayor was somewhat pathological, quoting him as having said that being Mayor of Venice was like being a cultivated mushroom—'You are kept in the dark, shit is poured over you at intervals and you end up having your head cut off.'

The Police Chief's good humour brought support from all but the far-left journalists, but his real strength lay in the support of the Defence Ministry official from Rome, who had

258

previously reported back that Fanti seemed to be handling the situation very expertly and had no intention of admitting that his judgment might have been at fault.

Rome was quick to exonerate Fanti or anyone else from taint of collusion, because the last thing it wanted was Palestinian reprisals, which could be aimed at the capital as they had been before.

As the hours passed and the diplomatic manœuvres multiplied, the protests were soon submerged in a welter of admiration for the sheer guts and daring of the Israeli effort. Success was paying off once again and what might have happened had the operation failed was quickly dismissed as academic. Remembering how rapidly the complaints against Kenya had subsided, the Italian Government convinced itself it had little to fear from the Arab and Soviet-inspired noises, and being beset with so many other problems, chief of which was remaining in office, the sooner it got rid of the Israeli embarrassment the better. An Italian citizen, one of the carabinieri, had been seriously injured, though not fatally it seemed from the latest hospital report, but that was a detail which could be dealt with later. Once the furore had diminished, a formula would have to be found for repatriating Yacob and the commandos, and both the Israeli and American ambassadors were hard at work on diplomatic devices for arranging it.

★   ★   ★

The reaction to the stunning success of Operation Ehud in Israel itself was understandably jubilant at both political and public levels. While the Government had appeared to be losing face through unforgivable surrender, it was suddenly seen to have given a tremendous lift to national morale through superlative triumph just when it was needed, the impact of Entebbe having been slowly eroded by domestic discontent. Surrounded by inveterate enemies, the Israelis needed regular opportunities to remind the world that the old image of Jews as grasping money-makers with little stomach for a fight was mythical indeed.

★   ★   ★

While Cardinal Talamini had been ordered to bed by his doctors, the euphoria of their deliverance had neutralized any shock suffered by Paul and Ruth, and after being given mild sedatives they were allowed to return to their hotel, the Gritti Palace, the Italian security men being satisfied that they were in no further danger. Kline senior surprisingly showed no symptoms beyond joyous relief, and was prevailed upon to transfer to the same de luxe establishment, which had once been the home of a Doge as distinguished in his time as Dandolo.

'The last thing I want is to play gooseberry on your honeymoon,' Sam protested, but Ruth insisted that they were only too sorry that her own father was not allowed to join them.

'You just can't get away from them, can you?' Sam laughed as he checked in at the Gritti reception desk. The desk was dignified by a bronze miniature of the Four Horses, which Italy's main hotel chain had adopted as its emblem.

★   ★   ★

At Sam's insistence they celebrated their freedom with a fine bottle of champagne, the questing newsmen being kept at bay by the vigilant management.

'Had you any idea what was going to happen?' Ruth ventured after her second glass.

Kline smiled and patted his daughter-in-law's hand.

'On that subject, my dear, my lips are sealed—even to you. All I'm prepared to say is that your father is a braver man than I am. I was pretty damn scared facing that thug.'

Ruth looked at her husband, who knew it was useless pursuing any matter once his father had made up his mind.

'I'm going to take a bath,' she announced. 'I feel unclean.'

'Me too, after twenty-six hours in that company,' Paul agreed, though it was the solitude of the bath he needed rather than the benison of its water. He still felt sick from the sight of the killings, more sure than ever that the Israelis' judgment was dangerously corrupted by the arrogance of military success and, with Ruth so elated, did not wish to disclose his sentiments.

As they ascended in the lift from the cool, elegant lobby Ruth said, 'I think he knew something, but how could he?'

'Made a few telephone calls, I guess. Or maybe some Israeli contacted him.'

While their baths refreshed them, the long build-up of adrenalin in their blood continued its excitation. There was only one activity at hand to abate it and their pleasure was ecstatic, as though in mutual celebration not just of their release but of a long and loving future together which, until their savage experience, they had taken for granted.

★   ★   ★

Kline's first move after settling into his suite was to telephone Frank Bozzoni.

'I'd like to thank you in person, Mr Bozzoni, and we do have a little matter to clear up.'

'Right, come here for a drink,' Bozzoni responded breezily. 'I'll send my boat for you.'

The Palazzetto Falier, a restored Gothic building on the right-hand side of the Grand Canal beyond the Academy Bridge, had been built in the fifteenth century by the patrician Faliero family, from which Bozzoni claimed descent. With its two projecting loggias it had always caught Kline's eye on previous visits. Caring for comfort and convenience as well as beauty, he saw it as just about the only private house on the entire Canal fit for modern living, a view reinforced by his first sight of the interior. Bozzoni, whatever his behavioural eccentricities, had taste.

As they shook hands Kline could see that his host was as elated by the events as he was.

'That sure was a great operation,' Bozzoni said. 'What a scenario! If I'd used it in one of my books the critics would have said it was too far-fetched. But who the hell cares about them! They pan all my novels and they sell for a million bucks.'

It took only a few moments to settle the question of the money now that the ransom had been restored to the Banca d'Italia.

'You were more than generous, Mr Bozzoni, to do such a thing. It made my position much easier,' Kline said as he took a bourbon and soda.

'You could hardly have made it easier for me, could you, Mr Kline? But tell me one thing: if you knew that the terrorists were not going to get away with it why did you care what anybody might think, as it would only be for a few hours anyway?'

There was a twinkle in Kline's eyes as he replied, 'Mr Bozzoni, like you I am an American citizen. Even if I had known any such thing I would have had to take every possible step to avoid involving my country.'

Bozzoni got the message. 'Well, I'm grateful to you, Mr Kline, for giving me the chance to play a small part in saving those Four Horses. You know if it hadn't been for one of my ancestors they wouldn't be here at all.'

'How come?'

'A few years after the Horses first arrived here, there was a proposal to abandon Venice and move the capital to Constantinople. It was defeated by only one vote—cast by a man called Angelo Faliero.'

'Then thank God for Angelo! Or there wouldn't be any Horses or any Venice. New Venice would have fallen to the Turks!'

Each took care not to mention Gideon Arad, not wishing to let the other know the extent of his involvement with the Israeli Secret Serviceman. Bozzoni had been of far greater use in Operation Ehud that he had imagined, particularly in dissuading Italian intelligence from probing too deeply. Had he known it, he might not have relished being used as a stalking horse in Harry's Bar.

Arad was not around for interrogation by the Italians. He had remained at Venice Airport throughout the operation in the Piazza and had left on the empty El Al plane. Bozzoni had already telephoned him at his headquarters in Tel Aviv to secure yet another bonus for his help. He had decided to write a quick paperback account of the entire episode, and was making sure of Mossad assistance when he arrived in Israel for research purposes at the weekend. With the film script, the book would be worth another million.

★   ★   ★

When Sofia, the wife of Filippo, the wounded carabiniere, went round to see her husband in hospital she learned that he was out of immediate danger. The high-velocity bullet from Santos's M52 automatic pistol had gone clean through his body, drilling neat holes in his colon, but prompt surgery had saved his life. He was in no condition to talk but Sofia was—to anyone who would listen.

Filippo was something of a hero to his relatives and to the Press for daring to take on such a deadly shot, but to his commander he was just a damn fool. No order had been given to fire and Santos would not have bothered with him had he not raised his gun first instinctively—and stupidly—the commander told reporters.

On reading what the commander had said, Sofia suspected that their chance of substantial compensation, which her relatives had told her would be assured, was already being prejudiced.

'He does his duty and what happens—he nearly gets killed,' she complained to reporters who went round to question her. 'You'll see, they'll find some way of getting out of paying him any compensation. Just because we are too poor to fight them. And what will happen to me and Alessandro if he does die?' she asked tearfully. 'There's no justice for the poor.'

Sofia was right. The carabinieri were controlled by the army, and the men who ran the bureaucratic machines in both Venice and Rome were averse to making any payments which might establish costly precedents.

★   ★   ★

Newspapers throughout the world had a field day with their stories of Operation Ehud and obituaries recalling the exploits of the dead Santos, but the follow-ups were not what they expected. Examination of the fingerprints of the dead terrorist

263

leader showed that he was certainly not the Santos wanted for murders in France, Vienna and London. They were of some person unknown to the finger-print registries of those cities and his identity became a matter of intense speculation, but not to the Mossad chiefs or to those Israeli statesmen and planners who had been involved in Ehud.

They had known it on receipt of Gideon Arad's on-the-spot report, which he had dispatched immediately after seeing the blown-up pictures of the man in the peaked cap in the Loggia dei Cavalli. The mortuary photographs and finger-print copies secured by his agent in the embassy in Rome had fully confirmed it to Mossad.

Publication of the man's name would have meant little to anyone outside that small Israeli circle, save for the Palestinian leaders who were only too aware of the loss they had sustained, but disclosure of his past deeds would have raised the general rejoicing of Jews throughout the world to ecstatic levels. The Loggia 'Santos' had been the most wanted subject on Mossad's death list—the man they knew to be most responsible for the massacre of eleven Israeli athletes at the Munich Olympic Games in 1972. That most emotive of all the outrages perpetrated by the Palestinians had bitten so deeply into the Jewish soul, that when Yacob and Kline had been told the true identity of 'Santos' they agreed to play their part in the bloody charade of Ehud, irrespective of the danger to their own and to themselves. Kline had entertained fleeting reservations but the General had reacted with enthusiasm to the chance of avenging the beloved Yigael.

The men and women in the Mossad hit-team had been hunting for the instigator of Munich in simmering fury ever since Golda Meir, then Prime Minister, had approved the destruction of all those responsible wherever they might be.

Over those years, while a dozen murderers had been eliminated from the list by booby-trap and bullet, the prime target's identity had been withheld; and Mossad had encouraged writers to point the finger at others, in the hope that the man might believe his commanding role at Munich had gone undetected and think it safe to take to the field again.

Now for different reasons the authorities in Jerusalem

decided that the mystery must be preserved, at least until General Yacob and the commandos were safely home, for their enemies and critics would claim with undeniable force that the prime reason for the 'San Marco Massacre' was glaringly apparent. It had not been to save the hostages or the Basilica and its treasures. It had been 'eye for an eye' revenge.

Of course, one of the numerous Palestinian agencies could reveal the truth but that seemed unlikely. Their natural response with their disasters was to play them down, and to take the spotlight off themselves by concentrating it on diplomatic difficulties created by their enemy's success. So far, beyond claiming the bodies of their comrades for burial, they had not even admitted responsibility for the events in the Loggia dei Cavalli.

Chapter Twenty-one

The Klines were surprised to find that the last thing they wanted to do after their ordeal was to sleep. The reaction of all three was continuing excitability and a long, leisurely dinner was a much more agreeable prospect.

They dined, with Luigi as their guest, on the Grand Canal veranda of the Gritti Palace. Facing them was the immense white pile of the Basilica of the Salute with its catherine-wheel buttresses, built in gratitude for the deliverance of Venice from a previous menace. To make it an occasion and for personal morale, Ruth appeared looking her best in an apricot caftan with Greek gold sandals and, almost as an act of defiance, wore the medallion retrieved blood-stained from Freya's slacks.

Over brandies they watched the brightly-lit serenade-boats with their bands and operatic singers, followed by the great rafts of gondolas carrying the tourists, and laughed nervously at almost anything. By intuitive agreement they avoided discussing the day's events over the meal, an aftermath familiar to Luigi, who in his war experience had found that killings, even of the most detested enemy, muted talk about them.

As they touched hands reassuringly under the table, Paul and Ruth had different reasons, each sensed by the other, for being grateful that there was no mulling over their shared experience. He was far from proud of his performance. Yigael would have put a braver face on it, as he was sure Ruth appreciated, while she was concerned with her private guilt at having felt relieved when Jerusalem had appeared to capitulate.

Sam had deliberately stimulated the small-talk because the less said about 'Ehud' in front of Luigi the better. He might be a dear friend but he was an Italian, and discussion might inadvertently reveal information which could strain his loyalty; for there was no doubt that the authorities would be

266

questioning him closely. But when, after ten p.m., Luigi suggested the ritual stroll in the Piazza, they could not resist the chance to indulge their curiosity in revisiting the scene of the massacre.

The traders were making the most of a beautiful evening to return quickly to normality, in readiness for the Festival. This was to go ahead the following day, except for the *Te Deum* Mass, which had been cancelled by the Cardinal because of the carnage. The arcade shops, offering tooled leather goods, jewellery, glassware and exquisite lace were ablaze with light; the souvenir pedlars and quick-portrait artists were touting busily; and at the open-air cafés, orchestras were in full swing.

The Piazza was thronged not only with those excluded all day but with sensation-seekers from the mainland. Hundreds who had never taken particular notice of the Four Horses were staring at them, while others concentrated around the areas where the terrorists' blood had been scrubbed away. Even Sofia had been unable to resist the morbid attraction of taking her mother to see where Filippo and the terrorists had been shot.

With commendable speed the night-tour guides had latched on to the Piazza's enhanced curiosity value, and held their rolled umbrellas aloft for recognition by their flocks as they led them to the points of macabre interest, particularly the spot where retribution had overtaken 'Santos'.

Nobody appeared to recognize Luigi and his party as they pressed through the crowd, but fleetingly Paul wondered whether their movements might be under watch by foreign eyes constricted with hate, perhaps burning with zeal for revenge.

The nearer they approached the Loggia dei Cavalli the more unreal the day's events appeared, particularly their personal involvement in them. As they stood looking up at the Four Horses, standing proudly in their floodlit stable, a modest tenor at Quadri's was rendering a verse of the Festival song:

> '*Stay mute in your den, leave us with our pretence*
> *That Man's nature improves through culture and sense,*
> *The fiction that learning will lessen his greed*
> *And make him more loving, from cruelty freed . . .*'

'We really will have to make that our tune, darling,' Paul said half-jokingly, putting his arm round Ruth's shoulders.

'Yes, dear, but not the words. We can't really accept that Man's nature will never improve.'

'I can,' Luigi said firmly. 'That song is right. I reckon that in the last two thousand years the nature of Man has probably changed less than those bronze horses.'

'After what we've experienced in the last two days, I'm afraid I have to agree with you,' Sam said.

'But surely we've got to assume that it won't always be like that,' Paul protested. 'Otherwise what's the point of it all? We must have faith in the inherent goodness of Man.'

Luigi shook his head sadly. 'I'm afraid you'll find that the belief that all will be well, provided enough human beings receive enough education, is a romantic delusion.'

'But education must help,' Ruth insisted. 'Isn't that what civilization's all about?'

'It's what civilization should be about, but each generation throws up fanatics capable of inducing enough "educated" people to convert their ideas into action, whatever the cost in death and destruction.'

'Like Santos?' Paul said.

'Like Santos, like Hitler, like Napoleon, like Alexander . . . The trouble is that God has organized things so that every generation has to make the same mistakes. Experience is not inherited. That is the human tragedy and there seems to be no way out of it.'

Luigi paused for a moment then added, 'Perhaps that's what God meant by making man in His own image. He makes so many mistakes Himself.'

They stopped by the central flagpole and looked more closely at the site of the young Klines' incarceration. The so recent past was taking on the qualities of an extravaganza they had witnessed as detached observers, rather than a bloody action in which they could so easily have lost their lives.

'It looks more like a stage-set than ever at night,' Ruth murmured.

'Yes, I was premature in saying there would be no more dramas here,' Luigi admitted. 'I should have touched wood.'

268

'To all those millions of viewers it must have seemed just like another Western ending in a shoot-out,' Paul suggested.

'One that the "goodies" won again!' said Ruth.

'I suppose so,' Paul agreed half-heartedly. 'But I wonder who'll get killed as a result. Folk we've never heard of?'

Sam looked at his son despairingly. He just couldn't understand his attitude.

'Well, one thing's for sure,' he said. 'Santos and his gang won't be killing anybody. Don't worry, son. You can be sure it was the right side that won. *Our* people won. And they sure deserved to. My God those commandos were brave. Cooler than any gunfighters.'

'They certainly were, but the terrorists had courage too,' Luigi reminded him. 'They always do. That's what makes them so dangerous.'

'I suppose that's true,' Kline admitted without enthusiasm. 'But, you know, the real heroes, the only ones sure to be remembered, are those four up there. Just look at them! You'd think that nothing had ever happened to them since the day they were made.'

Luigi nodded appreciatively, happy that like his friends the Horses were free again to continue their objective observation of human affairs. 'Yes, Sam,' he said reflectively, 'they do say a lot for the durability of bronze, but considering all they have seen they say infinitely more for the durability of the human spirit.'

From their surveillance platform the Horses would see much more. At that very moment there might well have been among that jostling, cosmopolitan throng, pickpockets greedy for easy money; lusting youths and lascivious old men ardent for gratification; a few inordinately ambitious and resentfully avid for recognition; and one, perhaps, as yet unknown, driven by the most malignant motive of all—greed for control over others.